NAKED LOVE BERLIN

Naked love Berlin

by: Jin De Luong

JIN DELUONG MEDIA INC

This novel is entirely a work of fiction. The names, characters and incidents portrayed in it are the product of the author's imagination. Any resemblance to actual persons, living or dead, or events or localities is entirely coincidental.

Paperback Edition November 18, 2023
ISBN 978-1-7381983-0-6

Dear reader,

Books about Berlin have focused on war, but that's a perspective from straight men. For gay authors like Isherwood and myself, the German capital represents not war, but freedom to love and lust after other men. Berlin is the greatest cultural and extravagant freedom you can imagine. Like many authors before me, inspiration came from myself, my life, and the lives that comprise Berlin. Details have been changed to protect the innocent and those up-to-no-good. Be prepared to experience this freedom.

Jin De Luong

As a thank you for purchasing this book, please visit jindeluong.com to download a short story of how Kay and Helmut met.

Contents

1. Kay

Keys jiggle at the apartment door, and I abandon my text message ("…*suck my*") with a frantic press of the home button. The hefty shake of German-made keys startles me, and I panic. Emails, I'm reading emails as I sit at the maple kitchen table. Helmut opens the door and enters with a bouquet of lilies. He grabs a black vase and places the flowers in front of me, and their green and pink fragrance mingles with the smell of vanilla cake baking in the oven. He bakes for my birthday.

"You look good in that shirt," he says, and squeezes my shoulder as I hold my breath. He goes to the oven and stands with his back to me. I breathe. Helmut is eighteen years older than I am, and we've been together for the last five. I met Helmut when his hair was still dark and his jawline firm. After fifty, the visible signs of aging are dramatic. His ass has no shape, his hair is long despite being Chernobyl-sparse on top, and the folds of flesh under his jaws are visible when he turns to smile at me.

Its screen locked, I set my phone aside. I go to the bathroom. With the door closed, I sigh. Is this how I ever pictured my thirty-third birthday? I am Canadian but live in Berlin. I live with a man who loves me, but his friends are older than he is, and they're dying. Cancer, last stages of AIDS, bad knees. Helmut coughs from years of cigarettes, and with each cough, I resent his love. I'm thirty-three and should be living a carefree life, not one saddled with aches and pains from semi-retirement.

Helmut is very German, his apartment is *typisch Deutsch* but modern. The bathroom is completely tiled, from the floor with black granite to the walls in white ceramic. In modern German bathrooms, the sink is white, the bathtub is white, and the toilet white. *Typisch Deutsch* bathrooms are clean, and to keep clean, German men sit down while urinating. A sign hangs by the toilet which shows a stick man standing while pissing, slashed with a red line. *Es ist verboten*. Fuck that. I unzip and let the urine splatter from standing height. I hate these shelf toilets, something so despicably German. They save water, but a platform is built into the bowl to collect urine and other excrement—and my waste sits there like it's on display in a shop window.

"Kay!" Helmut screams. I press the white button to flush and watch everything dissipate in the swirls of clear water. I wash my hands, and they're still wet when I open the door to see Helmut holding my phone and pointing it at me like a knife. "Who is this Georg?"

Shit. I forgot about notifications. "A guy who lives nearby," I say.

"A guy who lives nearby," Helmut says. "And loves the taste of your cock." He throws the phone at me. The screen cracks when it lands on the hardwood floor. "*Arschloch!*" German is powerful when barked in anger. Helmut's eyes are as wet as my hands, and his teeth are bared. Is he more disgusted by the sex or the betrayal? "Are there more?"

"Georg and Uwe," I say. They're men my age. I don't know if I should say more. Explaining my selfish reasoning won't help: That they haven't lost interest in sex. That I miss the feeling of young flesh against me. That their asses are perky and shapely.

"Were you safe with them?" he says.

Now I twist my mouth in disgust. "Yes, of course fucking yes."

Helmut covers his face with his palms. When his hands withdraw, his fingers leave pink trails on his puffy cheeks. His eyes narrow and he commands in slow and deliberate English, "Get out."

I stand still. What was I expecting to happen?

"Kay," he says. "Get out."

I panic. Get out? Where will I go? I moved from Winnipeg to Berlin for him. I don't have family here, and know only people from work. Without Helmut, I'm an alien in this country.

"Kay, I can't stand looking at you," he says. "Get out. Now! GET OUT!" Helmut screams the last two words, and his face reddens by rage.

I pick up my phone, and grab my backpack with its "University of Manitoba" stitching on the front. The door slams shut, and in the silence, I contemplate what I've done. Helmut's expression and twisted features mean he hates me because I'm the betrayer and I cheated on him. In the love story of Canadian boy meets German man, it has a sad ending, and they don't live happily ever after.

I'm outside. It's January in Berlin—trees are bare, sun is blocked by dark clouds, and the buildings' colours have faded to gray like black-and-white photos. Grey European buildings makes me feel nostalgic of the past, and grey Berlin evokes eerie echoes of films about the war. My next steps could mean life or death.

Turn right to hide in a basement café. I sit down and watch legs in leather boots walk past. I recognize the woman's gait. She's Helmut's friend and suffers from bad knees. She walks with hopes for a fun dinner party, but will instead find a crying old man.

A waiter comes to my table. He wears a white shirt framed in a black vest. "*Ein Glas Sekt, bitte,*" I say for my order. German sparkling wine. It is still my birthday.

A young woman wearing a backpack walks in. Her eyes scan the café, then sits down and pulls out her Berlin guide book. The waiter approaches her. "Do you speak English?" she says. He nods. "Coffee please." They spend a few moments discussing coffee options. "And a glass of water."

"Sparkling or still?" the waiter says.

"Tap water, I mean," she says. The waiter looks annoyed. Tourists from North America beware—one does not order tap water in Europe. That person used to be me. I used to be a naive tourist. I was a country bumpkin from Winnipeg. I marveled at churches and castles like the other hordes of backpackers bussed around Europe.

I receive a text message from Mike, another Canadian I met months ago at a party named Queer Beer. "Free for drinks at my place?" he texts. He doesn't know it's my birthday. Of course he doesn't. Only Helmut knows. What do I do now?

Another message. It's from Georg. "BF just left," Georg texts. "Your cock not only tastes good but feels good inside me. Come over and fuck me. Please."

When in doubt, fuck. "OK. I'll be there in 10 min," I text. After a pause, I add, "Today is my birthday."

"A special birthday blow job then ;)" he texts.

My sekt comes. My lips touch the rim of the champagne flute and my tongue tingles with soft bubbles. I drink the alcoholic melody without the glass ever leaving my lips. Foam clings to the side when I put the glass down. The tourist stares at me.

"Welcome to Berlin," I say, leave money on the table, and head out.

Minutes later, at Georg's building, I push the button beside "Schmidt/Fuhring" on the intercom, and push the heavy door open once it buzzes. We are in Charlottenburg, a wealthy part of West Berlin. The buildings that survived the war are opulent and hint at the former glory of the capital. This house has a front garden, and the entryway has a curved, domed ceiling with a chandelier. A wide spiral staircase leads to mystery and magnificence on the upper levels.

Georg, however, lives in the *Hinterhaus*, the nondescript building hidden in the back. These apartments behind the opulence were for servants who cooked and cleaned for masters living in the front. The stairwell here is narrow and dark. Georg's door is ajar, and squeaks when I push to enter. As I walk toward the living room, the floorboards creak under my shoes.

Georg sits naked atop a blue throw on the brown leather couch. We never fuck in the bedroom. He's tall, his arms stretched out to half the couch's length, and his legs are so long that not only his feet but also his calves rest on the floor. His torso, large and hairless, glistens in pink glory. His cock is very German, uncut and even rosier than the rest of his body.

I approach him. Georg purrs like a kitty when I'm close. He purrs like a tiger when he squeezes my pecs. I'm built like a rugby player or gymnast, my own calves thick and my forearms striated with muscle, and Georg grabs my biceps as he nuzzles his face into my crotch. I unzip my pants.

"Happy birthday," Georg says and wraps his lips around my engorged and veiny cock. Georg's own grows thicker and longer, the head a deep shade of purple. A birthday blowjob is definitely better than cake.

I grab the lube and condoms. I use my teeth to rip open the wrapper. The condom is snug when I slip it on; I'm a little over average length but thick.

Georg sucks me through the latex. His English is good but heavily accented, and I bite my lip when he talks dirty to me. "Your cock is beautiful. Fuck me with it please." I don't know whether I would sound any less awkward talking dirty in German. *Du blast gut.* Or is there an umlaut somewhere in that sentence?

I turn him around and he lays on the couch like a dog. I push inside him, and I'm greeted by the smell of sex. Georg's breaths turn ragged and I begin with slow thrusts. His tongue laps the navy-blue cloth, and his neck and back flush red. I now fuck with greater force at greater tempo. I'm consumed by a feeling of power as I fuck this tall specimen of a man. Fuck and groan. Thrust and moan.

"*Georg! Bist du da? Ich habe was vergessen,*" another man says from the hallway. It's the boyfriend. Oh shit. The boyfriend walks in. He has a beard, and is just as tall but with a belly camouflaged by a blazer. Thrust, thrust—I should stop, right? The sound of the boyfriend's shoes stop. "*Ein Asiate, Georg? Das hätte ich nicht erwartet.*" You never expected your boyfriend to be with someone Asian? Well, I never expected to be fucking your boyfriend, *Arschloch.*

The boyfriend walks to a desk on the opposite wall, pulls out an envelope, then steps out with a very prominent, "*Tschüuuss!*"

I've grown soft, and pull out. I should be peeved or angry, but instead feel like a popped balloon.

"It's no problem," Georg says. "We have an open relationship."

"Sorry, I can't," I say. As I put on my clothes, images of Helmut and our past flood my mind—the holidays spent by the sea, in the mountains, and in villages with all houses painted white. I'm homeless. I'm a single gay man seeking an apartment or room to rent. How many other homeless gay men in Berlin are seeking the same?

I'm back outside. The street lights flicker on, and fortunately it's not raining. What do I do now? I stare past the traffic and naked trees to find an answer. I then see the tourist from the café, this time carrying a smaller bag. She steps to one side to avoid a group of people chatting, but she blocks the red brick path reserved for bicycles, and no one is as rude with the rules as a Berliner on a bike. *Ting! Ting!* Rings the bike's bell. That's just enough time for her to jump out of the way—but she crashes onto the cobblestone sidewalk, the contents of her bag spilling out for all to see.

I rush over. Her face blushes, and although there are tampons and condoms on the pavement, she reaches first to pick up her guidebook, *Berlin Through the Back Door*. I smile.

"Are you OK?" I say, changing my lips to a pout of concern.

"Yes, just embarrassed," she says. She brushes the dust off her clothes. "Can you tell me where Wiesenstein restaurant is?"

"Good choice," I say. "It's straight down this street." After considering what "straight down" might mean to a North American, I add, "The street hits an intersection, and will curve forty-five degrees left. But it's still the same street."

"Thank you." She walks away, glancing every so often at the ground to make sure she doesn't step onto the red bicycle lane.

I'm not her. I may be homeless, but I'm no tourist. I'm a Berliner. I may have messed up, but life goes on—another day, another party, another moment to fuck things up.

I call Mike. "Hey. I'd like to join you. How long will you be there?"

"We're finishing up," Mike says, "We're going to GMF soon. Want to meet us there?"

"Sure," I say.

"Do you know where it is?" he says.

GMF. I know where it is. Not just a Berliner, a gay Berliner. "Yeah. See you in a bit." I'll check into a hotel, take a few days off work, and find another place to live. I'll email Helmut to arrange a time to pick up the rest of my things. Maybe I'll live with a roommate so I don't have to buy tons of furniture. It's Saturday, January 18, 2014 and for my thirty-third birthday, I've gifted myself a new life as a single gay man in the sexy big city. I walk toward the U-Bahn without any need for a map.

2. Alex

I look in the bathroom mirror and see red hairs sprouting through the black and brown of my beard like a weird type of carrot salad. I guess this is what happens when you get older and you have a mixed German-Japanese background. Some days, my brow bone appears more prominent, and people think I'm German. Other times, my eyes look more Japanese. That's usually when I've barely slept, and my eyes are half-shut and I'm tired as fuck.

The intercom buzzes. A guy is coming to see the room. He says he's Kay from Canada. He didn't speak with any "eh" at the end, but I'm going to pay attention to his "about."

I run into the bedroom and put on the first shirt I can find—a pink shirt I wore last night to a gay party. It's not only pink, it has a lazy pride of maned lions on the front, with a few even sniffing each other's butts.

I open the door for Kay. I'm surprised. I mean, he's Asian. I wasn't expecting this from a Canadian. I can say this because I'm half Japanese.

"Hi," I say. I don't see many broad-shouldered Asians. "Come on in."

"Should I take my shoes off?" Kay says. Of course he'd ask something like that.

"You can if you want, but I don't," I say and walk toward the living room, my shoes resounding on the hallway's hardwood floors. I still have boxes piled against the wall from my last move. "Your room is behind the doors. It's the bigger one, but no balcony." I open the doors to reveal a space empty except for a bed and mattress left by my last housemate. Sunlight shines in through the window, an unusual thing since it's January. The weather has been warm today, although last night was as cold as a Minneapolis winter.

"Nice," Kay says. His voice echoes in the large empty bedroom. He walks around, opens the windows. The room faces the courtyard so it's quiet except for the tweets of birds.

"When did you arrive in Berlin?" I ask him. He's the third person to inquire about the room.

"Five years ago," he says, looking at my shirt. He smiles. "My boyfriend and I broke up, so I need to move out of his place." Gay, Asian, and Canadian. I can't say I'm not intrigued. "Are utilities included?"

"The *Nebenkosten* yes," I explain, "but internet, electricity, and a few other things we would split. What job do you have?"

"I work at CoExcel," he says. "It's a company that implements clinical studies for pharma companies." Kay's a guy with a regular sounding job. That's a big plus for a roommate in Berlin.

We continue the tour through the bathroom and then the kitchen. He mentions that he likes to cook, and asks whether that would be a problem. Of course I say no, but seriously, what's the smell going to be like? Even though my mother is Japanese, she didn't cook. I've spent more of my life eating hamburgers than I have sushi or ramen. And don't fucking give me chopsticks.

I'm not sure I'm feeling it with Kay from Canada. I've decided to give him the whole spiel about having two more interviews before I can make my decision when his phone rings.

"Hey Mike," he says. His face changes. "How badly are you hurt?" Color is draining from his face as he covers his mouth. "Where are you?" More from the phone. "I'll come get you."

"What happened?" I say.

"Shit," he says. "My friend Mike got into an accident. He's been here for a year and a half, but he doesn't know German. He doesn't even know the number to dial for an ambulance. I said I'd pick him up, but fuck, I don't have a car."

"I do," I say. "We can go pick him up together." We head out of the apartment and walk down the stairs.

"What brought you to Berlin?" Kay says.

"I like your question," I say. "It's one of those vague, open questions that doesn't work on Germans."

"I know. You're American."

"With German citizenship," I say. "I came here to study opera. And to party. But I don't mention that to my parents." Partying in Berlin is so much cheaper than anywhere else. I sing him a piece from *Der Kaiser von Atlantis*. A neighbor pops open the door and quickly closes it when she sees me.

"At least you've learned something," Kay says. "I've met way too many students here 'learning' German," he does the air quotes around *learning*, "and when I start a simple conversation with them, their faces go blank like, 'OK. You've caught me. I'm really here for the drugs.'"

I point to where the hatchback is, a black VW. I'm glad I can get some use out of it since most of the time I'm too drunk to drive. "What kind of accident was your friend in?" I say.

Kay is putting on his seat belt. "He slipped on ice and fell off his bike. His right hand hurts, so something there must be broken."

"I once hit a curb and fell off my bike," I say. I was piss drunk. "It was near a square and I landed on grass. Otherwise these European cobblestones are painful. What brought you to Berlin?"

"The relationship that I'm moving out of," Kay says. "That, and the cheap booze."

He drinks. Good, thank God. I drive and Kay tells me where to go. The GPS navigates but the American voice is mangling the pronunciation of German street names. We arrive. There's an Asian guy pacing back and forth behind a fallen bike.

"Mike," Kay greets. "What happened?"

"Is my face scratched?" Mike says. His words burst out with hardly a breath. Kay shakes his head. "I was going downhill. I've taken this route for so many fucking months. I turn right like I've done how many fucking times, but today, there's ice. The bike slides and I fall. I hold my hands out like an idiot to stop. Fuck, my hand hurts." He looks at his right palm.

"Give me your bike key," Kay says. "We'll lock up your bike and then go to the hospital. You have your insurance card, right?"

"In my wallet," Mike says. In the back of the car, Mike looks at me. Two and a half Asians in my hatchback. This black car has never been sat on by so much yellow ass.

"I'm Alex," I say.

With another wince, he says, "Thanks for taking me."

This is my first time to an emergency room in Germany. I was once in an emergency room in Minneapolis to help a friend who drank too much. This waiting room is way smaller than an American one, and fairly empty with no one bleeding. Instead of filling out paperwork, Kay hands an insurance card to the receptionist, who hands it back only seconds later. Kay explains what happened. I listen, curious whether he speaks better German than I do.

"Mike doesn't speak German, so I'm here to help," Kay says. "He was riding his bicycle and fell. His right hand hurts a lot, so we think a bone is broken." I wonder if I would have explained it like that. When my friend back home was delirious and almost unconscious, I kept ranting about how they had to do something and we were just partying and how I had found him in the bathroom unconscious like that.

The receptionist asks us to sit and wait. Mike's weeping and supporting his right hand with his left, and Kay has his arm wrapped around Mike's shoulders. I pick up last July's copy of *Der Spiegel*, and along with old news, there is an article about the best vacation spots in Spain. Germans love Spain—Malaga, Barcelona, and Mallorca, *ja!* Madrid? Meh.

A woman wearing white pants and a white shirt comes to us. She's not wearing a lab coat. "Herr Mike Lee?"

We all look at her, but Kay says, "Mike doesn't speak German."

"I will take an X-Ray of Mike's hand," she continues sayig in German. "One of you can accompany Mike, but not both."

"I'll wait here," I say. They leave. She has a large round ass. I like big booty.

An hour or more later, my phone battery's dead. Kay comes out and sits beside me. "Mike's getting his hand in a cast right now. Thanks again for taking us, but if you want to go…"

"I'll stay," I say. "I like helping." I don't mention that I've got nowhere else to go, or that I don't have friends who would take me to the hospital here, so it's comforting to see people like Kay and Mike that do.

"Mike kept telling me how powerless he felt," Kay says. "And this is just at the hospital. What's it going to be like for him when he has to cook for himself, or shower, or even put on shoes?"

"At least you only need one hand to jerk off," I say with a grin.

"Or if he uses the cast hand," Kay says, "it'd feel like a gracious bottom doing it for him." We both chuckle.

Mike comes out. He has his jacket draped over his left arm because the other's in a bulky cast. "If only I had landed on my left hand," he says. "A cast on the left would have been inconvenient. But I'm right handed, and this," he says while lifting his cast while grimacing, "is life-altering painful. I have an appointment in two weeks. I could at least understand that much."

We head to the car. In one of those strange Berlin twists of the rules, I pay a fine of five euros because I hadn't paid for parking. If I had paid and had been late, it would have been fifteen.

In the car, Mike says, "I called my mom. After the surgery, she wants me to go back to Vancouver." His voice is rather whiny, but who wouldn't be after breaking a bone?

"Is that what you want?" Kay says.

"I think so," Mike says as he looks out the window, as if ashamed. "What's keeping me here? Sure, partying is fun, but I'm teaching English at a language school where there's always a guy who's a little too surprised that an Asian guy is teaching them English. I was supposed to write something, anything, but all I've managed to do is piss away all my money."

Shit sounds familiar.

"Although I've heard there's a new night at Lab for guys into casts,"

Kay says. He's talking about a sex club, one I'd only recently learned about. "Just imagine how popular you'd be. When it comes to fisting, you're a top, right?"

"Oh God," I say. I stop the car at the apothecary's green cross. After the pharmacy, we drop Mike off at his apartment. Kay gets back into the car, and I say, "You're a good person to help him out like that."

"Without family," he says, "we expats have to look out for each other."

I let that settle in my head, and realize it'd be nice to have an expat like Kay in my life. "When can you move in?" I say.

Kay puts on his seat belt. "Tomorrow?"

"When exactly?"

"About two?" Kay says. Yes, that about is fucking Canadian.

"As long as it's the afternoon," I say. "It's Chantal's House of Shame tonight. I won't be getting up before noon."

3. Timothy

Who's the bloody wanker who left his alarm on for a Saturday? And why are these walls so damn thin? I thought Germany was renowned for quality, but this furnished business flat is pitiful. It's a tiny one-room place with paper veneer furniture rejected from a motorway hotel. This is what happens when I accept the recommendation of a relocation agency. I was out way too late last night, and may perhaps be mildly hung over. I don't need this.

I try in vain to block out the noise with my pillow. The alarm's shrill and incessant beeping only intensifies my hangover. Exasperation sets in. I pull on a jumper and head to the balcony to light a cigarette. My lips encircle the fag and inhale smoke deep down my lungs while thinking of him.

Even though I only arrived home two hours ago, last night was worth it. His name was Orhan, and we met at the bar over our mutual like of vodka Red Bull. In truth, I hate the cocktail, but I had spotted this fine specimen of Turkish delight earlier in the evening, and had seen what he'd ordered. We met at the bar while ordering the same drink, I said hello, and after some small talk I carefully placed caresses on his thigh. Cut to me in his bedroom, he pushed me on my knees, and I was sucking on his stubby but oh-so-thick circumcised Muslim dick. It was almost painful when he bent me over and fucked me. I whimpered like a schoolgirl.

Who am I fooling? I relished every minute of my rosebud being ravaged.

I head back inside, where the neighbour's alarm continues to pulsate through the room. I lie on the bed and can't help but think about Orhan shagging me. I can still feel his girth inside me—like wounded soldiers complaining about phantom limbs, I as a power bottom can complain about phantom cock, especially Orhan's hard and fat monster.

I begin to wank, and with each stroke I desperately try to recall every detail. Not only his schlong, but his body pounding into mine, him olive-skinned and muscled, me with my pale and freckled limbs. But I was dreadfully pissed, and the details are hazy.

It then dawns upon me. After all our fumbling, he didn't use a condom. With my pathetic German, I couldn't understand all of what he said, or why he didn't want to. It was a strange sense of powerlessness conversing in German, and I couldn't think swiftly enough, couldn't speak swiftly enough. I was left mute. Did it matter? When it happened, when he was inside me, my breathing quickened, and all I could focus upon was the force of his body and the pleasure of sex.

An hour later the alarm stops. My eyes, however, remain wide open. The sun reflects into my flat from the face of the glass office building across the street. I watch the light shift as the hours pass, until I sit upright. A sharp tingling erupts on the left side of my chest. I rush to the mirror in the windowless bathroom, and in the paltry lighting, I see it—a swollen lymph node above my ribs, bulbous and squishy underneath my fingertips. As more hours pass, a rash of pink blotches bursts through my freckles.

Why is it taking so bloody long for this laptop to load? I smash my palm onto the desk.

With the web browser opened, I click on a page from the NHS entitled, "HIV and AIDS—Symptoms." The flu-like symptoms are signs that my body fights a battle for its life. I read further because it gives some vague sense that I'm still in control. My immune system musters all its strength to eliminate this invader. T cells, B cells, and macrophages are deployed at full power, and I suffer with a fever and rash in the hopes of continuing to live.

The page, however, also warns that these symptoms are unspecific, and could mean flu. Wasn't there a twat at the office who came to work feverish?

It's now Sunday. I hadn't bothered to bathe after coming home, and yesterday's half-eaten pizza gathers more dust by the foot of the bed. I'd been so daft. I wallow in self-hatred. How could I have been so stupid and utterly reckless after all the books and movies I've read about AIDS in the nineties? Yet this resentment leads to thoughts of Orhan's body, and I feel my cock stiffen—and despise myself even further.

I need to get out, to distract myself with other people, and forget. If I were back in London, there'd be a gaggle of other nancy boys I could join for early-evening cocktails—even if that meant a forty-minute ride on the Tube. But here in Berlin after three weeks, I only have contacts with investors. Except for one person. I dial his phone number.

"Hey Alex," I say. "How are you?"

"Still hung over," he says, "but otherwise functional. What's up?"

"I'm bored out of my mind from work," I say, "and was wondering whether you'd be free and fancy a drinkette?"

"Right now?"

"If you're free," I say.

"My new roommate moved in Friday," Alex says. "Saturday was a Swedish shopping spree and we're still assembling shelves and other shit."

I let out a moan. He's busy. Try not to sound too despondent, Timothy.

"What the fuck was that explosion? Wait a sec." I hear Alex press the phone against his shirt, and there is muffled discussion. "Kay popped open a bottle of Rotkäppchen, and we've had enough for one day. You're welcome to join. Kay's Canadian, so we can have an Anglo threesome."

"It'd be prudish of me to decline a threesome," I say. "Where are you located?"

We clarify details. I shower, and avoid shaving because I just can't look at the rash below my collarbone. I need to be the most bubbly me, so I pour a finger of whiskey in a used glass and gulp it down. My father would chide me that it's improper not to savour a drink that's aged twenty years, but he isn't here. I head out and onto the U-Bahn.

From the U-Bahn station, I stop off at a convenience store before I walk to Alex's place. He lives in an old turn-of-the-1900s building with five floors and ornate balconies for the front facade. I push the button for "Anders/Hung" and the main door buzzes open. There's no elevator and I walk up and up and up and up until I see the wooden door left ajar. I enter the flat. It amazes me how quickly Americans welcome a stranger into their homes even if it is slightly dreadful inside. The flat certainly looks like someone has recently moved in with boxes piled high, but there's also a layer of dust that dates from before Friday.

"Welcome Timothy," Alex says. He opens his arms for a hug, and I hug him back.

"Since you were celebrating with Rotkäppchen," I say, "I brought a couple of bottles to contribute. You must be Canadian Kay."

"From cold and humble Winnipeg," he says as we hug.

"Isn't Winnie the Pooh's name inspired by Winnipeg?" I ask.

He takes my jacket. "It is. There's even a statue at the zoo."

"Winnipeg is on the map," I say. I hope he doesn't see me as a snobbish Londoner.

Kay walks to the kitchen. "Interesting tidbit: I've seen tons of weather reports in various countries, and whenever they show North America, they always show Winnipeg. I think it's because there's no other city around it for a thousand kilometers, and this spooks the weather reporters."

We have three glasses of sekt filled to the brim. I suppose when one celebrates with four-euro bottles of bubbly, it's all about quantity. "*Prost*," Kay says.

"Well, cheers and *prost*," I say and raise my glass. "Are you new to Berlin like myself?"

"I've been in Berlin for five years," he says. "But boyfriend drama is making me move."

"Easier to organize a sex date when you don't have a jealous boyfriend looking over your shoulder," Alex says. We head to the living room.

"Is that something you two have agreed upon in the rental contract?" I say after a sip. "That random boys will be walking through those doors and depositing their DNA somewhere in the, um, apartment?" I must speak American English.

"The boyfriend took all the jewels in the divorce," Kay says. "I'm not worried about being robbed if Alex entices a boy over."

"Or girl," the bearded Alex says. "I'm actually bisexual."

"Truly, darling?" I say as I purse my lips. "Or is Bitown just a stopover until you catch the next train service to Gayville?"

"The discos are so much better in Gayville," Kay says. "Plus you can eat gluten-free cupcakes."

Alex suddenly gets up. "Assholes. I'm going to piss."

When Alex is out of the room, Kay asks, "Do you think he's really angry at us?"

"This is only the second time I've met him, so I haven't a clue."

Kay then looks at me. "You're new to Berlin. Has the city changed you yet?"

"How do you mean?" I say.

"In a city so debauched and raunchy it's debaucherous," Kay continues, "where the clubs stay open for days, beer is cheaper than cola, and you can fuck a guy at home before going to the sex party and getting gang-banged in a sling—does it change a person?"

The image of Orhan followed by the rash on my body floods my mind, and I feel my entire body grow hot. Would I have done that in London?

"I'm still new to Berlin," I say, "But it changes you like a potted plant that grows to the shape of its container. Or one of those outrageously priced square watermelons from Japan."

Kay gulps down more sekt, looking away into the distance as if he's deliberating. "Those who chose to live in Berlin," he says, "aren't innocent and naive. Those who choose to stay are happy to be n the poor but sexy capital. I don't think Berlin changes you. The city just awakens a part of you that was already there."

"You chose to stay," I say.

"I did," he says, and winks. "Will you?"

I stare at Kay through the translucent fizz of the glass. From the kitchen, I hear Alex pop open another. "To my blossoming debauchery then," I say and down the rest of my glass. I can't help myself. After three glasses, this Rotkäppchen is splendid.

The party continues at the obscenely named Ficken 3000, at a Sunday event called Pork. *Ficken* was one of the first words in German I learned, and I dare not imagine the protests that would converge in any other city at a bar named "Fucking 3000." It has the look of a 1990s bar, with black tables, a mirror as one wall, and a banner in red LED lights flashing drink specials. I love tacky when tacky's done right.

The cellar has even more love—porn on the telly, and a dark room with men fucking. This definitely takes fucking to the next level.

I climb down the spiral staircase and decide to sit on a fluffy black leather couch in front of a screen playing porn. Of course I think about my mistake, my terrible mistake, but lust compels me. My erection rages against my trousers, but I'm also hyperventilating. I know that once I leave this first chamber, there is another world in the darkness. My hands shake and I can barely inhale from my fag. Of course I'm nervous. I'm a dark room virgin, and despite all the schooling I have undertaken, no classes at Oxford prepared me for this. No class, but there was that rarely frequented WC of the English faculty also located in the building's cellar. I throw the butt onto the ground and walk into the darkness.

After my eyes adjust, it's not absolute blackness, just poorly lit with shadows hiding the filth. I wander through the place, at first only observing with more than my eyes. In the darkness punctuated by the silhouettes of other men, my nose flares to inhale the scents of man musk, cigarette smoke, and the lingering smell of poppers.

A score of men stand and linger. There is a blond twink with a poor excuse for a beard, and when a fat old man lingers too closely, the twink gazes away. Denied. In another corner, a bear in dark clothes stands in front of one of the few sources of light, an indoor window to the first room with the porn. He appears as a massive, bulging shadow. Another bear walks past, and they make eye contact. The bear mating call is answered. I hear the sound of a belt being unbuckled, a zip's teeth being drawn slowly open, and the soft thud of knees on the ground from the second bear. A moment later, his head bobs in front of the other man's crotch. Sex is that easy below in a bar's basement.

I walk to another chamber. Enough light enters this room for me to discern the face of a short but well-built man—his features are stern although his face is narrow, he has a beard, and he looks Middle Eastern. I approach him from the side, and look at him. He doesn't look away.

He unbuckles his belt. That clinking resounds among the shadows, and the sight of his cock entices me and my mouth waters in anticipation. He has a massive member, so massive and long that it curves downward under its own weight.

I have a brief moment to taste his cock before he fucks my mouth and gags me. He's rough and I struggle to breathe between thrusts. He moans, "*Du Sau, du Sau...*" My cock is erect and I resent myself that I'm hard from his oral abuse.

He takes himself out only so he can flip me around and pull my trousers down, pants and all. I feel his cock nudge against me, already lubed with my saliva. It tingles, and I want him inside. "*Fick mich.*" My breaths are heavy. I wait and feel my insides relax.

"*Scheiße,*" the big-dicked man says. He's coming already, and I can feel the sticky heat on my perineum and inner thighs. Before I can even turn around and catch my breath, his belt clinks frantically like his disappearing footsteps. I am left bare-cheeked. I pull up my trousers and feel cum dribble on my fingers. Unlike everything else here, it smells fresh and clean. I'm tempted to taste it, but smear it on the wall instead.

I head upstairs, gripping the railings tightly. Alex and Kay are where I left them, but their beers are almost empty. Do I tell them what happened?

"I hope you enjoyed yourself, and took fucking to the next level," Alex says.

"I'll take a cab back to Mitte," I say.

"Come on, one more drink," Alex says. "My treat."

"Fine, if you're buying." I rub stickiness from my fingertips with the inside of my trouser pocket.

I sit down. When the beers are almost finished, Kay offers to buy the next round. This is when another dark-haired man enters the bar and stares at me as he walks past towards the cellar. I feel another stirring. But this time, I whisper, "Do you have a condom?"

Kay hands me one. I bolt downstairs without waiting for the next round.

4. Thomas

Today is my first time at a medical conference, and I present my poster, "High prevalence of genetic markers DIKY3 and DIKY5 in patients hospitalized for major depression." The suit is Hugo Boss, my one and only suit, but I had bought it when I had thirty kilos more, and it is simply too big. Drinking before 16h should not be done, but at this moment, I wonder what is the point of "should." A drink would calm me.

The poster session is at a large hall of the congress. A woman with glasses even thicker than mine stares at the poster. The printing job is last minute. Whereas the other posters from drug companies are glossy and printed on huge poster paper, my poster is printed on A4 sheets pinned together to regulation size like a jigsaw puzzle. Where is she from? Will she ask a question? She reaches the end, scrunches her nose, and then moves on.

It was a terrible morning. I cut myself shaving below the jaw line. There is a pink bandage covering it, and I am certain that everyone who passes by can see it. I mean everyone. I am the tallest person in this room, so when people look up to talk to me, they will see a two-meter giant of a man who shaves like a teenage boy.

It is 15h30 and one of the drug companies sets up a wine reception. Is that allowed? The conference program states that evening receptions should start no earlier than 17h.

"How did you hone in on the DIKY genes?" says someone.

I look down. There's an Asian man in a neat suit and rimless glasses smiling at me. He has a preppy, safe-to-take-home-to-your-parents appearance, but his jaw is square and strong. I don't see that often—and I have forgotten his question.

"Your question again please?" I say.

"How did you know to look for these particular genes in the millions of genes on a human DNA, Dr. Urning?" he says and smiles.

"The genes are linked to serotonin receptor expression," I say. "A paper had published that earlier." Although not that many people ask questions about the poster, many ask questions that are answered in the poster. *Can't you read?* I want to say. There are personality types, and a major determinant is whether a person is extroverted or introverted. I am introverted. It exhausts me to be with new people, especially if they are superficial and can't talk about anything important.

"It's a paper you wrote," the man says. "I find it remarkable that you could find the needle in the haystack." He actually read the citations list?

"The honest truth is that my mother has severe depression, and out of plain curiosity I got my family's genome sequenced," I say. "After countless hours of scanning, one late night I noticed a sequence that only my mother had and not me, my father, or my brother." I can't think of any other answer to give.

"This fascinates me about science," the man says. "How scientists get these hunches. In your case, a personal connection."

I nod. I don't mention how severe my mother's depression was, and how awful it was to be motherless for weeks on end. I look at his name tag. "Kay Hung from CoExcel in Berlin?" I say.

"Yes, and I had to write some creative emails to get approval to be here," he says while he extends his hand. "Dr. Urning, nice to meet you."

"Just call me Thomas," I say as I shake it. "I haven't gotten my PhD yet." Asian and in Berlin? I want to ask where he really comes from but he continues.

"I know some of the people at the GKS booth, the ones sponsoring the wine reception," Kay says. "I can probably get us a glass now. Do you want to be bad and leave your poster?"

"Yes," I say, before adding, "Everything is online now anyway." Being with this Kay from CoExcel makes me want to break the rules.

Wine leads to dinner.

At first, dinner is new and interesting. I meet pharmaceutical men and women in suits, and medical academics in sweaters. The food and wine is paid for, and I'm glad because one meal in this restaurant costs enough for a week's worth of groceries. I order steak. The conversation centers around safe heterosexual topics—work, children, and more work. The most interesting topics were vacation spots, but I have nothing to contribute. I've never traveled farther than Amsterdam. I grow bored.

Kay touches my shoulder when people order coffee. "We should go," he says. Where? But Kay says to the table, "Dinner was wonderful. Thank you, but Thomas and I are expected somewhere." We leave the restaurant without paying anything, and hail a taxi.

In the car, I ask, "Where are we expected?"

"Someplace gay," he says. He squeezes my hand. How did he know?

We enter a smoky gay bar in Prenzl'berg. On a Wednesday evening, Marietta is packed with clean-cut and respectable gays. The crowd is mostly German, and although I am still the tallest, the men here are taller than at the international men at the congress. Kay comes back with a *Kristalweizen*, and hands it to me. It is the first drink we've had to pay for.

"How did you know I was gay?" I say.

"You were a tough one," Kay says. "I asked my standard questions—why did you move to Berlin, what do you think about Berlin's nightlife, or what do you for fun—my gaydar wasn't going off." My answers were the following—PhD, never been, video games. "But then you were talking to my female colleague and a cute guy walked past, you looked at him like she was invisible." Oh yes, him, I remember. He was a dark-haired Mediterranean man with bulging biceps, a waiter for another table. "And then I asked what your favorite movie was. That was irrefutable evidence," he says.

"Chicago?" I say.

"You might as well have said, 'My favorite movie is Buttsex.'" We clink glasses, and in unison, say, "and all that jazz." It surprises me how comfortable I feel doing that.

I excuse myself to go to the toilet. Kay isn't like other Asians I've met. The Asians I have met growing up in Hannover were shy and seemed as though they were never truly comfortable in Germany, even if they spoke perfect German. Is it different for Asians growing up in Canada?

As I urinate, a guy uses the urinal beside me. He's skinny and twenty centimeters shorter than me. He cocks his head down to stare at my penis.

"That's big," he says. Did he really say that? "I love to suck on a big dick. Want to go to the stall and I'll give you a fantastic blow job?"

I shove my penis back into my pants. I'm in such a hurry I don't even flick the last drops of urine off. He frowns, shrugs his shoulders, and continues to piss as if nothing happened.

I rush out of the bathroom. When I sit down, I say, "You wouldn't believe what happened to me. A guy—" I struggle to find the best English word, "propositioned me at the urinals."

"How exactly did he 'proposition' you?" Kay says while he raises one eyebrow.

"He was urinating beside me, and commented on my penis," I say. Why is this important?

Kay smiles and finishes his beer. "At least he waited until you were in the bathroom. Last summer, there were two guys here. One was pulling his pants down on the street and showing off his cock, and another guy pulling down his shorts to show his ass. Like baboons on the African Savannah disturbing the peace of a gay pride of lions."

"This is Berlin gay nightlife, or?" I say.

"It can be," Kay says. "But I think those guys weren't from the area, because the regulars were shocked, and one guy whispered, 'We don't do this in Prenzlauer Berg. There are children here.' If only he knew that the children's café down the street was once a sex club."

My eyes stare at the guy as he leaves the toilet and passes by us while acting completely normal, as if he didn't offer me a blowjob.

"You have a deer-in-the-headlights look," Kay says.

"I don't understand this expression," I say.

"Wide-eyed and shocked," he says. "I'm sure this didn't happen in Hannover, but I would take it as a compliment, since he's a pretty good-looking guy. I'm not surprised. You're a good-looking guy yourself."

I cross my arms across my chest. There's a mirror across from us, one of those brass-rimmed mirrors that my grandmother had and we threw out when she passed away. "I know I'm tall, but good-looking? Look at my eyes." They bulge out of their sockets from the magnification of my thick lenses.

"You may need contacts for that," Kay says. What does he mean by 'may'? "Stand up Thomas. I want to check something."

I do as told. I am still wearing my suit and say after inhaling the thick cigarette air, I say, "I will need to dry clean this."

"And have some tailoring done." Kay reaches to touch my shoulders. "But the shoulders fit, and the arm length is still good. You just need to reduce it around the waist, and that isn't expensive to do. Open your blazer." I do. "You could probably also get the waist of your pants narrowed. They wouldn't fit perfectly, but it would look a lot better."

My beer is finished, and Kay wants to take a taxi to drop me off. But we live in opposite directions, so it doesn't make sense. I say I will take public transport. How does one say goodbye in these mixed business and social situations?

I reach my hand out for a handshake. "I think we're past that," he says. "Gay artists are a dime a dozen, but gay scientists are rare indeed—we have to stick together." He opens his arms for a hug. I bend down to hug him, and am surprised that I can feel his pecs through his shirt.

Kay touches my chin. It tingles, and my face feels hot. "Your bandage was falling off," he says. He waves goodbye.

Later that night, when I step out of the shower, I look at myself in the mirror. Good-looking? I take off my glasses, but when I get close enough to the mirror to see my features clearly, all I can see are parts of my face. My nose is not bad, but face? I will have to trust Kay on this one.

I put on my glasses and look at my body. Broad shoulders. I have blond hair everywhere, although it's odd that my chest hair is darker than the rest of my body. I still have stretch marks around my armpits and belly from when I was fat, but at least the skin doesn't sag.

I look further down. One good thing about walking around while fat is that my legs got a good work out, and they still look like tree trunks. Then there is my cock. Big? Of course I measured my dick before, but it wasn't gigantic, only bigger than average. But my body was something that always disappointed me, and I tried my best to avoid looking at myself. Until now.

I haven't measured since losing weight, and now it does look bigger. It dangles low. I take a tape measure from a drawer. I look down, see my thighs, hold my cock in my left hand, and press the yellow tape measure against it with my right. Soft and flaccid, I measure seventeen centimeters. Wasn't the average erect penis in Germany fifteen?

I am big. As I realize this, the blood rushes to my dick, engorges in the palm of my hand, and it protrudes from my body like a tree branch. My eyes scan up on the tape measure— seventeen, eighteen, twenty, twenty-one point seven. Round up to twenty-two. Losing pubic fat gave me three extra centimeters. The foreskin doesn't retract, so it looks like the end of a sausage link. A *Blutwurst*. As I stand and stare at myself, I jerk off and roar when the orgasm erupts. My semen makes a mess of the mirror. I'm ashamed, like how I felt this morning cutting myself. I touch the wound. Kay touched me here. It tingles.

5. Kay

My favourite bar is closing. Sharon Stonewall is a casualty of the ever-increasing rents in a gentrifying Mitte, and as implied by the name, is a campy gay bar with divas as decor. Drawn on walls painted pink, in chalk lines pixelated by the rough drywall surface, is the eerie portrait of Sharon Stone. The face looks like her, and it's not bad, but something's off. It's the eyes. The whites encircle the irises like halos, like she's days into a cocaine binge. Cray-cray crazy.

For her last weekend, Sharon goes all out with half-priced booze to clear the liquor cabinet. Mike and I arrived here early, too early for anything good to happen. "What's Queer Beer going to do once this place closes?" Mike says.

"I hope the organizers find another bar," I say. Mike and I met at Queer Beer, a party for expats, and bonded as gaysians. I knew he was Canadian when I asked him what his favourite grade in high school was. Americans say "eleventh grade" but Canadians say "grade eleven."

Mike leans on my shoulder for support, holding his pink drink with his left hand since his right is still in its cast. Cranberry-something pink. "Queer Beer saved my sex life. I was living in Bremen for six months before I moved to Berlin. I had no luck approaching German guys," he says.

"Flirting with a German guy is like playing fetch with a lazy dog," I say. "You throw the tennis ball and he only stares as the green glob bounces down the driveway."

"It'll be English every day in Canada," Mike says with a smile. He has already moved out of his room, and is fully packed for tomorrow's flight to Vancouver. He has been sleeping on our couch.

"Even in Hongcouver?" I say.

"Especially in Hongcouver," he says.

I had invited the guys here. Alex had been trimming his shaggy beard as I passed the open bathroom door, and had told me over the shaver's buzz, "I may show up if my date sucks, but if you're a real friend, you'll hope that I don't show the fuck up." He gave me a sheepish grin. Timothy had said he'd come, but I hadn't heard from Thomas.

As always, the music at Sharon's is loud. Tonight it's even louder than usual, with speakers distorting Kylie's pop voice. The bartender is a blond twink wearing a pink tank top, and he extends his arm outward to grasp at something invisible.

When the twink's arm drops, I see the entrance. Timothy walks in. A draft blows his brown coat, and it billows around him like a superhero's cape. Or a supervillain's. Alex follows behind, sporting a leather jacket with the collar turned up around his neck. The crowd parts and opens a path toward us.

"Gentlemen," I say and hug Timothy and Alex in turn. They greet Mike.

"I've had to endure a taxi ride without a drink," Timothy says. "This round is mine. Beers for all?"

I gulp the rest of my beer, and we all nod. "Alex, should I be worried that you're here and you've lost your mojo?" I say.

"I've still got it," Alex says. "He was hot. Full lion-mane beard. But he also had terrible halitosis."

"So you made a quick getaway?" Mike says.

"Yes, but only after he sucked my dick," Alex says.

"Was that such a great idea?" I say. "You probably have halitosis dick right now."

Alex's nose and mouth twist to one side in disgust. "Excuse me a moment," he says. "I'm going to freshen up."

Timothy arrives with beers. I take one and say, "We shouldn't wait for Alex. He's washing his dick in the bathroom because he's a considerate gentleman."

"Cheers," Timothy says and stares at Mike's pink glass before clinking bottle-to-bottle with mine and mine alone. "Aren't we all gentlemen?" he says. "I'm freshly prepared for any encounter tonight."

I toast Mike, and whisper, "We probably shouldn't have eaten Chinese. And we definitely shouldn't have ordered the squid dumplings."

"I've already resigned myself to a sexless future after I get fat from too many carbs," Mike says.

Alex returns and downs his beer then says, "I hope I didn't miss anything important."

"We were talking about sex," I say. "So you didn't." We chatter and babble about the crowd but before long, though I'm not sure how late it is, I struggle to keep my eyes open.

"Wake up, Kay," Alex says as he jabs an elbow into me.

I glance at my watch. It's midnight. "Can you watch my beer? It's my turn to head downstairs," I say and wonder whether I should go home as I descend the stairs to the basement bathroom. I piss and flush.

I then wash my hands and I see my tired reflection in the mirror. I'm tired, really tired. I should go home. I ascend the stairs to the party that's pop music. Timothy and Alex are chatting with each other, and Mike is at the other side of the bar with two blond Americans wearing glasses.

Timothy hands me the beer. "Bottoms up," he says.

"*Prost!*" I say and down the rest of it. Mike returns.

"This bar's too pink with too many twinks," Timothy says. "There's no one here I'd fuck. Gentlemen, time spice things up?"

"It's Snax tonight," Alex says.

"What's that?" Mike says.

"A big fetish party where Lab and Berghain are connected," Alex says. "Men only."

"Would that mean even my prissy ass could get into Berghain?" Timothy asks. Alex nods. "Good. I tried twice already, and was denied entry both times by that eight-foot-tall dragon of a bouncer."

"And what fetish are you wearing?" I say.

Timothy lifts up his shirt and pulls up the thick red strap of his jock. "That's a thing, isn't it?" he says. Alex and I nod.

"Do you need a Red Bull?" Alex asks me.

For some reason, I'm starting to have more energy. "No. Second wind," I say. Not second wind—second horniness. I jerked off already today yet I want more. A rumbling vibrates my crotch, and I answer my phone with a peek at the caller ID. "Hey Thomas."

"I'm sorry I did not call back earlier," he says. "Are you still at Sharon Stonewall?"

"We are, but we're going to head to the party at Berghain," I say. "What have you been up to?"

"Just in my apartment," Thomas says. That's a poor excuse for a late reply, but he adds, "I was trying to put in contact lenses and they weren't going in. It took me two hours, and now that they're in, I'm afraid it's going to take another two hours to take them out. My fingers are too big to do this."

"You might as well head out," I say. "Why don't you meet us at the entrance to Berghain?"

"OK," he says. "See you later." He hangs up.

"Thomas is going to join us," I say to cheers from the others. "Our token German!"

"Considering how tall he is, he counts as two, doesn't he?" Timothy adds.

As we head out and wait for a taxi, Mike says to me, "You go on and enjoy tonight. I'm going back to your place. I don't want to be too hung over for my flight tomorrow."

"As long as you promise to wake me up before you leave, hung over or not," I say. We hug, and he walks off toward the U-Bahn.

When we're inside the taxi and on our way, Timothy asks me, "How are you feeling, Kay?"

"Good," I say. "I want to dance the night away."

"Just dance?" Alex asks. "And I'm only going to meet friends and chill."

I rarely take a cab to get anywhere since the U-Bahn network is extensive, but whenever I do, I'm amazed at Berlin's beauty. We pass Alexanderplatz and the former East's TV tower, with its top resembling a disco ball. Even at night it glitters. Around the area, government officials planned the buildings as a showcase for Soviet architecture, and there is something beautiful in the repetition of simple windows stacked one on top of another like blocks in a game of Tetris. The lights mask the emptiness of the buildings inside—a hallmark of Berlin, where communist-era buildings stand unused because of walls insulated with asbestos.

We head deeper into the East. In the late 1800s, factories lined the banks of the Spree River, and after 1945, the northern part was sectioned off in communist Berlin. As opposed to Alexanderplatz, there was no grand government plan here, so it looks like an architecture student puked up schemes for these streets, with factories ruined by Allied bombing, nineteenth-century homes destroyed to build the Wall, and massive communist apartment blocks mixed in with capitalist big-box stores that rushed in after 1989.

At the center of this mess is a former power station turned club. I see the massive concrete edifice through the taxi front window. I'm not a size queen normally, but Berghain is massive and industrial like a German *Fabrik* would be. I'm impressed.

We get out of the taxi, and walk the long dirt path to Berghain's main entrance. No billboard is displayed because Berghain needs none. Normally there would be a massive line of hopeful Berliners and tourists trying to get into the hottest club in Europe. Though the line usually of men and women stretches a city block, it takes only twenty minutes to reach the front because the bouncer rejects everyone but a select few who know the secret of getting in.

Tonight, the line comprises only men. This weekend, we know the secret. Snax is a fetish party where men from all over the world descend on Berlin in leather, rubber, or nothing but boots. We don't use the main entrance but we go around the side where we wait in a deep corridor painted black, with the words "LAB.ORATORY" in red. Standing in line with hundreds of other men, I realize this party is a big fucking deal.

I text Thomas that we're in line and he should find us.

As we wait, Alex laments that we didn't stop off at a *Späti* and buy a pack of gum and some beers for the wait. "But that would make us look common," Timothy says.

"Who gives a fuck," Alex says. "I want to be drunk."

We're not the last in line anymore, and I see a straight couple in their forties walk past, scanning the partygoers' faces in confusion. They leave without trying to get in our line and turn the corner to where the main entrance would be, if it weren't for Snax.

They're back a few moments later. The woman says hesitantly to the gay guy behind us, "Do you speak German?" In the German capital where a third of Berliners aren't Germans and there are countless hordes of tourists on any given day, this is a legitimate way to start a conversation.

"Yes," comes a high-pitched reply from a man who looks much gruffer than his voice would suggest.

"Is this the line for Berghain?" she says.

"No," he gay man says. This is the beauty of dealing with Germans in German —one answers only the question posed, nothing more.

"What party is this, then?" she says. Only she is asking, and I wonder whether she or her guy has noticed that only men wait in line.

"Snax," the gay man says.

"What's Snax?"

There's a sigh. "If you need to ask what Snax is, this isn't the party for you," the guy behind me says. "The entrance to Berghain or Panorama Bar is around the corner. This line is only for men, if you haven't noticed."

The woman gasps, apologizes for disturbing, and rushes away, holding onto her man's hand very tightly.

"When a couple in their forties is looking for Berghain," I whisper, "you know the club is getting mainstream."

"They're not from Berlin," Alex says.

A few minutes later I feel a tap on my shoulder. I turn around and have to look up. "Hey Thomas," I say. "Glad you could make it." Thomas isn't wearing his thick glasses, and without them he's handsome in very German way—blond, blue-eyed, and square-jawed. He's clean-shaven.

"Hey Kay," he says and bends down to hug. I'm aware of how good his body feels, and he smells like freshly laundered clothes.

I realize I've been silent for too long. "How do the contacts feel?" I ask.

"Uncomfortable," he says. "My eyes feel itchy, and I have to keep massaging them every now and then."

"At this party, be careful about touching your eyes," I say.

Thomas' brows rise. "What do you mean?" he says. Even though he looks more like a Berliner than me, I've been in the city longer than he has.

Alex explains. "If you want to dance, there's an upstairs dance floor the size of an airplane hangar. If you want to have sex, and the sleaziest sex you can imagine, well, there's a never-ending Alice-in-Wonderland maze for that too."

When we enter, we each grab a giant polyvinyl bag to store our stuff. We sit on benches and change. I wasn't necessarily planning on going to this party, but thank the morning divas that I decided to wear my sexy underwear today. I tuck condoms and lube in my sock; like a gay credit card, I never leave home without them. As I'm stuffing the rest of my clothes into the bag, I check out two men across from me. One is a muscular guy wearing leather pants, the other a tall twink in athletic shorts and sneakers with hairless legs. Seeing me staring, he says defiantly, "Sportswear is a legitimate fetish," and storms off.

I hear you, sister. Those rugby shorts, knee-high socks, and pecs bulging through a tight jersey are legitimately sexy. Actually, staring at all the men changing is sexy, and my mind wanders to when I'm in the locker room of the gym and stealing discreet glances, but here, I don't have to be discreet. By entering Lab, as gay and bisexual men, we are given and have given permission to gaze.

Timothy sashays in front of us in his black boots and red jock. "What do you think, gentlemen?" he says.

"Looks like a baby's bum," I say. "Which is surprising, considering how much mileage you've gotten out of that thing."

Timothy caresses one cheek then says, "A daily skin-care regime shouldn't be just for your face."

Alex seems to have anticipated the possibility of going to Snax this weekend, because he's wearing a black leather harness over his hairless chest. When Thomas joins us, he has taken off his jacket, but still has his shirt and jeans on. He looks at us with unflinching eyes.

"Darling, you could be going to church in that outfit," Timothy says. A man in his sixties walks past us completely naked in all his sagging glory, belly, tits, and balls. "Granted, you don't have that nude."

"At least take off your shirt," I say.

Thomas crosses his arms.

"I thought Germans were supposed to be OK with nudity and their FKK," Alex says.

"Not all Germans," Thomas says. "I'm from Hannover.'

"How about this?" I say. I begin to lift his shirt, and he doesn't stop me. "You hook your T-shirt into your belt, and if later you don't feel comfortable, you can always put it back on." I lift his white T-shirt past his belly button, and he gives in, pulling it off completely himself. His torso looks like something from one of those 1950s physique magazines—hairy and barrel-chested with a bit of a gut.

"I don't have a body like you," Thomas says to me, "so I'm not used to showing it. But OK. I can agree to this."

We wait in line to drop off our bags. The guy behind the counter scrawls a number in black marker onto each of our shoulders in turn. When the guy marks my shoulder, the marker's felt tip presses into my deltoid and I feel as if I've been branded like a piece of meat. As we head to the bar, I say, "Whoever got 69 has the easiest pick-up line ever."

"Considering I have 2124," Alex adds, "he was also here way too early."

We buy beers and gather near the bar. "Since it's Thomas' first time," I say, "we should each toast to something. I toast to the party never ending."

"To self-discovery," Thomas says.

"To forgetting all our troubles," Alex adds.

"As the power bottom," Timothy says, "I hope my asshole is still intact after all of this."

Thomas downs his entire beer in less than a minute then says, "I need another. I'm not drunk like you yet."

The club is as dark as a student's basement apartment. We meander through a maze of shadowy tunnels to arrive at a green-lit room with a dance floor and another bar. Moans erupt from black crevices hidden by concrete.

"A few pointers to the uninitiated," I say to Thomas. "Early on, men walk around and check things out. There's always the hope that someone better is around the corner, and no one wants to commit. Later on, desperation sets in, and it becomes a free-for-all. Get close, and if he doesn't move away, start touching."

"It's a bit more complicated than that," Alex adds. "But that's the gist of it."

"Timothy, you could just crouch on all fours and present your assets like a stock portfolio," I say.

"Is this the main dance floor?" Thomas asks. "It's not as large as I had imagined."

"You get the next round and we'll show you more," Alex says.

Which beer are we on now? We walk past the dark corner where faceless bottoms are on all fours, asses lined in a row like loaves of bread at the neighbourhood bakery.

"Is he getting fisted?" Thomas says.

"Worse things happen here," I say.

We head for the main chamber where a giant steel stairwell leads upward to thumping music. Berghain's main dance hall is high above us and we climb the wide metal stairs. Each silver-steel grate reverberates with every heavy step up we take. The beat grows louder the higher we go, and the scent of sweat grows thicker as we rise. Our ascension to techno heaven booms with pungent notes.

We reach the top and the orgy of men. Sometimes, the hype deserves the hype. The hall is the size of a church with giant speakers overlooking the housands of shirtless men like a crucified Jesus. We merge with the other men, and together, our near naked bodies dance while our hands supplicate to the rhythm. I do and feel the music. Unlike other clubs that pretend to be cool and play music too loud for their speakers in a distorted mess, the speakers at Berghain pump out techno that's loud but clean. Null distortion. The bass resonates deep within my thorax, through the muscles of my pecs and through my ribcage. I feel it there, that deep. Above me, lights glow and pulsate blue from the ceiling like they float in the air, as if their power emanates from space. I dance with my fellow gay and bisexual men, our naked chests heaving and sweating. Our musk and pheromones thicken the air, and I breath in to taste the pungency. I've always imagined what a gay party on steroids would be like, and this is it—thousands of men from all over the world pumped full of testosterone, drugs, or everything.

"This may be the last time we're together tonight," Alex says. At these parties, who you come with is rarely who you leave with.

"I've got to piss," I say.

"It starts already," Alex says, winking.

I head back down. Down from techno heaven to descend into the basement of LAB.ORATORY. The air is thick here, but not from dancing. I walk to the bathroom down a long corridor. At the far end, there's a shower room, and to my right the wall is lined by a row of sinks with four-litre buckets of soap dispensers. Opposite the sinks, a naked bald man lays spread eagle in a bathtub, one leg dangling over the side. Is he waiting for someone to piss on him? The answer comes when another naked man with a long flaccid cock sprays the bald man with a golden shower, and some of it ricochets to the floor. The wet floor. Wet and soiled bathroom floors disgust me and make me want to burn my shoes. Here the pungency arises from more than just urine.

The urinals in the piss room are guarded by men sat on the soiled floors with their mouths gaping open. I really need to go, but I have enough difficulty peeing with someone pissing beside me. I peek into the area with stall toilets. The line is crazy long. A door opens and three men walk out while looking very happy.

I can't wait anymore, so I go to the urinals. I think about going swimming when I was a kid, something innocent to distract me as I unzip my fly and—actually, the guy beside the urinal is kind of cute in a teddy bear way. He looks at me with big eyes, and I decide, fuck it. I pivot, and start peeing ever so slowly on his tongue and throat. This is polite etiquette, right? He holds the urine in his mouth. Like a sommelier judging a new wine vintage, he savours it, sloshes it across his palate, but in the end, spits it out.

He smiles, and I say, "Thanks."

"No, thank you," he says. I zip up and leave.

A bull of a man walks down the corridor, his skin tinted crimson from the light. His back is a massive expanse of muscle, his arms thick and covered in black-inked swirls. The tattoo surges from his forearm and encircles his biceps but leaves his left shoulder bare. A perfect circle of peach skin with a single Chinese word written in its center: rabbit in red.

I follow the red rabbit, shoes sloshing through puddles, but when I turn the corner after him, he's gone. Fuck, I've lost him. But I'm horny, so I wander. Hundreds of men and dozens of flaccid cocks pass me, and in a matter of seconds I judge whether each is fuckable. Just like they judge me. I imagine the countless other men who have wandered through countless other venues in search of one memorable moment of sex—bathhouses, parks, the video stalls of adult bookstores. Tonight, I wander through them all. Am I wandering only for sex, and these men as well? Or are we hoping for something less fleeting?

I once had something less fleeting. Saturdays with Helmut on the leather couch. I had comfort while laying my head on my old lover's lap. Moments pass as I lean against a wall, and not a friend, alone in the crowd.

A muscle bear approaches me from the left. He's in his forties with a beard and shaved head. Although he has a belly, he also has huge pecs. I unbuckle my belt, and he falls on his knees. His mouth is warm, and his beard ginger, but more blond than red.

"I want to fuck you," I say. I guide him to a corner and roll a condom on my cock. His pants are assless. He's taller than me, so I push his knees in so his ass is level with my crotch. I ease myself in. He's pre-lubed. He moans *"Fick mich!"* and I grunt. I'm not the first to fuck him tonight, but the feeling of fucking and dominating this taller German man is exhilarating, like I'm a pilot in the Allied forces bombing Berlin into submission.

A crowd gathers, and I give them a show. Fuck yes, fuck yes, take my cock. I'm transfixed by his ass jiggling after each thrust. I'm close, and I fuck as furiously as his hand jerking his cock. The smell of his sweat and my sweat, and then he roars. As the scent of his cum wafts up my nostrils, I feel his sphincter squeeze around my own cock, and it's so damn tight. I erupt inside him. Fuck yes.

I'm careful with the condom when I pull out. I kiss him on his neck. I cradle the small of his back, and he turns around with a grin on his face. He kisses me on the cheek, and before I know it the crowd around me has disappeared, and he with it. My nose sniffs. I'm left with only the specter of his scent.

I should be tired. But as the parade of soft cocks flop past, I can feel myself stiffen again.

The speakers crackle, and for a moment, silence punctuates the techno. Then the music blares again, and at that exact moment, I see the bull with the red rabbit tattoo. I almost sprint toward him, but he turns a corner again.

I turn into the darknes. His face is hidden in shadow as he leans against the cement wall. He's wearing leather shorts and boots. I approach him from the side, like I'm nearing a horse or other beast. He doesn't move as I draw close, so I reach out and touch his chest. He grabs my wrists and pushes me against the concrete, and his chest heaves against my back. He's not only taller than me, he's stronger. He breathes on my neck, and my skin tingles.

"I'm going to fuck you," he grunts in German, his breath reeking of cigarettes, beer, and something fouler.

"No, I don't get fucked," I say.

He laughs. He pulls both my wrists high above me, locked tightly in his left hand. His hands are twice the size of mine. My arms grow numb from the strain and submission. With his other hand, he rips my underwear down past my knees.

"What a sexy tiny ass," he says. His cock slides between my cheeks. It's long and skinny like a worm.

Is this happening to me? Is this what I want? And if not, why is my cock so hard?

He spits on his dick with a frog-like croak—and rams his cock in me. My insides tear and pain radiates from deep within.

"No! *Nein!*" I scream. His huge palm smacks my mouth closed. His violation is an assault yet as a fag, I feel I deserve this.

"*Schlampe,*" he says between ragged breaths. I focus on the grey wall, on the cracks and bubbles in the concrete, on anything but the pain. "*Du Schlampe. Deine Fotze. So eng.*" He grunts and his body convulses, each of his muscles flexed, and he pounds one last hard thrust. His orgasm splatters inside me, heat burning with pain.

When his penis shrivels and he deflates out of me, he spits in my face. He grabs me by the neck and throws me off to the side like a cigarette butt. I crash onto the dirty floor. There's too much moaning, darkness, and fucking. He struts away and no one notices.

I notice my underwear and crawl toward it. It's tattered and black with dirt. As I pull it past my calves, I realize—better naked than torn. I walk to the changing chamber with everything exposed. I try to walk normal but each step feels stiff. Past the bathroom, the maze of corridors, past the green-lit bar, past the men who stare at me, now completely naked. Finally, waiting in line for coat check, my eyes staring down my hands, I know I need all strength to say my number. I stare and see my dick, and see a white glob dangling. Did I come again? From him?

"*Nächste bitte!*" The man at coat check is skinny with a nose ring.

"2120," I manage to say in German.

"Your ticket," he says. Of course I need to present my coat-check ticket. It's in my sock, and as I bend down, intense pain radiates from my ass and rectum. I squeeze my eyes shut, and pull out the laminated ticket. He grabs it and returns with my clothes in a clear plastic bag. I sit on a bench and grab my jeans. I pull them on and stand, no longer naked. Paper towels are everywhere, and litter the ground like tumbleweeds in a western movie. My cock feels the cold metal zipper.

"Kay," Alex says in surprise. He stands beside me and touches my shoulder, his palm resting on the 2120 writ in faded black ink. His friendly touch is the most comforting feeling in the world.

"Hey," I say. I put on my shirt.

"Look at all these paper towels," he says, and rips a few sheets to wipe sweat from his chest. "I wonder what brand they use."

"What?"

"I mean," he adds, "maybe they have a sponsorship deal. Can you imagine if Zewa had a deal with Lab, and after the eight o'clock news, an ad came on that said, 'Don't use any paper towel. Use the paper towel trusted by sex clubs all over Germany.' And there were testimonials of guys saying, 'It's so absorbent I only need one sheet to wipe the cum clean from my face. It's bukkake strong!'"

"Sometimes you're very American," I say.

"How was your night?" he says without looking at me. "I fucked this guy with perfect chest hair. I'm in love." He grins but I don't grin back. We're fully dressed and head to the exit. The security guards open the door for us and say goodbye. I can't make eye contact with them.

We're outside now. It's raining. Crows caw through the pattering raindrops. I reach into my pockets. Shit—only change. I just want to go home. This is all I want in the world.

"Do you have cab fare?" I ask.

"Yeah, this weather is *Scheiße*," Alex says. A line of cabs wait outside Berghain. We get in a beige Mercedes station wagon. "I hope you didn't try to call me. My phone's been dead. I lost Timothy and Thomas. I think they're both still inside. No surprise, but Thomas was pretty popular. I saw him being worshiped by two boys of a darker persuasion."

Where did my watch go? Another thing lost. I check the time on my phone instead. It's ten in the morning. We drive past other beautiful buildings, and Alex describes another beautiful man he may be in love with. I say nothing. I can only focus on the striated pain from the fissures inside me. We arrive at the apartment, and my heart sinks when I realize that this may be my apartment with the bed I sleep in, but at a time like this, I'm not home. The smell is off.

We're inside the hallway when I remember that Mike's supposed to be here. But he isn't. There is a note where his luggage was. "Dear Kay, thanks for letting me stay the last few days. I didn't want to be late for my flight. Canada beckons me. I hope we can meet again soon. Maybe sushi on English Bay? Love, Mike."

"Have you seen my charger?" Alex yells from his room.

"It's here," I say. "Mike must have borrowed it." I take the charger to Alex. When he bends over to plug it in, his body wobbles, and he holds onto my shoulder with one hand for support.

I hear my phone ringing and head back to my room. I check it and see it's Thomas. "Hello?" I say.

"Kay? Can you help me?" he says. His voice is frantic.

"What is it?" I ask.

"I can't see," he says. "My contacts fell out, and I can't see anything. They helped me get outside, but I haven't enough euros for a taxi, and I don't have my EC card. Could you come get me and help me home?"

"OK. Wait there, and I'll pick you up. It could be more than a half hour."

"Thanks. I am really grateful Kay," he says. "I feel so lost and I'm just happy you're coming."

I walk to my underwear drawer, where I keep an emergency hundred-euro note in all its green glory. I sigh. I don't want to go out. It's not safe. But I think about the tone in Thomas' voice, and shove the large bill in my wallet. Its edges peek out. I change into a fresh pair of underwear but I don't have time to shower.

I tell Alex I'm leaving as he walks into the bathroom. When I get downstairs, the cab that dropped us off is still there. "Berghain please."

"The party there never stops, or?" he says. I nod.

Arriving, I see Thomas standing like a lighthouse as the rain soaks his hair, jacket, and jeans. I approach him. "Hey, it's Kay." I imagine he sees me as no more than a human shape with black hair. He rushes to me and places a hand on my shoulder. The rain hasn't washed away the smell of sex on him.

I wonder if he can smell sex on me. Not sex. Rape.

Back in the cab, he says, "I don't know what happened. I was in the bathroom, and my face was sweaty, so I splashed some water on my cheeks—and then everything was blurry. I started to hyperventilate, and a guy asked me what was wrong. He helped me to the exit."

We reach his place. "I'll get you to your door," I say.

The taxi driver waits. Thomas holds onto the railings of the entrance stairwell. He lives in Wedding, a neighbourhood that was in the West and has always been touted as an up-and-coming part of the city, in a 1970s building that looks anonymous from the outside. Inside, fluorescent lights reflect from dark blue floor tiles with walls painted a pale yellow—but there's an elevator, a luxury in Berlin.

The elevator is tiny, and only a sliver separates Thomas' head and the elevator's ceiling. It rumbles as it ascends, and then slides open. Thomas unlocks his door. "It smells like my apartment," he says. The right smell at the right time is comforting. He turns to me and says, "You're my hero, Kay." He bends down and kisses me on the cheek.

The right words at the right moment give strength.

"We both had eventful nights," I say. I stroke his cheek and kiss him on the lips. I taste him. His breath tastes like beer and the bodies of countless other men. "Goodbye for now."

"*Tschüss*," he says as he closes the door.

When I'm back in the cab, the driver asks me, "Back to Berghain?"

"The apartment on Lychener street," I tell him.

I call Mike. Maybe he hasn't boarded the plane yet. When he picks up, I notice the rain has stopped. "Hey Kay. I guess you had a crazy night," he says.

"I did." Two words, and I start to sob.

"What's wrong?" Mike asks.

I peek at the cab driver, but he doesn't look my way. "I feel like such a fool," I say. "There was this guy there, and he—I don't know how I let this happen, but he raped me."

"Rape?" Mike asks. My silence is his confirmation. "Did he use a condom?" More silence.

"Shit. They're boarding my row. This is terrible, and I wish I could be there for you. You're not thinking right, but the number-one priority is to get to the hospital. You told me about Post-Exposure Prophylaxis for HIV. You need that. You can't blame yourself. If you go to the hospital, you'll take control of the situation. I'll call you as soon as I land in Frankfurt."

I say goodbye. I stop my crying.

"Change in plans. Charité hospital," I say. The taxi driver nods. As the sun peeks through the clouds, we drive from West to East Berlin, past a wall that no longer exists, and through a checkpoint that once claimed lives and is now just a traffic light. A moment of red before it flashes green. We accelerate.

6. Timothy

When I stumble outside, I'm greeted by the stench of fresh air and the incessant chirping of birds. It rained recently, and all that is putrid has been washed down the gutter. Where am I? I thought I was in the city. Right, Berghain in Berlin, a city known for its greenery. What time is it? Of course my mobile's dead, but it doesn't really matter. I had no plans for the rest of the weekend.

This is less than brilliant. My hand fishes into my trouser pockets and I feel only coins. I brought a wad of blue and pink euro notes with a bit of orange mixed in, and I've got only coins left?

"Drugs, darling," I say to myself as I walk in a semblance of a direction. It's the BVG for me. I have no idea where the station exactly is, but I can see the train tracks in front of me. There's a bloody fence in the way. I decide to walk along the fence and hope for a gap to cross.

A voice inside my head wonders whether it's pitiful that I'm fumbling home alone. But between buying drugs and going to the stalls to use them, to finding a dark gentleman to shag me senseless, I knew I would not be leaving with Kay, Alex, or Thomas. Shudder. Thomas is dreadfully German. Even if I did see his humongous schlong being serviced in stereo by two enviable Mediterranean cock whores—it's not only his personality that's stiff, now is it?

Fuck—this tingling in my ass, like a company of firemen sliding down my poop shoot, is divine. Eight men fucked me. Two were from behind, and I don't remember their faces, but one of them had the largest cock of the night. Three thought I was spunkworthy, and let loose their load either in me or somewhere on my person. I came twice, and once without touching myself, from being fucked by a defined Turkish guy with an average cock thrusting like Fuck Machine 3000. I've lost count of the number of cocks in my mouth. My blood pulses with lingering euphoria—this feeling is absolute heaven, and this feeling obliterates any distressing thoughts of rashes or poor cash flows.

I cross a muddy patch littered with glass bottles. A mixed group sits around fire. An actual fire burns inside a metal drum. They listen to music from a phone. A few of them are women. Berghain rejects? "The party is still going on in Berghain," I say. I jiggle my backside for their amusement. I stop abruptly when I feel a rumbling, an undesirable byproduct of being gang-banged. I clench my arse. At least that's still intact.

"When we finish our beers," one of them says with a Spanish accent. He takes out a pack of American Spirit cigarettes.

"You've fantastic taste in cigs," I say.

He looks up at me with eyes the size of an anime cartoon. "You want one?" he asks.

"A hint of a puff, if you're being so kind," I say. Even from crappy phone speakers, the music is good. I dance and notice this Spanish man gazing at my ass. A girl with a pierced brow pours orange juice and cheap vodka into paper cups. After more than a hint of a puff, I say, "If you place your phone inside a paper cup, the sound will be much better." She looks confused, so I grab a cup and set it on the ground far away from the flames, and drop the phone inside. The paper cup amplifies the sound, and everyone cheers.

I head back to the Spanish guy. "We owe you one," he says. He sits on a rock and my crotch is at his eye level.

"Another cigarette and we'll call it even," I say. More puffs and more dancing. I wonder if Alex is still inside. The last I saw him, he was fucking a man in a sling.

I decide to test the waters. "You know there's a massive gay party this weekend at Berghain?" I ask.

"We're here for the long weekend and didn't know," dreamy-eyed

Carlos (or whatever his name is) says. He opens his mouth and wets his lips, and I swear he's salivating over my cock. Even considering the gaseous unmentionable, I'd still shove my cock in his mouth.

"I've got a stamp on my wrist," I say. "Want to go inside Berghain, warm up, do a little dancing?" I edge closer to him. Come on, bury your face in my crotch.

He suddenly gets up from the rock and pushes my chest then says, "Get away from me." Everyone else looks at us.

I throw the rest of the cigarette on the ground. "Enjoy the rest of your stay in lovely Berlin." I take a few steps and am tempted to kick the metal drum over. Instead I unclench my poop shoot by a sliver, and as the silent stench spreads, I say, "Good luck trying to get in." I walk away, and it's only when the music grows faint that I hear their groans of disgust from my silent but deadly stink bomb.

I run. There's a bridge, and then I recognize Warschauer Straße station, a busy cluster of multiple train lines, hordes of people, and a dizzying array of beer kiosks and Turkish shops. I'm acutely aware that it took a mere five minutes to run here, but it felt like a horror movie—like running down a long corridor towards a door shrinking perpetually into the distance.

Drugs, darling. Drugs.

I'll hide in the crowds. The noise around me is confusing and frustrating at once, and I imagine the voices as white specks in a snow globe being shaken by an epileptic having a seizure. Drugs, bitch.

I look back. There are scores of faces, but none belong to the Berghain rejects.

I'm famished. I count my change like someone from council housing. Five euros twenty. Brilliant. That leaves me only three euros after a BVG ticket. I crack a smile. That's all I need to get a *Döner*. As the grilled chicken laced with garlic sauce touches my lips, I feel like I'm in heaven. Wasn't I in heaven earlier? Heaven needn't exist in singularity.

I grip the handrail on my way down to the train platform towards the ticket-vending machine. *Einzelfahrschein.* The display reads "€2,40." Wait, you must be toying with me. When did they raise the bloody fare? I insert all my coins in the vain hope that I miscounted earlier, but with empty pockets, the display still asks for another twenty cents.

I contemplate my options—either I appeal to the sympathy of others, or embark on the train and take my chances.

My train arrives, and when the doors open, I risk walking in. Through speakers, the train conductor says his *"Zurück bleiben bitte"* in a disgusted tone, like he's herding school children. The *bitte* is said in half a breath, like an exasperated afterthought with no vowels.

I find a seat. One stop later, a drag queen enters and sits opposite me. It's Sunday afternoon, and no one bats an eyelash that she rides in full regalia, obviously showered but wearing last night's clothes: a white shirt and a pink miniskirt, the shirt's cartoon-rabbit face distorted by her breasts. Her hair is damp and frizzled, and without makeup, she looks haggard as she clutches her purse with outsized hands. Yet, despite the obvious outward catastrophe, she has a dominating presence, as if the sheer power of her bitch shield prevents anyone from mocking her. Perhaps it's due to her being monstrously tall.

When the doors close after the next stop, I hear the worst words one can hear in German at a moment like this: *"Die Fahrscheine, bitte."* This time, the *bitte*'s vowels are drawn out.

A twenty-something man of Turkish extraction is moving from seat to seat inspecting tickets. My heart races. At any other time, I'd relish having my heart aflutter in the company of a dark-haired gentleman. Any other bloody time.

Then the ticket controller stands beside me, and as I desperately attempt to think of an explanation in German, the guilt evident on my face, a rumble of a voice says, "He's riding with me." The dark-eyed man glances at the drag queen who produces a subscription ticket that enables another person to ride with her on weekends.

The ticket controller walks away. Now that I'm safe, I let my eyes linger on his ass.

Where are my manners? I look at the drag queen and say, "Thank you." In English, like a twat. *"Tut mir leid. Dankeschön."*

"You're welcome," she says in English.

I rise and sit beside her. "I'm Timothy."

"I'm," she says and looks at her skirt, "still in drag. I'm Heidi Klo."

"I'd like to buy you a drink," I say. "You saved me forty euros and a lot of embarrassment. I'm English, so it's almost as if you've saved me from being run over by a lorry."

"I'm often at Schwuz, so you can buy me a drink there," Heidi says. "You are gay, or?"

"Gay and a power bottom," I say. "Next stop is my stop."

"I'll be performing next Saturday," Heidi says. Heidi Klo. Maybe I'll look her up when I'm in front of my computer.

I leave the station. I walk past more communist-era buildings and a plethora of construction sites to turn down my street. It's mostly offices so on a Sunday, I'm the only one to walk among the chirping birds. I hear my footsteps and feel each step, through my leather shoes, through my socks, and deep into the soles of my feet. My skin relishes the sun's warmth. I smell the air, and it tastes clean. After an epic night with my senses heightened through sex, I feel this peaceful moment with everything, and wish I could live this forever.

When I arrive at the front steps of my flat, however, I feel empty. The feeling's worse than when I stay at airport hotels. I sleep here, but without things to call my own it's a soulless and characterless sleep. When I step into the lift, I shake my head. What am I thinking? It's the aftermath of a drug binge. I am not suffering an existential crisis. I am not suffering anything.

After a glass of water and two paracetamol tablets, I lay in my bed with my boxer briefs on. Fuck. I want to sleep, but I'm staring at the fascinating ceiling with eyes wide open. I should sleep—I have an early meeting tomorrow morning. Investors will tour the office and decide whether to increase their financial stake in the company. We need the cash.

I then remember—my chemist friend in London gave me a pack of Xanax for when I might need to calm down and sleep. I rummage through my toiletry case and find the blister pack with my condoms. Yes, I still live here like it's a hotel room.

I pop out a tablet and grab another glass of water. One tablet looks lonely and forlorn. Two tablets are in order. Maybe three. Back on the bed, I wonder where Kay ended up. I hope he appreciates the boost of energy from the G I dripped into his beer. Drugs, darling. They're wonderful.

7. Alex

I get into bed. After a night like Snax, all I want to do is sleep. I'm hung over as fuck, but I try to close my eyes. Sleep will make it better.

Buzz. Buzz. "Silent" mode can be louder than a ringtone if it's vibrating against a wooden floor. Shit. I shouldn't have plugged in my phone in my bedroom. From the side of the bed, I grab my phone. It's mom. Isn't it three in the morning there?

"Yeah, Mom?" I answer.

"I've been trying to call you all night," she says.

"I was out and the phone battery," I say and stop talking when I understand that she's frantic.

"Your dad was in an accident," she says. "It's serious. I'm in the ER." She's crying, and the rhythm of her sobbing is like a rapid drumbeat. "I'm alone here. Can you come?"

Accident? "What happened, Mom?" I ask.

"The doctors think it was a heart attack while he was driving," she says.

"OK. I'm going to find a flight and be there as soon as I can." We say goodbye, and I sit up in my bed. Everything spins.

"Kay?" I call out. He's still not back. I'm alone here, and it's depressing. I'm dizzy, everything's spinning, and all I hear is silence in the apartment. I fucking hate silence.

Nine hours of silence on the flights from TXL to AMS to ORD. By the time I get to my layover in Chicago, I've at least gotten some sleep. Flying isn't fun when hung over.

Coming back here, I always find something sad and wrong about America's airports. Even in the dump of an airport that is Berlin's Tegel, men wear suits and women wear form-flattering slacks. At Chicago's O'Hare, it's all about comfort, with everyone in sweats and sweatshirts with sports-team logos. I imagine the photos of American airports from the 1960s and wonder why we as a nation stopped trying.

After clearing customs, I switch SIM cards and turn on my phone. "Hey Mom. It's me. I just landed in Chicago. How's—"

"Why didn't you take the direct flight to Minneapolis?" she asks me.

"That flight only had business class left," I say. "And you were the one who said I could only get three thousand a month, remember?" When I booked online, it was scheduled to arrive only an hour earlier.

"Dad's still in the ER," she says. "Alex—"

The phone's dead. What the fuck is wrong with it? It was half-charged when I turned it off mid-flight.

At least today I have my wrist watch. I thought I had ninety minutes for a layover, but I've only got twenty minutes until the connecting flight takes off. Fuck, fuck, fuck! My luggage may not arrive with me, but at least I can be on the plane. I rush through the airport. I'm wearing jeans and a blazer, and as I run, my laptop bag swings back and forth, and my carry-on doesn't just squeak, it screams. But I jog every other day, so this is nothing. I can do this.

When I get to the gate, I don't see the plane. They're already showing the sign for the next flight to Winnipeg. Why is a flight to Canada in the domestic terminal? Fuck.

I go to the counter. "Hi. I was delayed from my Amsterdam flight. Could you rebook me, please?" I say but I'm still catching my breath.

"I'm sorry sir, I don't have that kind of authorization," a twink with blonde hair says. "But if you go to the customer-service desk, they'll be happy to help you."

I'm doing all I can to hold in my anger at this useless piece of shit. I walk away and make my way to the United desk, and wait in line. The woman in front of me speaks on her phone with a southern drawl, her yellow neck pillow dangling by her fat ass. Precious minutes pass, then it's my turn. "I was delayed, so I need to change my connecting flight to Minneapolis." I hand my ticket to a woman of some type of Asian descent. Diversity in America.

She takes my boarding card without a smile. I'm a Gold Medallion member. Where's that customer service, bitch? She types, and the sound of keystrokes is almost melodic unlike in Germany where people peck at the keyboard with two fingers.

This woman makes eye contact with me. "Mr. Anders, in your flight class, the 3 p.m. flight is full, but there is a seat on the 5:19 or the 7:27," she says. "Which one would you prefer?"

I look at her name tag. "Suzie, is the 3 p.m. flight really full?" I ask.

"No, Mr. Anders," she says. "But we only have Economy Plus seats or business class left for that flight. I see you have sufficient miles on your Medallion account. Would you like to be upgraded for a fee of 20,000 miles?"

I'm angry now. "What kind of customer service is this?" I yell as I grip the desk with extended arms. "It wasn't my fault that I was delayed, and..." I imagine what my mother is going through right now. She had a big fight with Dad's side of the family last Christmas, and I'm not sure whether she called them about the accident. She's by herself.

And then there's a moment when I look into Suzie's eyes and imagine what she's seeing. I look like a jerk.

"I'm sorry," I say. I retract my arms and clasp my hands together like I'm praying. "I'm upset because my father is in the emergency room. I live in Europe and am trying to make it back to Minneapolis as fast as I can. A few hours can make the difference between seeing him still alive or..." My voice trails off. I sigh and I close my eyes.

"I see that you have an American Express Platinum card," she says. "I can upgrade you to Economy Plus at no charge." She prints out a new boarding pass and hands it to me.

"Thank you," I say. We say this so often, but this time, I'm truly grateful.

"I hope for the best, Mr. Anders," Suzie says.

I walk to the gate for the 3 p.m. flight. I sit beside an electrical outlet. One good thing about America is that there are outlets everywhere. I take out my charger and travel adapter and plug in my phone. For the next five minutes, I stare at the battery icon filling up.

The battery is still full when I land. I call Mom. "I'll grab a cab and meet you at the ER. How's dad?"

"I'm still in the waiting room," she says. "Hurry."

I say goodbye and head to the taxi stand. The driver is a white guy in his fifties. I tell him to go to the University of Minnesota hospital on Riverside. In April, spring is in full bloom, and there's something beautiful in the perfectly manicured lawns and trees planted at regular intervals along the boulevard. We enter the Crosstown Highway, and in this world of vehicles, everything looks and sounds the same.

I think about Dad. Our family owns Anders Trucking, and although he had drivers, he was never home. One of the fondest memories I have of him is from when a touring production of *The Nutcracker* came through town. I was nine, and he bought me a suit for the show. Just because we had blue-collar roots didn't mean we had to stay that way, he said. Mom was too sick to join us. We drank hot apple cider during intermission, and he tucked me into bed that evening.

"Where'd you come from?" the taxi driver asks me. He has the typical Minnesota accent that I have worked very hard to wipe clean.

"Berlin," I say. "Jet lag is crazy."

"Berlin, Germany?" he says in surprise, as if I might truly mean the tiny town of Berlin, Wisconsin. "My wife's half-German but we've never been."

Distract me. "Berlin is a fun place, but different from the rest of Germany. Kind of like the drunk uncle who's an artist in a family of engineers and doctors."

"I can relate," he says. "My two brothers are dentists. I guess you live in Berlin?"

"Yes, but grew up here."

"Do you miss it here?" he says.

"No." We exit the highway. "The winters are warmer in Berlin, but if I wanted to live in a warm place, I would've moved to Los Angeles. I never seemed to fit in here, I guess. My dad was born here, but my mom moved here from San Francisco. As soon as I started looking at colleges, I couldn't wait to leave."

We are at the hospital. "It's a certain kind of person I normally take from the airport to the hospital," he says. "Pharma industry types—but you don't seem like a drug-company guy."

"No, my dad's in there," I say. I gulp down a lump in my throat.

"I figured it was something serious," he says as I hand him my credit card. He also takes out my carry-on luggage, and before handing it to me, he holds out his hand. "I wish you the best," he says.

"Thanks." I shake his hand. For a moment, I'm glad to be back in friendly Minneapolis.

I enter the ER with my luggage rolling behind me, the wheels squeaking. I hear a lot of chaotic noises. Mom sits in a corner, the only woman with jet-black hair tied back into a bun, and her face in her hands. I get close, and she looks up. No makeup. No pearls. Just puffy, red eyes. I walk closer, half afraid she'll say something. I'm late.

She stands, and when I'm close enough, she collapses into me. I almost fall back, but regain my balance. Her tears smother my neck. I feel her heart beating against my chest, and she smells tired, like a mixture of days-old Chanel Number 5 and the scent of an old lady in a retirement home.

"Is Dad gone?" I ask when she stands on her own.

She tries to dry her eyes with the sleeve of her blouse and shakes her head. I'm relieved. She sits down, and I sit down with her. "I told the doctors your dad donated a lot of money to the hospital, and he knows people on the board, so he better get the best care," she says.

A few minutes in silence, and then a doctor comes to us. She's white and in her late thirties, blonde hair in a ponytail, and very short. She's holding a tablet PC, staring at the screen. "Mrs. Anders?" She looks up from it, and notices me.

"I'm the son," I say. "Can you tell me what happened?" I look at the name—Dr. Bjornson.

She doesn't look at the notes when she speaks. "Your father had a heart attack while driving and swerved into oncoming traffic. The good news is that it wasn't a head on collision. The bad news is that your father continued to careen down a ditch. Although paramedics arrived within minutes, they had to wait for firemen to free him, which delayed treatment. Although his chest and lungs are badly injured, he has no obvious head injuries." She looks at my mom. "We've been successful in operating on Mr. Anders' lungs, and did a bypass in order to restore blood flow to the heart."

"That means?" I ask.

"He's stable, conscious, and out of immediate danger. We'll transfer him to intensive care, but the next twenty-four to forty-eight hours will be important. We have him on blood thinners, but there's been a lot of clotting and that's the danger right now."

"Can I see him?"

She nods her head. "He'll be coming out of anesthesia soon and may be groggy. Nurse Garcia will show you the way." An even shorter Hispanic man with dark curly hair walks toward us. Why are only short people taking care of my dad?

As Dr. Bjornson is about to leave, I ask, "How's the other driver?"

She seems startled by this question. I'm surprised myself that I've asked. "He was driving an old car and didn't have airbags. He was twenty-six, and died from head trauma."

As we're being led, Nurse Garcia adds, "He was an undocumented worker." We head into the room. "Your dad will have bruises on his face, but they're just superficial, from the airbag. It's shocking but they will heal." He leaves the room.

When the nurse is out of earshot, Mom whispers to me, "Why did you have to ask about the other driver?"

"I don't know," I say. Maybe this time I can see the world from the other perspective.

We close the door, and there is the familiar beep of a monitoring machine, and I feel like I'm watching an episode of Chicago Hope. But it's different in person, different when it's all attached to your own dad. The bruises cover his forehead and cheeks. He looks sick. Bandages peek out from the collar of his hospital robe, and the pink skin of his overweight six-foot-two body glistens with a layer of sweat.

"Dad?" I say. His eyes open to reveal their blue, and slowly look at me. How I've always wished I had eyes like his instead of like my mom's.

"Alex." He winces with each breath. "Thank God you're here."

"Tobias, dear," Mom says.

"Sweet Keiko," he says. She kisses him on the cheek, and I see tears coming from both of them. "I shouldn't have eaten those donuts."

"For like the last twenty years, Dad," I say.

"Why are you teasing your dad now?" she says and slaps me on the shoulder. "Dear, I called your sister, and she was yelling at me on the phone before I could even get a word in. I can't believe she's still angry—she can sure hold a grudge, but I shouldn't be so surprised, since you can too."

"Keiko, is she coming?" he asks.

"They were in Chicago for Greg's big match, but they're on their way." She looks at me, and seems to see my luggage for the first time. "You just landed. You must be hungry. I'll grab something from the cafeteria and be right back." She kisses Dad on the cheek and whispers, "I love you."

"I love you too, honey," he says.

Once alone, I ask, "Dad, can you up the monthly amount from my trust fund? Mom got all over my case about not being here earlier, but I could have if I'd bought the more expensive ticket."

"Jesus, Alex," he says. "Shut up for a sec." When I do, he continues. "I'm not out of the woods yet. What would you do if I wasn't around?"

Shit. I've never thought about it. "Help out with the business?" I say.

"The summer after your senior year," he says. "I gave you a job at dispatch and you spent more time playing on your Game Boy than learning about the business. When you dropped out of psychology at college, I offered you an entry-level management job—and you spent more time on long lunches with Todd Erikson than on learning who our key accounts were. Don't think I was so blind that I didn't know." I'm fucking embarrassed. "You can do what you want with your love life, I couldn't care less. God knows I took a lot of shit when I married Keiko, so I'm not going to do that to you. But I do care what you're going to do with your life, son."

"I like to sing," I say. I'm gripping my luggage really tight. I want to fly back to Berlin.

"You've got a great voice, and I support you in this, Alex—but remember that your trust fund comes from Anders Trucking profits, so if the business goes, or they close this tax loophole, you'll be getting a lot less."

"What do you want me to do, Dad?" I ask.

"If singing is what you really want to do, and once you graduate, you can live off it, good. But if you're going to drop out before you finish to go backpacking through South America and 'find yourself' or, I don't know, become a writer—think long and hard. You're twenty-nine and have nothing to show for it."

"I have my BA in English," I manage to say.

"Look what," he says, then breathes like he's choking, "you're doing with it."

Mom comes in with a bag of sandwiches. "Food isn't going to fix things, Mom," I say, and walk out.

My luggage squeaks as I go down the hall and out the door. Outside, I call Vicki. Her lips are luscious, and she blushes when I make her laugh really hard. I get her mailbox. "Hey Vicki. It's Alex. I'm in town for … a week maybe. Call me." I light a cigarette, but then realize that this is fucking America, and I need to be fifty feet away from the door.

Squeak, squeak. I take a drag and grin when I see a small pile of butts in the bushes vandalizing the pristinely manicured hedges. I feel my phone vibrate.

"Hey Vicki," I say. "It's great to hear your voice. The best thing about coming to Minneapolis."

"Welcome back." There are children screaming in the background. "I'm free tomorrow night. Want me to pick you up?"

"You've got Josh?" I remember what Josh looks like. He has his father's eyes.

"And two of his friends. I didn't feed them sugar, but they're still a handful. I wish I could be in France, like I've heard, and give them wine in their juice to calm them down."

"I did see a mom in Bordeaux dip a finger in her wine glass and shove it in her toddler's mouth," I say. "The toddler made a face and the whole table laughed." There's a loud crash. "You gotta go? Are you sure you can't meet now?" I want to hold her in my arms and feel her breasts pressed against me. I want to feel something soft and tender.

"I gotta go," she adds. "I'm looking forward to tomorrow."

"Tomorrow." I finish my cigarette and wish I had rented a car and could just drive. Where would I drive to? Someplace warm and sunny like Florida, where I'd get wasted drinking at the pool. Or maybe hiking in the Appalachians. Didn't Kay say that Minneapolis was the closest city to Winnipeg? So close to the border, yet I've never been to Canada. I wonder if booze is just as good there. The beer should be stronger.

I hear my dad's voice. God damn it. Squeak, squeak, squeak. I'm back in the hospital. More squeaks and then I hear the beeps of the heart monitor. Mom is holding Dad's hand, and I place my hand on theirs.

"Dad, I'm sorry," I say. For what, I'm not exactly sure. He looks up at me, very slowly this time. There's drool on the side of his mouth. "You were ..." There's a faint smile on his lips, but then there's a loud, flat, and incessant tone. Nurses rush in and push us aside. There's frantic activity like a rising crescendo. But it's too late. I've already seen it—the exact moment when his blue eyes went blank. My dad's dead.

8. Thomas

Any good experiment needs a control. In this case, I have one Gay-romeo profile named *Wissenschaftler* that shows my face and lists my hobbies, and another one with only a dick pic and my sexual interests named *SchwanzXL4U*. *SchwanzXL* was already taken. All other height and age details are the same.

Which profile will get more responses? My hypothesis is that *SchwanzXL4U* will get more.

It starts off as expected. After three days, however, the difference is shocking: five messages with *Wissenschaftler*, and one hundred twelve with *SchwanzXL4U*. Thirty percent of these messages include an unsolicited dick pic.

Yuri walks into the lab, and I quickly close the browser. What's he wearing today? He has a pastel yellow T-shirt that doesn't quite cover his stomach, so whenever he raises his hands up in the air, one sees the rainbow underwear he is wearing. Yes, we know you're gay. The janitor knows you're gay. The cafeteria staff know you're gay.

"Good morning, Doctor Urning," he says as he walks to the lab station behind mine.

"Good morning, Doctor Genkin," I say.

"I visited most interesting website last night," he says as he leans on the counter beside me. "I did not know you were gay *Wissenschaftler*."

"I don't advertise it with my clothes,but if someone asks, yes, I am gay," I say.

He leans closer to me, and I can smell the fruity and floral cologne. "Is your dick really XL and is it for me?" I lean back. He rests his chin on his hands and smiles at me with a twinkle in his eyes. "Same age and height—and there's a red towel in background of both profile pictures. Don't deny it."

"I won't, then," I say. I feel ashamed, like when my mother found the DVD *Spanish Tutors Teach Best In Bed*. "What's your profile name?"

"*Bellyshirt*," he says. "Can you believe it wasn't already taken?" He twirls around and heads to the coffee room.

I log on to the website and delete *Wissenschaftler*. I want to delete the other one, but Yuri is quick to return.

When he is by his lab station, he says, "We gay scientists must stick together." Even though we both applied for the same grant? "We should go dancing," he adds.

"I've been to Berghain," I say.

"Schwuz moved to a new location," he explains. "Hardcore Neukölln, in former warehouse. Industrial, gritty, fabulous—all at once."

Does he sound this gay in Russian? "Sure. One day."

"I know DJ on Saturday," Yuri says. "I get you on guest list."

"OK."

At 10h30, the delivery guy comes in with his trolley of mail, reagents, and things we've ordered for our latest experiments. His name is Peter, although I think he changed his name when he arrived in Germany. Peter hands me an envelope. He is unshaven today, with stubble all over his chin and jaw, and I try hard to place where he is from. I have heard he is from one of the "Stans"—Kazakhstan, Uzbekistan, Turkmenistan, or other-stan. He has brown hair that is really dark, but not East Asian dark. His eyes are thin, almost Chinese, but without the eyelid fold. He has a prominent jaw like someone European, but large cheekbones like someone Asian.

"Thank you, Peter," I say, and he quickly leaves without saying anything. That is unusual, because normally he at least says, "You're welcome."

I open the letter. It is a reminder that the presentation for the grant committee is next week.

Later, after I return from the canteen and Yuri is still chatting away at the lab technicians' table, I log into Gayromeo. I want to delete the profile, but I check the messages first. None of them are interesting. I check the visitors page, and aside from those that have left boring messages, one in particular stands out—just a chest picture, but with the intro text, "My name is Peter, and I come from Kyrgyzstan." I check his profile, and no surprise, he is a bottom. Before the timer runs out, I click on the button to "Hide my visit." Delete profile. OK. Maybe I am more private about being gay than I believed.

The next morning at 10h30 when Peter comes by to drop off mail, I can't even say thank you. Yuri isn't around. The following morning, he is early in the lab with his coffee already drunk by the time I arrive. I must say something to Peter, otherwise Yuri will know something strange is happening.

Peter does not stop by our lab. "No mail today," I say.

"All important stuff is by email," Yuri says. "Whenever I get snail mail, I know is spam. Or lab equipment. If I am awarded grant, I will get new cell line to investigate whether certain anti-HIV medications inhibit tumor growth." He is wearing a pink shirt today—it is a button-up shirt, yes, but it is pink. Not salmon, not coral, not fuchsia, but hot pink. "What will you get?"

"Computer modelling software," I say. "And a fast computer to run it." I have already illegally downloaded the software from an online student forum, but my laptop is too slow to run it.

My PhD supervisor also gave me an ultimatum: I have to make my gene discovery patentable. In Germany, this means an application of the gene discovery. If I can't do this, Professor Dr. Schäffer will not approve my dissertation.

"Any plans for this weekend?" Yuri asks me.

I called Kay earlier but I only got his mailbox and didn't leave a message. "No."

"Silly Thomas," he says. "You're going to Schwuz with me. Where do you live?" I tell him my address in Wedding. "I come over Saturday evening and we have a few drinks before going. Nine p.m. OK?"

"OK." I don't know what I'm getting myself into.

After the gym on Friday, I spend the rest of the evening deciding on whether to open a new profile. If I had a smartphone, I'd use Grindr instead, but no, I only have a Nokia with a black-and-white screen from eight years ago. It still works, so I won't buy another one.

Saturday arrives, and after I finish grocery shopping, I get a text message from Yuri. "I bring vodka. See you tonight :)"

Shit. He probably knew I'd never go if I just told him I'd meet him there. I try to call Kay again, but there's no answer. Reluctantly, I shower and change. How does an extrovert like Yuri become a scientist?

When I open the door for Yuri, I am surprised he is not wearing anything different from the lab—I have seen him wear this exact "69" T-shirt, and these exact baby-blue pants that sit so low on his hips that whenever he picks up a fallen pen, we have what Kay would call "a plumber situation," except this plumber wears a thong.

"Herr Doctor Urning," he says as he walks in.

"Hello Yuri," I say. I see he opens his arms for a hug, but instead I walk into the kitchen and say, "Do you want a beer?"

"I've got vodka," he says. "Cold like Siberia."

I have one of these salted Goldfish platters, and serve it with my breakfast cold-cuts. I know better than to drink vodka with a Russian on an empty stomach—and although I have been counting my calories, I didn't eat much yesterday, so it should make up for the binge drinking today. Bread and potatoes are foods I avoid.

"Shall we play a game?" he asks me.

"What game is that?"

"I guess something about you—if true, you take a sip. If wrong, I take a sip."

"Sounds like you want to get me drunk," I say.

"I like my boys hairless," he says, peeking at the tufts of blond hair sprouting from the collar of my T-shirt. "So this isn't complex game to get into your—big pants. You can take little sips too." I nod in agreement. Yuri begins. "You started drinking later in life."

I sip. "You started early." I nibble on a cracker.

Yuri drinks the entire shot glass. He pours himself another. "You were popular in *Hochschule*."

I shake my head. "I was tall, fat, and shy. I spent most of the day inside my head." This time, Yuri sips his vodka. "You had sex early in life."

He sips again. "I was fourteen and it was friend from same building." I can see his eyes glisten with the memory. "In winter, we built snow forts and hid inside so we could kiss."

"What happened?" I ask.

"Every snow fort destroyed," he says. "Bullies found us one day inside and beat us. He never came by again."

I raise my glass and so does Yuri. Sometimes, one has to celebrate the sad moments.

"My turn," he says. "You had sex first time after eighteen years old."

I drink the entire shot glass. I had tried the internet, but was too shy to post a photo. There weren't many responses to me in Hannover, and the only interesting one was a guy who said he was thirty-two. I was seventeen, and when he opened the apartment door, I ran away. It wasn't until I was twenty-four, still fat, that an exchange student from South Korea invited me to his room for dinner. Hyun wasn't short and parted his hair in the middle. After lots of BBQ and soju, he said I was too drunk to go home, and he insisted I sleep on the bed— but only after helping me out of my clothes. I still remember the look in his eyes when he saw my cock grow hard and he fished it out from the underwear slit and sucked it. He swallowed when I came, and masturbated with my flaccid cock still in his mouth. He fell asleep, and I felt something weird, so I got dressed. I left him and the mess in the kitchen. I was the only person on the night bus. I could not name these strange emotions, but being alone felt much better. Hyun never spoke to me afterwards.

"You miss Russia," I say.

Yuri's eyes narrow. "I hate Russia. I hate Moscow. I hate Putin." He slams his fist on the table before drinking a shot. He barely notices that I drink my shot for being wrong. "Everyone called me names, and I had to run from subway station to home. When bullies beat me, make me lose teeth." He pulls loose his two false front teeth. "I know what people think. I dress very gay. But I dress very gay because I can. In Russia, I dress like normal yet still bullies beat me. In Germany, in Berlin, I dress as I feel and no one beats me. I become fabulous." We drink another shot to that. We have drunk half the bottle.

"If we drink more," I say, "I won't be able to speak English."

"Me too," he says. "You speak Russian? Many Berliners speak Russian."

"My mother does," I say. "But I grew up in West Germany."

It is 23h30, and we decide to leave. I change into a tight T-shirt with a high collar. I have contacts on, but I put a spare pair in my pocket. The U-Bahn is crowded with very loud people, and I hear more English than German. Is this really Germany? It occurs to me that my life is spent more in English than in German in Berlin. My work is in English, I have no German friends, and the only time I hear German is when I grocery shop and watch TV. Even then, Kay lent me *Will and Grace* DVDs, and when I heard Karen's voice in English, I thought this was funny—the German actress' dubbing was horrible.

"I spend more of my life in English," I confess to Yuri.

"Because your English is perfect," he says.

We leave the U-Bahn station, and as Yuri promised, it's a bad neighborhood. Or as Kay would say, "It's up and coming." North Americans are too positive.

Schwuz is an old warehouse turned into a club. For a gay club, there are a lot of straight guys as security. We walk through a long corridor that probably used to be the shipping and receiving area. There is nothing that would make me think it was a gay club until we get to the cash desk, where a drag queen in a blue dress and blue hair looks at me from top to bottom. She's tall, and I do not think she is used to being the smaller one.

"I wish we charged by the meter," she says. "Then it'd cost you a hundred euros to get in, and you'd want to blow me to get in for free." She points to the sign that says entry is ten euros.

"Yuri, we're on the guest list, ja?" I say.

He points to his name on the list. "Sorry, Thomas. Just me." He walks off. I have to pay, and wonder about my colleague. I hand over my jacket to the coat check, and don't know who I hate more right now, the drag queen or the man who lied to me. Yuri walks beside me and says, "Beer and then dancing?" I can hear pop music as we wait for our beers. I then notice the bartenders.

"They're twins," I say. There was a video online with Czech twins and one very lucky man in between. These twins had dark hair and wore sleeveless shirts to expose defined forearms and biceps.

"One's active and one is passive," Yuri says.

"I want to be the center Lego piece," I say.

"What's Lego?" Yuri asks. But then he sees the way I look at them and says, "I've seen that look in your eyes before... Peter! You like Peter, yes?"

I ignore the question. "Let's dance."

There are three dance floors at Schwuz. There's a small dance floor for variety. There's a dance floor that plays techno and is the smoking room. The main dance floor is a huge place, but smaller than Berghain's. There's a stage to one end. When we enter, I see the crowds of twinkish gay men and their women friends.

It takes me a while to get in the mood for dancing. This is one gay thing about me—I like to dance, and I have danced alone in my apartment. Sometimes in only my underwear. This time, just as I really get into it, the music stops, and spotlights shine onto the stage with smoke billowing from the sides.

"Ladies and gentlemen, welcome to Schwuz!" says an announcer.

A phalanx of shirtless guys parades onto the stage, all wearing retro swim trunks in various colors. They form two columns on either side of the stage, followed by a drag queen in a sparkling black dress, wearing a massive blond wig.

Is that Timothy there, shirtless?

The drag queen throws kisses to the audience. "I'm Heidi Klo. Isn't Klo Klo Clock at Schwuz the best party?" The audience cheers, but I find it to be shameless self-promotion. "Let the show begin!" she says, and Timothy walks behind her. Suddenly, he rips her dress to expose a pink leotard underneath.

Hung Up by Madonna begins. Heidi Klo lip-syncs like her life depends on it, and does not miss a word. For a moment, I forget that it's a man in high heels. I forget that it's not Madonna on stage, only a reasonable doppelganger. Near the end of the song, the crowd of boys encircles her, and instead of the usual fade-out, there's a thunderclap audio effect and we see four twinks lift Heidi Klo in a chair and carry her off stage.

Cheers, screaming, and even I can't help but clap for minutes. I start walking closer to the stage.

The phalanx of boys leaves, and a large curvy drag queen takes their place, wearing a sparkly silver dress and black lace gloves. There must be more drag queens here than beer coolers. "Thank you, Heidi Klo," she says. "You always make us happy when you come on stage—but, girl, you make us happier when you leave." She speaks German with an American accent, and walks to the front of the stage. "Ladies and gentlemen, and those still deciding, I am Delores Clitoris, and unlike the real clitoris, you can spot me from a mile away.

"Tonight, I will be your host for 'Top or Bottom.' I'll ask a lucky volunteer three questions, and from his answers, we'll guess which side of the pumpernickel he prefers to butter. Just like life, there's no in between, so if you say you're versatile, we know you mean bottom. Any volunteers?" There are no hands. "You get free drink tickets." A few hands go up.

The spotlight goes to one boy, and he walks up to the stage. He has perfectly tweezed eyebrows, and as he walks on, his lips purse into a half kiss. He wears very tight jeans. Delores Clitoris looks at him and with a flick of her hand shouts, "Bottom. Please. Don't waste our time." The crowd laughs, and the boy opens his pouty mouth in shock. Delores hugs him. "What's your name?"

"Johannes," he says, his cheeks slowly becoming less red.

"What kind of guy are you looking for tonight?"

"A sporty top," he says.

Delores turns Johannes around so we can see his ass. "Look how firm this ass is, like a ripe apple ready to be bit into whole." She slaps him on the ass and he exits the stage through the back.

"Next victim?" Delores asks. "Come on, there must be more guys who are alcoholics and want free drinks." She scans the crowd and sees me. Of course she sees me. "You, the tall drink of water." I shake my head and start to step back, but I feel someone pushing me from behind. "Look, he's shy," Delores says. "Can we get some applause to encourage him to get on stage?"

The entire club is clapping and cheering, and when I feel everyone's eyes on me, I begin to sweat. Shit, what's worse? Getting on stage or having them look at me all-night long?

I walk on stage. Delores Clitoris' makeup, upon closer inspection, is patchy and powdery. There are holes in her lace gloves. Is this common among drag queens? She smiles, and says, "Precious, what's your name and where are you from?"

"I'm Thomas and I am from Hannover," I say.

"I was in Hannover once," she says, looking at me. "More beautiful than people say." She looks at the audience. "Not much more beautiful. A piece of shit is still a piece of shit." The audience laughs. "So, I have three questions to ask you, Thomas. First—what is your favorite movie and why?"

I remember what Kay said about my love of Chicago, so I lie. "Contact," I say. "From Carl Sagan, so it is very realistic."

"Oh my, we have a gay nerd, ladies and gentlemen," Delores says. "I've asked this question more times than I can count, and it's either a musical or if it's an older gay man, something with Meryl Streep. I don't know how to interpret this answer—can you just twirl around for a moment until I figure this out?"

I do. When I expose my ass to the crowd, there is a huge cheer. I smile at that.

"Next question," Delores begins. "How do you stay fit?" She rests her chin on her fist while raising one eyebrow.

"A good diet and lots of cardio," I answer.

"No free weights? No grunting when you do your bench presses?" she asks.

"Just machines then," I add.

"You work out like my mother," Delores says. "OK. Last question. If you were stranded on an island, and could only bring one porn actor to fuck for the rest of your life, who would that be?"

Porn stars? I watch them but I don't remember their names. Then I remember the one who lives in Berlin and checked me out once while I was shopping for milk. I looked him up online to find out the name. "Brent Bravo."

"Brent Bravo—he only tops in his films," she says. "Well, ladies and gentlemen, what do you think? Is Thomas a top or a bottom?" As she says this, she winks and points to my ass. I turn around, because I can't believe what's happening. It's a game, it's just a game. A shitty and stupid game.

The crowd cheers, "Bottom! Bottom!"

Delores walks closer to me, and I can see from the corner of my eye that she bends over to take a closer look at my ass. "I'll have to agree with the audience. Are you a bottom, Thomas?"

The idea comes to me in an instant. I unzip my jeans, and before Delores can get up, I turn around with my massive semi-erect cock gripped in my hand. In this split second, her eyes go wide at the sight of my dick, and she gasps.

That's when I slap her face with my cock. I swaffle her not once, but twice.

"Is this the cock of a bottom?" I yell.

There's a moment of silence from her, from me, from the audience—until she falls on her ass. The crowd becomes crazy. Cheers, applause, howls, and laughter.

I put my cock back in my pants. Delores Clitoris stands up. She smiles and says, "I've been wrong before, but I've never been so glad to be wrong. Ladies and gentlemen, I present to you Thomas, the biggest-dicked top I've ever seen!" There's more applause, and Delores adds, "Let's give it up for Thomas for being such a sport. And Johannes, I think I've got the top for you!"

I stare into the crowd and see only silhouettes in front of the spotlight. But I hear the cheers—and the cheers are for me. For the first time in my life, a crowd cheers for me. I wave at the audience and they cheer even louder. I take my bow.

Exit via the back. The cheers quiet, and in the dulled silence of backstage, the contrast is stark. The room is lit with pale fluorescent lights, and Timothy is on a lumpy black leather couch. On either side of him are the twins with dark curly hair. Timothy is kissing one of the twins while the other nibbles on his nipple. While his lips are still locked, Timothy looks at me.

"Have you met my new Greek friends?" he asks after the twin stops kissing and moves down to nuzzle on Timothy's crotch. "Demetrios and Demetrius. Quite a brilliant performance you gave there, Thomas. It inspired the Double Ds here to get a little frisky with me."

"Have you seen Kay lately?" I ask. "I've been trying to call him or Alex, but there's no answer."

"Alex is in middle America somewhere," he says. "Kay, he said he didn't feel well and stopped answering my calls. He must have had a bad trip."

"Trip? Where did he go?" I say, my brows furrowing.

"Down the rabbit hole, darling," Timothy says. I don't understand Timothy and he annoys me.

The twin who had been working on Timothy's crotch turns around and starts nuzzling mine. "You look sexy like that," he says. My cock gets hard, almost hurting as it strains against my jeans. "I'm Demetrios." He unzips my pants and pulls out my cock, his eyes wide. His tongue touches the sensitive area just below my piss slit, and tingles surge through my body.

"He's the passive one," Demetrius says, pulling down his pants to expose his own hard dick. Timothy tugs his pants all the way down and sits on Demetrius' cock without a condom.

My cock goes limp.

"Need Viagra?" Timothy asks. His hips start to move, and he moans.

"No condom?" I say. Demetrios has stopped sucking on my cock.

"It feels … like heaven…" Timothy barely says through heavy breaths. "I don't give a fuck." Demetrios puts a house key in front of Timothy, and he snorts white powder from it.

That startles me. I reach out and hold Timothy by the side of his face while looking deep into his eyes. His pupils are dilated. "Why don't you give a fuck?"

He sniffs deeply and stops moving his hips, but his face and shoulders are still red from the pleasure of sex. "I missed my investor meeting. Overslept. Since the company has no cash flow, it's in administration."

"Administration?"

"I'm bankrupt, you twat." Demetrius pushes Timothy onto the floor and begins to pound furiously into Timothy's pale buttocks. In between moans, Timothy mutters, "So, yes ... my dear friend Thomas... I don't ... give a fuck. I just take them." His hands clench into fists. "Now piss off."

I zip my pants and walk out of the back room, the bar, and Schwuz. I ignore the cheers and the cat calls. I receive a text from Yuri asking where I am, but I ignore it and walk to the U-Bahn. I get a compartment to myself, and as the rhythmic bumping of the underground tracks lulls me, I think about what this all means.

I spend the rest of the weekend in my apartment, and don't see Yuri again until Tuesday morning. He smiles at me, and says, "What happened to you at Schwuz? Did that little display of yours get you action?"

"One of the bartender twins," I say.

"I'm jealous," he says. "You must tell me more, but I just saw Peter in hallway."

I saw Peter on Monday and it was the same awkward silence between us. As Peter enters the lab this morning, holding a big package this time, Yuri gets a phone call. He has *Hung Up* as his ring tone, and it blares through his phone's speakers—and for a moment, I see Peter strutting instead of walking. I am reminded of Schwuz, and the rush as the crowd cheered and all I could see was the blinding spotlight.

I walk to meet Peter halfway. "Is this big package for me?" I ask. The cheers echo in my head, and I smile.

He smiles back and his cheeks flush red. "Yes, Doctor Urning."

"Thomas," I say. "You saw my Gayromeo profile." He nods. "Then you know I've got a big package for you." I can still hear the cheers. My cock grows and it snakes along the left pant leg, engorged and angry. "Meet me after work?"

"What about now?" Peter looks around. Yuri is still busy on his phone, his back to us. Peter massages my cock through my pants, wetting his lips with his tongue. "Storage closet is private."

The cheers are deafening. I nod. I follow his lead, and he opens the storage closet with a key. Inside, with the door locked and the lights on, Peter wastes no time going to his knees. "I didn't think I was your type," he says. His breathing quickens when he lays his eyes on my dick. It is the same look that Demetrios gave me.

He opens his mouth, and I take that as a cue to shove it in him. He makes an unintelligible noise, and tears form in his eyes. Maybe he wanted to say something more? It does not matter now. Peter is a gay bottom and transfixed on blowing me, and once we develop a rhythm, he unzips his fly with his free hand and jerks himself. He tries to take all of me, but can get only half of it in his mouth.

"I'm going to come," I say, and instead of letting go, Peter's lips hold on even tighter. I grip his head as my body trembles, and with a couple of quick jerks his cock spews too. Peter swallows every drop of mine, and when his mouth withdraws and he is able to speak again, he says, "Yuri told me you were into me, but I didn't believe him."

"Yuri told you?" I ask.

"But then you acted so remote yesterday," he says.

The door clicks. The cheers are only a faint echo now.

As I turn around with barely enough time to stuff my cock back inside, zipper drawn down, the door opens and I see my supervising professor, Dr. Schäfer, staring at me. Of course he has a key. He shakes his head, and his eyes go wide enough that I can see the whites all around his irises.

"I will see you at your grant meeting," he says, and walks away. No. Runs away.

I see Yuri. We're competing for the same grant. Asshole. He has a grin on his face. My hands clench into fists, and my breathing is heavy. I take very large strides to him.

"I think the grant is mine," he says. "I'm ..." I grab him by the neck and push him against the wall. He squirms, sputtering. But I have his fucking neck in my hand, and I squeeze. I want to see this asshole suffer. I bare my teeth and force a heavy breath out, spit flying through the tiny gaps of my teeth into his face.

He makes more noise. His face is purple. He looks around desperately.

There's a crowd around us. What am I doing? The blood rushes from my head, and I feel dizzy. I unclench my hand from Yuri's neck and he drops onto the floor like a crumpled sheet of A4 paper.

"Your fly... is open," Yuri spits back at me in between ragged gasps.

My colleagues are silent. The hallway is silent. I zip up my fly, and that's all I hear. Then my footsteps as I walk out. The walk becomes a run.

9. Kay

He chokes on my cock. He is an East Berlin bull of a man and his gagging excites me. I am powerful and his suffering is my revenge. His real name is irrelevant, but his online nick is Pruegel which means punished and beaten. He looks like a skinhead except he is the one on his knees. I grip the back of his shaved head. I force his lips to my base, feel his beard stubble graze my balls. He gurgles, cheeks blush crimson, and as the veins on his thick neck bulge with purple, I let go.

He gasps for air. Tears well in his eyes. His gasping lasts more than a mere breath but he then lunges for my cock again. Pruegel likes to submit.

This afternoon was my last submission. This afternoon was the last dose of my four week Post-Exposure-Prophylaxis, one tablet twice a day. I had started at 17:13. I remember the white display on the microwave. Each time the blue, oblong tablet hit my tongue, I could taste *his* breath and that odour of beer and cigarettes. I could feel his sweat on my back. I had wanted to scream, to bite the flesh off his hand, but I submitted. I had submitted and I resented each day. Wallowing in resentment meant wallowing in my own sloth, and days turned to weeks.

Two weeks in, I looked at myself in the mirror. The sloth meant I hadn't shaved and the beard was growing in. I was an Asian man with a beard and a moustache that didn't quite connect with the rest. Not many Asian men have facial hair, and I no longer looked kind, or meek, or like the Kay who was raped. In the gym, I trained like my masculinity depended on that one last rep.

Three weeks after, I set up a new online profile for sex. There were only photos of me viewed from someone on his knees and never of my face. I marked myself as "Top Only" and displayed a dick pic, but as a protruding silhouette on a white wall like Mapplethorpe had taken the photo: firm ass, beefy thighs, and a dangling thick cock. In seconds, messages filled my inbox.

I had eight men in the span of seven days. Markus, the muscle bear who had chips after getting fucked on all fours; Florian, a deaf guy whose apartment was bold with colours and only made a sound when he sat on my dick and moaned; Uli, a closeted football player on the B roster, who at the last minute didn't want to get fucked, and I had to come from grinding between his thighs, but how wonderful those long and sinewy thighs were. Another Markus, Daniel, Andreas, Lutz, and Sascha. I fucked without submission.

I squeeze Pruegel's shoulders and feel muscled deltoids then guide him up. He stands and is taller than me by a head. He turns around and leans against the heavy kitchen table with windows open. His back is a massive expanse of V-shaped flesh. His ass comprise mounds of perfection coated in blonde hair. He knows what I want.

My pants are discarded by my feet, and I reach down to grab packets of lube and a condom. I fuck him. I am in control. My hands grip him by the sides of his stomach, and thrust slowly at first. His moans, deep and gruff, are just as slow. Then, I build momentum. His groans grow louder, become grunts, then shorten to breaths like he's sprinting. I really fuck him now. Around his shoulders, his pink back flushes with blood from the pleasure of the fuck. His moans escape out the window. When I'm ready to come and lose control, my thighs and arms flex in one last thrust. I moan like being a man depended on this fuck and my orgasm erupts within latex.

I breathe through my teeth. I'm still inside him when I wait for the sweat to drip off my face, and he masturbates. He's only silent then turns around to kiss, and I see a puddle of sperm on the cherry wood table top.

"Would you like a drink?" he says as he takes the condom from me.

I nod.

He bends down to the freezer section of the fridge. "My mother's Polish so we'll have vodka." He rests the bottle of Polish vodka on the table beside the puddle of cum and the glass frosts up like a window in winter. I've never had vodka served like this.

We clink glasses while making eye contact, and the vodka tastes clean going down. There's no aftertaste. A digestif after sex is better than awkward chit chat about the weather. We kiss good-bye. I walk down the stairs and as I go through the courtyard to the main building, there are two elderly ladies with empty canvas bags. "Did you hear that?"

"The moaning?" says the other.

"Close the window if you're going to have sex," says the first. "Otherwise the noise echoes through the entire courtyard."

I walk past them and they briefly look at me but continue their conversation. The Asian man couldn't be guilty. Sometimes, it's good to be assumed innocent.

"Did you hear a woman moan?" says the first woman.

"Don't be so naïve," says the other. "We're in Schöneberg."

Along the main street, I'm swallowed by the crowd's hustle and anonymity. I see bars with European flags across their windows—Eurovision will happen tonight. In principal, Eurovision is a song contest started in the 1950s with entries from all over Europe to celebrate peace. In practice, it's a proxy war with national pride at stake, and the weapons are cliché lyrics, costume changes, and dance choreography from the wonderful to the insane. There was the song from the Turkish singer Sertab Erener with her pop rendition of a belly-dance ballad, and the quartet of women who tugged at her corset until she was set free and her belly exposed for all of Europe to see. There was *Hard Rock Hallelujah* performed by a Finnish band dressed as monsters, and the lead singer sprouted bat wings by the song's end. Dima Bilan, a Russian pop singer, graced the competition with a beautiful ballet dancer emerging from a white piano to sprinkle rose petals; when Dima didn't win then, he returned two years later with an Olympic gold medallist who skated on stage in the world's tiniest ice rink. He won with a flamboyant upright spin in Europe's gayest battle.

I head to the U-Bahn. I haven't been this far west since moving out of Helmut's place. In five minutes, I could be back and say hello. Or pass by the house and see if the name on the doorbell has changed. Is it just Rieger or Rieger slash another name, maybe from a new boyfriend? I can learn so much from reading a slash on the front door. No, I need to rush home where the door reads "Anders/ Hung." When the U-Bahn's door closes, I wonder if I smell like sex. I see my faint reflection in the window, and realize I have messed up hair from fucking. I watch the other passengers. A couple in their fifties holds shopping bags from KaDeWe, the department store of West Berlin. An Asian woman stares at her phone with gold grocery bags written with large red Chinese characters between her feet. No one notices me. We then pass Zoologischer Garten, and the crowds swarm in. People sniff around with suspicion in their eyes. They smell it. I'm sure of it. There's sweat and santorum in the air.

Seconds before the doors close, a grey-haired man in a blazer and scarf rushes in. He holds the hand of a woman wearing pearl earrings. Her hair is pulled back and her makeup is flawless. She holds a Louis Vuitton bag in her hand, and it's the real thing. Her eyes, though, betray her, and she looks tired or hung over since her eyes crawl around in her sockets.

"I should have just stayed in the hotel," she says. "It would have been better than dragging me to another photo exhibit."

"I don't feel guilty for wanting culture in our lives," he says. "Anyway, we'll head back to the hotel, grab our luggage, and you can rest on the train back to Düsseldorf. I'll make sure to read the newspaper."

"Where's the water bottle?" she asks.

"In your bag," he says, and with a sigh of disgust, reaches in himself and grabs it for her.

As she drinks water, another tourist holding a guidebook entitled "Berlino" stops sniffing and stares at me with righteous fury burning in her eyes that only an Italian Catholic can muster.

The woman with the designer bag and pearl earrings drinks the entire bottle and says, "That's better." As she puts the empty bottle back in her purse, there's a heave, a wretch, and she empties the contents of her stomach onto the U-Bahn floor. Splatter and swish.

No one is thinking about the smell of gay sex now.

The couple look at each other, and not a moment too soon, we arrive at the next station. He pushes the button repeatedly to get out. The doors open and once on the platform, they stroll toward the exit dignified as if coming out of an opera. In Berlin, rich or poor, straight or gay, we are human—puke, sex, and all.

Back on the train, the tourists squeeze to the other side of the wagon. I stay where I am because it's only water. It sloshes around my sneakers scuffed black. They serve as scars from various late nights in establishments of low moral standing.

At the apartment, I shower with door open. I walk down the hallway dry and naked, and pass a large suitcase. "Alex?" I ask.

"Living room," he answers.

I go through the living room to get to my bedroom. Is this the first time he's seen me completely naked? "Hey Alex. I'd hug you but my nakedness would make it awkward."

"Impressive," he says, "but then again, I haven't seen dick in a month."

"How jet lagged are you?" I say from the bedroom and dress. Today I'm showing my pro Deutschland stance with a red, yellow, and black striped belt.

"Very," he says, "but better I stay up until at least nine."

I head to the kitchen and bring back a bottle of red wine. "Tell me about your trip," I say as I pour.

He drinks the entire glass in three gulps. "More please."

I refill his glass. "This is the twenty euro Spanish one, so savour it a little."

He raises an eyebrow and sips instead. "My trip was awful." He looks off in the distance. The room across from us is the page-23-catalogue living room where a single woman spends evenings watching television with take-out. Alex clears his throat. "My dad died."

"Oh shit." I swallow a large gulp, and wonder what I'm supposed to say. "I'm sorry to hear that."

"I managed to get there to see him alive," Alex adds, "but he tells me that I need to do something with my life. I'm so pissed off that I go out for a smoke, and when I come back, he flatlines. I saw it in his eyes, that exact moment—and fuck, each time I try to think of him, I can only see his blank look on the hospital pillow."

"To your father," I say as I raise my glass.

Alex drinks the rest in another gulp. I pour him more. "My mom goes fucking haywire. The nurses shove us out, and there's an organized commotion as they do something. But I still hear that flatline noise once the commotion stops."

"How do you feel about it?" I ask.

"Pissed," Alex says. "At first, I was like, 'No, he's going to be OK. Get up Dad.' But then just fucking pissed when the flatline noise didn't stop. Mom's screaming and starts beating me on the chest. I have to grab her hands and restrain her, it was starting to hurt." Alex has finished another gulp and I pour him more.

"Thanks," he says.

"How was the funeral?" I ask.

"The funeral was a pain to plan," he says. "Mom got anal about every detail. We had the reception at the house, and all the flowers had to be white. Vicki brought beige flowers and my Mom took them and threw them in the trash. At least she waited until Vicki was away, but I saw it."

"Who's Vicki?" I say.

"My saving grace," Alex explains. He takes out his phone and sends a message on it. "We used to hang out in our senior year. I was in the glee club and she was in drama, and wore nothing but black. She even dyed her hair black, and I joked that she wanted to be Asian."

"You two got together?" I say.

"How do you know?" he asks.

"Your face changed when you talked about her," I say.

"We got together, yeah," Alex admits. "I spent more nights at her place than in my bedroom during this trip. She has a boy named

Josh—he's not mine—and he and I would play video games while Vicki was making dinner. It was awesome."

"How about your Mom?" I ask.

"A week after the funeral, we're in the lawyer's office reading the will," he says. Part of me is jealous that Alex comes from a family with money. "Mom was still angry, but this time because the lawyer didn't get back from his business trip earlier. She was threatening to change firms and bullshit like that." Alex grabs the bottle and pours himself the last drops. "So basically my Mom gets everything—the house, majority rights to the company, the investment portfolio. The trust fund is still mine, but there is now a clause which says I can only get it if I 'pursue education valuable to the family business'—and my mother gets to decide whether my music education is valuable. She's threatening to cut me off. Fuck her." He drinks the rest of his glass, and when he tries to pour himself more, the bottle is empty.

"What will you do?" I say and finish my one single glass.

"Sue," he says and heads for the kitchen. Alex says it in the same tone as if talking about the weather.

When he comes back, I change the subject. "Will you head out tonight?"

"Anything special?" he asks.

"Only Eurovision," I say in the gayest valley tone I can mimic. "There's a bearded drag queen this year."

"That's so gay," Alex says. "And I'm bi remember."

"Fine, go and watch the football or something," I say. "Timothy will be coming over though. He allows himself this indulgence."

I leave the door open for Timothy when he buzzes, and continue with drinks in the living room. When he enters, he says, "Well, what do you gentlemen think?"

Timothy wears a dress, a wig, and has a faux-five-day stubble. "Douze points for Austria?" I say.

"*Dankeschön*," he says. He's tall in his high heels.

"Marvellous," I say, walk to him, and pretend to kiss each cheek. I don't want any of that makeup on my face after all.

"You're not going to get laid in that," Alex says.

"Tonight's about the music darling," Timothy says. He looks at us with our beer. "Would you happen to have anything uncarbonated? I fear getting bloated in this sparkly thing."

"Vodka orange juice?" I offer. No one understands screwdriver in Europe.

"Splendid."

After drinks, Timothy and I take a taxi to Schwuz. As we walk out, I'm nervous. I'm not in drag, but I know that whenever I see a man in a dress, I look. Even if the man is in a terrible dress with terrible make up, I look. Maybe even more so.

"Help me walk over these cobblestones," she says. Tonight, Timothy is Conchita Worse as a tribute to the Eurovision contestant, Conchita Wurst. "Once I'm inside, I should be fine."

As we're walking, I notice Conchita's bulge through her dress. "No tuck?"

"No," she says. "There's only so much suffering a lady can endure." It's only the pre-show, and I see the line up as a forty-minute wait. Eyes stare at us, and the straight security staff scrutinize as well. "Heidi said she would put us on the guest list. Walk with me." We go past the line, and it amazes me—in drag, no one questions that this Conchita has special access. Fraulein Conchita Worse serves paparazzi-face realness. Her eyes appear determined, and she says in her British accent, "Conchita Worse and guest."

The door man is a bear with dark glasses. He replies in German, "I don't see your name on here."

"Heidi Klo is a friend of mine," Conchita says.

A drag queen comes. She has blue hair and a silver dress. She takes Conchita off to the side, and I see the regular guests continuing inside. Conchita returns to me, and almost trips but I grab her midfall.

"Let's go," she says. "This club is dead to me."

"What happened?" I ask.

"Heidi found out that I fucked the twins," Conchita says, then smiles as we walk out. In a louder voice, "How silly of me to forget our party favours."

A group of party goers leave a taxi and we stumble in. "Where to?" the taxi driver asks.

Conchita gazes out the window, and resembles more like Timothy now than the sugared version earlier. "There's Hamburger Mary's," I say. "The owner of the place is from Chicago and I know him."

"Bloody yes," Timothy says. It's one of those strange expat things—when things go your way, you are excited to be here. When a little problem happens, you scream in your head, "Fuck this city!" and want to find solace with people of your own kind. I assume this is what Timothy is feeling.

I call Thomas. No answer. I text him, "Sorry I haven't been replying. Heading to Hamburger Mary's in Schöneberg. Maybe see you there?"

"Fraulein, selfie time," I say as I hold the phone with outstretched hand. Timothy looks at the camera. His eyes don't move, and a crack on the screen dissects Timothy's face in two. At the very last moment, I kiss him on the cheek. I've ruined his makeup, but he smiles something genuine, the wrinkles around his eyes folding like they applaud. Timer finishes. Click.

Hamburger Mary's is located in the Axel Hotel. In the summer, there is a rooftop bar with showers because why not? This is a gay chain of hotels. The walls are painted black, and a gym and sauna are on the sixth floor. After nine o'clock, the lights turn off so that boys can be boys in the dark. On the main floor away from shenanigans, Hamburger Mary's serves hamburgers with sweet potato fries and a side of sass.

Sassy and flamboyant Pecan Pie Pam rushes to us in her high heels, and the oversized plastic glasses with rhinestones almost fall off her nose. Although the place is decorated like a traditional American diner, it doesn't have fluorescent lighting so when Pam greets us, soft lights hide that Pam is a broad shouldered farm boy from America's mid-west with a man's stern brow.

"It's so good to see you Kay," she says.

"Likewise," I say. "Pecan Pie Pam, let me introduce you to—"

"The bearded lady from Derby," Timothy says without missing a beat. "I'm Candice Cunt. The T is silent."

Pam looks down at the bulge. "But the D isn't." They hug and I remind myself the British say the C word almost as often as darling. "A round of shots on the house?"

Candice, formerly Conchita, says, "Absolutely darling. American hospitality and humour—like much needed sunshine in Berlin. And a pint too please. I want to sit down and bloat. It's time to kick off these heels." As Pam is about to leave, Candice adds, "Do you have any brownies?"

"Fresh batch this afternoon," Pam answers. "I'll get you two pieces."

"Vanilla ice cream with mine," I say.

"I need something sweet right now," Candice says.

There's silence once the show starts. I feel anticipation, like when I open a birthday present, or when I get a guy home and pull that zipper down. The silence is fleeting. The opening sequence roars on the screen with bikers and water skis riding through the streets and canals of Copenhagen. Raucous applause erupts in the Danish stadium as well as at the American-German restaurant here. Customers call out catty comments for the song's composition, costumes, and choreography.

"I used to hide in my bedroom while watching this," Candice says.

"You didn't watch this with your family?"

"Heaven's no," she says. "I was afraid to be seen as too prissy, and all that would have implied."

"There's no need to worry about that implication today," I comment.

"I wouldn't dare do this in London," Candice says. "One of my parent's acquaintances may see, and then we'd finally have to confront the issue."

I furrow my brows. "You mean your parents don't know?"

"It was one reason why I wanted to move out of London," Candice says. "That, and the Turkish men." Berlin's largest minority is from Turkey, and were originally guest workers invited to Germany after the war. Their apartments dot districts like Wedding and Neukölln with satellite dishes by their windows pointing toward Istanbul.

Pam comes with our order, and I invite her to sit with us. "You expats in Europe just rave about Eurovision, like it's the best thing since sliced bread. This is my first time so the hype better be deserved."

"Gay Christmas darling," I say and manage to hold my tongue about sliced bread. "Shhh. Conchita Wurst is on."

Silence settles as the ballad begins. The song builds to a crescendo, and I look at Candice and Pam briefly to see tears forming in their eyes. A drag queen singing about rising like a glorious phoenix from the ashes of abuse—it's a message we can relate to. A man with the freedom to be in a dress stands for values that Europe holds dear.

When the song is over, Timothy rises. "Douze points for Austria!" he exclaims, and waves to the crowd. The restaurant bursts with wild applause.

"Did it live up to the hype?" I ask Pam. The songs are over, and we have a few minutes to vote by calling a number. Candice is outside for a cigarette. I see her through the window, and she speaks on the phone. She waves at us.

"Oh god yes," Pam replies. "I think I'm a little wet from it."

"Who will you vote for?" I say.

"I can't vote for Germany?" Pam says. I shake my head. "Austria of course, silly. Us drag queens have got to stick together."

"I heard that in the past, people voted by turning their lights on or off and someone would read off the electrical usage," I say.

"Past? How far 'past' are we talking here?"

"This show's been going on since the 1950s," I say.

"You mean American Idol wasn't the first?" She smiles and notices something at the bar, and leaves me. Candice comes back at this time, and her face is flustered. "I need to leave."

"But the voting hasn't finished yet," I say.

"Sorry, I can't, I just can't," she says. "I hate to impose, but may I ask you for a favour Kay?" I nod. "May I borrow money for a taxi back, and could you settle the bill?"

"Of course, yes." I hand Candice thirty euros, and check that I have a couple of blue bills in my wallet. This is a cash only country.

"What's the matter?"

"I'll tell you later," Candice/ Conchita/ Timothy says. "Please let Pam know that I am grateful, and I'm sorry to leave without saying good-bye." With that, Timothy shuffles off in her high heels like a geisha.

I check my phone. Nothing from Thomas. Maybe he's mad that I only called him a week ago.

When the voting happens, I'm excited. The voting runs the gambit from Conchita getting nothing from spiteful former Soviet bloc countries like Belarus and Armenia, whereas Western EU countries shower Conchita with twelve points. I'm elated and wonder whether this is what straight guys feel when their sports team wins. She is declared the winner, and when she walks to the stage, she's victorious but in tears. In her soft and almost fragile speaking voice, Conchita Wurst says, "This is dedicated to those who believe in peace and freedom." She raises her trophy, shaped as a glass microphone, into the air.

Peace and freedom means I can dance. "Want to go clubbing Pam?" I ask.

"I wish I could but I've got to stay here," she says.

I don't want to go dancing alone. I guess I'll head back home. As I walk outside, and make my way to the U-Bahn station, the excitement doesn't abate. I'm almost skipping with each step. Europe is fabulously sassy.

Excitement and euphoria morph into horniness. I stand in front of Tom's Bar, one of the first stops for tourists seeking sleaze. I'm tortured by the images of Snax—of the cement wall as I lost control, yes, but I also remember the man with the red beard, his body bent over, of the power and pleasure I felt when I fucked him. I want to go inside and feel that again. This time will be different and I'll be more careful.

Tom's bar is a dark place, and unlike other bars, not smoky because there is a closed-off room for smokers. It feels like it could be a typical North-American bar under strict smoking bans. A row of beer coolers branded by Mega-International Beverage Corp banks one side, walls painted black enclose the rest, and halogen and neon signs of more brands serve as limited lighting. The downstairs, however, is very Berlin.

I have a beer in one hand as I descend. The darkness is broken by faint red-tinged light bulbs. Catacombs await for the adventurous to explore. I turn to a tunnel with cubicles off to the side. I wander, and see the outlines of bodies. It's too early for men to feel desperate and there's no sex. I enter even darker caverns. There's a beacon of light here where the young and attractive guys stand close and bask in its incandescent glory. I stand by a wall hidden in shadow so I can observe those that meander around like rats. I sip my beer and lose track of time.

How does the mood change? I now smell sex's pungent odour, and moans mingle with the distinct sound of thighs slapping against ass cheeks. My cock responds and strains against my pants.

I go to the source of the sounds. Men have already swarmed here. I can't take a good look, but a man nuzzles against my erection. I unzip my fly, and he pulls my pants down further, and fishes my cock out. As my eyes adjust to the dark, I see him. He's in his thirties, blond, stubble but no beard, and broad shoulders. He's a good cocksucker, and swallows me down to the base. He flicks his tongue on my head when he withdraws—only to plunge down on it again. Hands grope all over me, but I only care about this man and the warmth of his mouth. He withdraws with more tongue.

He then plunges his mouth once more, and I thrust into him at the same time. He gags, and it sounds like from more than just cock, and suddenly—he pushes himself away from my dick, head swings to the side, and pukes.

He's puking. And I feel globs of the half-digested ooze drip from my shaft onto my balls.

The guy stands and stumbles away. Maybe I should follow him and see if he's OK. No, most likely he's embarrassed and wants to forget. People flee from the vomit, and as I pull my pants back up after trying to wipe my dick clean, the only ones that remain are the two guys still fucking and oblivious.

I dash to the bathroom upstairs. I go first to a urinal and inspect my dick. Yeah. It's caked in crud but I need to piss. I urinate. A guy beside me strokes his cock. It's big, like twenty centimetres big, but it seems more spongy than hard. I avert my gaze to see his face and body, and this man is in his sixties. I walk away. No thank you.

I go to the sink, and with soap, wash my dick. Cleaning another man's puke off my penis is a new low. I can't imagine anything worse. When I finish washing my hands, I pat my pockets and realize—oh shit. Oh shit. My wallet's not there. My phone and keys are still in my other pocket. Relief, but where's my wallet?

Maybe it just dropped out. I return downstairs. I use my phone's flashlight to look at the ground. Beside the puddle of vomit, I see condoms, lube packets, and more condoms.

I retrace my steps but find nothing but condoms.

Let's keep trying. Maybe it's in one of those other catacombs I haven't been to. One catacomb—nothing. Second catacomb—nothing. The third catacomb is large, and fuck, I just got pickpocketed and there's no way I'm going to find my wallet, and I'm already desperately thinking about what credit cards I'll have to cancel and how—and in between another pile of condoms, I see my precious wallet.

My hands grope the leather. I thought washing the puke clean from my dick was the lowest I could go. I can't get any lower than picking up my wallet from the dark room floor at Tom's Bar. The cash is gone, but at least my cards remain. I breathe in relief.

As I shove my wallet back into my pocket, my phone slips from my other hand and falls onto the putrid floor. Shit, shit, shit! The light shines through greasy latex specked with brown, and I fish my phone from the pile of squishy used condoms.

My palm cleans the phone's screen, and notice the light points to another wallet on the ground. The thief must have stolen another and after taking the cash, threw away our wallets here. I grab the other wallet and head upstairs with better light to see whom this belongs to. And to wash my hands for a second time.

The best light is in the bathroom, and as a person is pissing behind me, I read the ID. Thomas Urning. I see Thomas' face covered in his glasses, and his cheeks are puffier than now. This must be an old photo.

Maybe Thomas is still here. I check the bar and the smoking room but know with dread that he's downstairs. There is one side tunnel further in, and I see him—this very tall man slumped onto the wall, eyes closed within his thick glasses.

"Thomas?" I say. No response. I walk closer. "Thomas?" I say as I touch his shoulder. His eyes open, and he reaches for my cock. "Thomas, it's Kay." He stops halfway and looks up at me. He blinks and smiles when he recognizes me.

"*Hallo,*" he says. "*Lange nicht gesehen.*" He's slow with his speech, and his consonants are slurred.

I reply in German and it's the first time we speak in his native language. "Are you OK?"

"Good. I drank." He looks fragile, like a small child, and I touch his cheek. He presses his face into my freshly cleaned palm, and whispers, "That feels good Kay."

I stroke his cheek as I speak. "Get up. We're going home."

Thomas stands up. He wobbles. "Home is a good idea," he says.

"How much did you drink?" I ask.

He purses his lips. "I forget."

"Come on," I say, "You can lean on me."

It takes us a while to get up and go through the bar. There's a taxi and I want to get in, but I don't have cash and I don't want to use my credit cards. I may have to dispute charges. We head to the U-Bbahn. It runs twenty-four hours on weekends. In a city known for all-night partying, a cheap ride home is fundamental. We wait on the U2 platform above ground and exposed to the night time air. We are alone and the next train arrives in twenty minutes.

"It's cold," Thomas says. It's ten degrees, and I don't find it chilly at all, but that's the Winnipegger in me. "Where's my jacket?"

"I forgot it," I say. "Do you want to go back?"

"No," he says. "It wasn't expensive." He hugs me. "You're warm." The minutes pass in our silent embrace.

The train arrives with a rumble and we enter. The compartment is empty, and when we start moving, Thomas falls asleep on my shoulder. He has a faint smile as he breathes in and out. I cradle his head with my left hand so it doesn't snap back at each stop. We transfer to the U6 and arrive at the underground platform just as the train doors open. Thomas falls asleep on my shoulder again and I cradle his head a second time. From Stadtmitte north to Wedding, we pass stations that used to be guarded by East German soldiers before the subway line returned to West Berlin. Living in the German capital, I'm always reminded how much history has happened here.

Thomas still leans on me as we ascend from the station toward his 1970s apartment building. Everything is quiet except for our footsteps. He takes out his keys and fumbles with the lock. The keys fall onto the ground with a clinking crash.

Helping a drunk person home means I need to think for two. I stabilize Thomas on the wall like I'm a police officer frisking him. He slurs something I don't understand. I pick up his key, a handful connected by a simple ring. There's an unusual brass skeleton key.

"The silver key," Thomas says. I slide the key with teeth facing down. This is Germany and all keys open this way.

Inside, I push the button to call the elevator, but Thomas takes the stairs. His place is on the second floor or third floor in Canada. "Cardio," he mumbles. He holds onto the railings and I climb. One step after the other. I look up. Thomas' ascent in tight jeans is sexy.

"Silver key," he says as he leans against the door. The same key to open both the front and apartment door. I open. "Smells like my apartment." He stumbles inside and leaves the door open.

I close the door and take off my shoes. We enter into his kitchen. Thomas wasn't expecting guests, yet it's orderly. He sits by the table to take off his shoes. I rummage and pour a glass of water and hand it to him. "Thanks," he says. I drink a glass myself. He lays his head on his arms. I've fallen asleep like that.

"Bedroom," I say. He rises but leans on me.

We walk through the hallway with bookshelves to my left. He has rows upon rows of books, some leatherbound and etched with Gothic font. I have no books in my place because they're too heavy to move.

Light from the hallway helps me guide Thomas to his bed. His arms are wrapped around me and when he falls onto his pillow, I'm pulled down with him.

"Kiss me Kay," he says.

"You're drunk," I say. But he smiles with wrinkles around his eyes.

"And so are you," Thomas says. "Kiss me. *Bitte.*"

I kiss him. I taste his lips. I taste his tongue. I taste the lingering beer, only beer with no cigarettes. His arms wrap around me tighter, and I cradle the sides of face. I go from kissing his lips to kissing his neck. My tongue tastes salt and sweat. I lick his earlobes and he lets out a moan as goosebumps form.

I need to see him naked.

My hands glide underneath his shirt and feel the curly hairs on his belly. I lift up the white cotton, and see his chest. It's broad, massive, and coated with blonde hair darker than his head. I pull off my shirt in one fluid motion.

"*Schön*," Thomas says as he runs his large hands up my stomach and pecs. He smiles like he is the happiest man on earth.

I unbuckle his belt and slide off his jeans. I feel his meaty ass and thighs as I get the pants off, and he lies in his white briefs. His cock snakes to the left, and its length and girth are so massive that the head peaks out from the leg opening. His foreskin doesn't retract.

Thomas tries to unbuckle my belt. He fumbles, and without experience, it's not easy. I help him, and I'm in my boxer briefs. A faint voice whispers self-doubt about the size of my own cock compared to Thomas', but before the voice could get too loud, Thomas pulls down my underwear to my calves, bends forward, and sucks my dick.

He slobbers on it, and in between breaths, moans, "*Geil. Sehr geil.*" He's playing with his cock through his briefs.

I kick off my underwear. Thomas lies flat on his back as I pull his briefs down his thighs. His penis pops out and waves at me. He pulls his legs up to allow me to remove his briefs completely. When he puts his legs down, they're wrapped around my waist. His legs are open for me, and my cock nestles against his asshole. I tease him with my cock, rubbing in gentle circles. He nods.

He reaches for condoms beside his bed and gives one to me. They're the normal sized condoms that gay charities give out. I roll the condom on and squeeze lube on it. He keeps nodding as I aim. I nudge the head in, and he squeezes his eyes shut. I meet resistance and wait. This is the internal sphincter and is under involuntary control. After a few moments, the muscle relaxes and I push myself deeper.

Thomas' eyes go wide. "You're in." His breathing is shallow.

I stroke his cheek. "I'm all the way in."

"You're the first one," he says. "Oh god yes." His breathing becomes moans that urge me to be careful.

My thrusts are slow and tender. Thomas stares into me and I look back. I push his legs further up his chest, and bend down to kiss him. I build the tempo and Thomas syncs his own moans to the rhythm. Sweat drips down the side of my face, and I kiss him again. I fuck him at full speed, and the room echoes with the sound of my thighs slapping his ass. I jerk his cock. My hand can't fully encircle his shaft, but I squeeze and jerk him with each thrust.

"Oh fuck, fuck me," he moans before one last moan escapes his lips—and his cock spurts cum over his thighs and my chest. His entire body spasms. With his orgasm, his asshole constricts around my cock. I've been holding off my climax but I now come with him and inside him. All of my body's muscles contract in pleasure and my moan is a roar.

I'm careful with the condom as I pull out. How is sex different this time?

Thomas rolls onto his side, and I spoon him. I stroke his chest and kiss the back of his neck. Lying on the bed, our heights don't matter and he can be the vulnerable one. He turns around. I stare at him for minutes. I study the lines of his eyes and lips. We have not broken eye contact, and tears form in his eyes.

"Something happened to me," I say slowly and softly. "When we went to Snax. I lost control and a man forced himself on me. That's why I didn't call you back."

"Something happened to me," he whispers. "I've been expelled from my PhD program."

I kiss him again. I want to ask him more questions, but that can wait.

"Can you hold me until I fall asleep?" he asks.

"Yes Thomas," I say. "And also in the morning." This is how it's different with Thomas. In a city where public transport runs twenty-four hours on weekends, I'm not forced to spend the night. Tenderness and intimacy makes this moment different. I pull the cover over us, even if German bedding is only ninety centimetres wide and designed for one person, so it barely covers both of us. "Good night."

"Good night," he says and rolls over to be the little spoon. I press my lips against the back of his neck, and when I close my eyes, I feel my tears squeeze out and drip onto his skin. This is beautiful, holding him—but do I deserve this? I'm the one who has betrayed, and I'm the one who was discarded after being ripped open. I squeeze Thomas tighter. I fall asleep with the hallway light on.

10. Timothy

The difficulty in unwritten and unspoken rules is that they may be broken. All manner of unknown and unfathomable consequences ensue. Thus, when I answer a call from my mother, on a Saturday no less, my teeth grind while I try to sound sober and tolerate her.

"Of course everything is well here," I say. The traffic around the hotel is atrocious, and my hand encircles my mouth and the mouthpiece to dull the ambient noise. A friend from Hong Kong showed me this brilliant trick.

"I'm so glad to hear that," mother says. "I was a little worried since we missed last week's chat." In other words, she found my excuse for not calling her unsatisfactory.

"I simply forgot my SIM card PIN," I try to explain again. I've disabled that but kept screen lock on. "I rarely turn off my phone —"

"Timmy," mother says, "Let's not go over this technical mishap again." There's a loud honk. "Where are you?"

"On the balcony," I manage to say. "A close call between two BMWs."

"At home? You were never home on a Saturday living in London."

Of course I can't tell her I'm dressed in drag at a gay hotel. In a stroke of genius, I pander to her preconceptions, and the lie is more beguiling. "I'm still settling in. It's awfully difficult to meet Germans with whom I can relate, mother."

"Right, of course." Speaking of preconceptions, she pauses and I can hear her sip her glass. "You must be wondering why I'm calling at this late an hour."

The idea did cross my mind. "I hope nothing terrible has happened."

"Nothing of that sort," mother says. "Your father is already reading in bed. He has an early flight tomorrow."

"Really?" Relief washes over me. As dreadful as it is to talk to mother, I can tolerate father's judgemental tone even less.

"He will be on the first flight to Hamburg," mother explains. "There's an issue with the proposal for the client meeting on Monday morning, so he's going to straighten that mess out. He and I were thinking, since he's already on German soil, he may as well take one of those high-speed trains and pay you a visit in Berlin. Would you be able to greet him at the central train station in the afternoon?"

"I could meet father in Hamburg instead," I offer. "Deutsche Bahn customer service is a travesty, and I wouldn't wish that on my worst enemy, let alone father."

"No," she says. "He'll meet you in Berlin. He'll bring some proper English tea and would like a cup at your place, and then he'll take the evening flight from Berlin back to London."

I've been cornered. "I can't say no to proper English tea," I say.

"Brilliant, it's settled then," mother concludes. "Good night Timmy."

"Good night mother," I say. I haven't had a chance to smoke my cigarette, and it's burnt to the filter. I reach into my purse and grab another cigarette, and realise I haven't any more cash.

I wave at Kay. He waves back. Pam is with them. I pretend I'm still on the phone, and light another cigarette. I wait until the American girl is gone and rush inside. "I need to leave."

"But the voting hasn't finished yet," Kay says.

"Sorry, I can't, I just can't," I say. "I hate to impose, but may I ask you for a favour Kay? May I borrow money for a cab back, and could you settle the bill?"

"Of course, yes." As I take the euros, Kay asks, "What's the matter?"

"I'll tell you later," I answer. "Please let Pam know that I am grateful for her graciousness, and I'm sorry to leave without saying good-bye."

I head outside, and as a cab approaches, it dawns on me. I will need to buy a semblance of groceries for my flat. I check back inside, and Kay isn't paying attention. I rush across the street, and walk toward the U-Bahn station.

When I enter the train, I notice vomit on the floor. I walk to the other side of the carriage, and at the next station, I change to another compartment. The crowds of people as we past Bahnhof Zoo are rowdy, and I am suddenly painfully aware of wearing a dress.

A burly man looks at me, and I think—you either own it, or they own you. "Handjob is twenty euros," I say, and pretend to toss him, but as I look deeply into him, tongue wetting my lips, I pretend to toss a tiny little schoolboy cock.

His face flushes bright red, and looks away. You've been owned bitch.

My feet hurt and are cramping by the time I return to my building. I kick the heels off, and the cool tiles are somewhat comforting. When the doors of the lift open, a woman exits holding a basket of laundry. I peer at her in shock and pity because who does laundry on a Saturday night?

She looks at me and how I'm barefoot while holding high heels in my hands. "How we suffer for fashion," she says. I can't place her accent.

"The high heels aren't the most painful part of this ensemble," I say.

Her gaze lowers to my nether region. "I bet." She continues to the laundry room, and the doors close.

I almost want to cry when I'm back inside my flat and see the mess. Of course my father's visit is a test. I need to clean. I contemplate whether to clean in the morning after a good night's sleep, but I might as well clean while I'm a little tipsy and the buzz will make this less sufferable.

I think about the woman doing laundry—and I pity myself, on my hands and knees cleaning as opposed to on my hands and knees lusting to be gang banged. I'm naked, and haven't bothered to wipe the eyeliner and lipstick from my face. Conchita continues to reside there, serving desperate housewife realness.

With the buzz gone, I've filled two rubbish bags full. I haven't sorted anything, and managed to only drop a beer bottle but that thing fortunately did not break. I head for a much deserved shower, and scrub my face clean. As the colours swirl down the sink, relief washes over me. I sleep naked.

In the morning, there is still work to do. There's a layer of grime, and I need to do another load in the dishwasher. I have a tiny forty-centimetre wide machine like a baby dishwasher. I check my phone and father hasn't yet called.

It's a shame to disturb the pristine bathroom after cleaning it but I need another shower. I had forgotten to wank last night, and the soap suds awaken my dick, like it's bitter from abandonment of the attention it duly deserved. Little Timothy does deserve at least a hello. I stroke, and slip a finger inside my bum.

When I orgasm, it's one of those disappointing ones, like a perfunctory climax. My toes aren't involved, my skin doesn't prickle, and I stare at the mess my jizz made on the shower door thinking it wasn't worth it. At least my prick is no longer bitter.

I'm about to finish showering when my mobile rings. "Good morning father," I say as I see wet footprints on the just-cleaned floor.

"Good morning Timothy," he says. "There's a fast train in five minutes. Would you be able to meet me at the central station in an hour and forty minutes?"

"Certainly," I answer. "I'll meet you at the train platform."

We say goodbye. Shit. I wanted to grocery shop and come back so father would attain the illusion that I am capable to take care of myself. It's bloody Sunday and the only places open are at the train station.

I'm dressed in my church best as I wait at the platform. I wait at the section for first class because I know father wouldn't have it any other way. At least I managed to fill my sports bag with groceries.

The train arrives in off-white and red glory with a distinctive metallic smell from braking. Father exits like a gentleman. As much as I hate his judging me, I judge him at this very moment. He's not a tall man at 5'10"—I'm taller than he is by an inch—but he has a full head of hair that's only greying at the sides. Although not fit, he's trim in his tailored suit. Before he steps off the train, I know he's already surveyed the platform. Each step is poised, deliberate, and unhurried. Father walks with the confidence of a man whose consultancy is worth millions, and not the cash hole that is my listed company.

He greets me with a pat on the shoulder. "Good afternoon Timothy."

"Good afternoon father," I say. He has a rolling carry-on, and detests the squeaking noise of the tiny wheels so would only use this if he plans to stay for longer than a day trip. I point at the luggage. "Mother said you were flying back to London tonight."

"I brought additional things in case I'd need to be present at the meeting tomorrow morning, and as it turns out, I do. I put too much faith in the new hire, although Derrick's been with the company for six months. I suppose people do disappoint."

"So you'll be spending the night in Berlin?"

"No need to fret Timothy," he says. "After dinner, I'll take the train back to Hamburg. I've already made a reservation at the Atlantic Hotel there."

As we walk to the taxi stand, we discuss business news. It's certainly better than discussing the weather. We arrive at my building after I've gained information on possible stocks to buy—and if I weren't broke, I'd buy them all.

"So tell me about why you chose this place," he asks.

"It's furnished and central," I answer. Is that answer good enough for you? He stares at the blandness of the building and says nothing. "It was originally a temporary solution, but I've been preoccupied with building the business."

Father nods. "Your mother and I have considered buying a flat here, and we could let it out to you," he then says. "Although I believe prices are inflated because of Southern Europeans hedging against the breakup of the Euro, we'd do this for you. Rent would be a token gesture."

I wonder if it was he or mother who wanted to do this. "I'll look for a flat and let you know."

"A two-bedroom place," he adds. "In a building with character." As opposed to this place, I know father.

We are on my floor. I am nervous about letting father into my space, and as I open the door, my next door neighbour departs. It's the woman who had done laundry last night. She smiles at the two of us. "So you're not the one who left the alarm on this morning?"

"No," I say, "but that annoys me too, those Monday to Friday residents."

"I'm Anna," she says.

"Timothy," I say. "This is my father, Edmund Goodall."

My father and Anna shake hands. "Pleasure to meet you," he says.

"Father?" she says. "I would have thought you two were... business associates." I think my father is staring too much at Anna's low cut blouse, and he didn't appreciate the subtle jest. "Nice to meet you as well. I better go."

As she enters the lift, I scream, "Wear ear plugs on weekends!" She smiles at me with soft and twirling blonde hair, and blows a kiss.

"Where do you think she's from?" I ask when we enter my flat.

"Holland," father answers. "I've dealt with many Dutch in my life." My father inspects the place with bed, desk, and TV in one room. "This flat is definitely furnished."

"Feel free to take a look around."

He drops his luggage by the bed/sofa. "You mean there's more?"

"The bathroom," I say. He walks into the bathroom, and I hurry to the kitchenette to unload groceries. I boil water in the kettle, and when he comes out, I say, "Mother said you'd bring proper English tea."

Father says, "Not English, but Scottish." I'm perplexed. He enters the living room, and I hear rustling as he rummages from his luggage. "I knew you'd appreciate whisky much—" There's a pause, then a groan as father rips open the duty free plastic wrap. I grab two glasses and put them on the table. Father enters the kitchenette and sits around the tiny table. His face is flushed and immediately pours both of us two-fingers' worth.

I raise the glass to my nose, and the bouquet of peat flavours awakens my nostrils. "Cheers," I say.

He blinks, then stammers, "Cheers, son." I pour him another two-fingers' worth. "Tell me what's really going on Timothy. I heard you missed an investor meeting."

Of course he knows—they were his contacts. But he need not know that I missed the meeting because I took too many sleeping pills. "I emailed them and said I was ill and if we could reschedule," I explain. "But no one has returned my calls or answered my follow-up emails."

"Were you truly ill?" he asks me. He's the one now pouring.

"No," I say.

"Was it nerves? You've given more presentations at investors' meetings than I can count."

The best lies germinate from a grain of truth. "The projections in my business plan were too optimistic. Even if the investors would have given me extra funding, my burn rate would have left me cashless in three months."

"An unviable business," he concludes. Yes father, I'm a failure. I'm not like you. "One missed investor meeting is not the end of a business, but if the numbers aren't supportive, investors will not return." Father, through a Dutch holding company, was a major investor.

I feel warmth in my cheeks. I think about all the times I worked like mad to gain his approval, and he dismissed my accomplishments with a nod. "I've failed and I am a disappointment." I gawk into my empty glass.

I feel father's hands on my chin, and he lifts my head to look at him eye to eye. "Failure is part of starting a business. As long as you learn from it, you have not truly failed. Understand Timothy?"

There's a softness to the wrinkles around his eyes, and I've never realized one only acquires these particular lines from smiling. I nod.

"So what have you learned?" he asks.

"Be more pessimistic with sales," I say. "Anticipate more outlays at the beginning."

"Why were your sales lower than projected?" he asks.

"My product was another Twitter clone, wasn't it?" I say.

"Your product did not possess a competitive advantage, certainly," he says. "Twitter could serve the entire market and had network effects, so your company had many hurdles."

My cheeks are hot again. What will I do now?

"Did you mention that your security protocol was unique?" father prods.

"It's secure and compresses data at the same time, and can work on dumb phones."

"It's a rare combination and may just be the security protocol for mobile banking, especially in developing systems in Africa," he says. My father is a genius.

"Brilliant!" I jump from my chair. "I'm going to work on another business plan."

"Hold on," he says as he pours more whisky for me. "Drink. I'll be honest with you Timothy. I wouldn't invest in your new venture. You have insufficient experience in the mechanics of banking."

I sit back down and drink. The buzz now numbs. "What do I do?"

"It's valuable," he says, "but not in your hands. Sell the rights to it." He pats me on the shoulder.

"Are you proud of me father?" I try my best to restrain myself, but the tears come. "When I was thirteen, I failed a math test and you berated me about how failure was not a possibility for us Goodalls. I never felt I could live up to your expectations or accomplishments."

"That was prep school," he says, and waves his hand like he's dismissing foul food served at a restaurant. "Prep school is pathetically easy, and you were too brilliant to fail then. You weren't applying yourself, and tough love motivated you. But life and the business world, that's something else entirely. I am proud of you."

I wipe away the tears like I'm in a bad telenovela. "Thank you Dad."

"This is your first foray into entrepreneurship," Dad says. "There will be others. You have a passion and drive that borders on the obsessive, and after you've had a chance to take stock of the lessons learned, we'll work together to find something new." Dad pours more whisky. "One more before dinner, my treat."

"Did you ever fail?" I ask.

"No," he says before looking away. He drinks the rest in one gulp. "I'm sorry Timothy. I lied. I did fail. Twice. Once in my first business. Second on your mother. I was very distraught. But it was inexcusable." He rises. "Let's go to dinner. I'm famished."

Dad treats me to steak at the Grill Royal. We reminisce over our family trip to Dublin when I was eight and we ate Irish filet mignon steaks for the first time. "Your eyes lit up like you were in Willy Wonka's chocolate factory," Dad recollects. "For months, all you wanted was Irish filet mignon steak, even for breakfast. We were all amazed by how much you wanted it, even your sister." Dad rubs my head, something he has not done since I was thirteen.

At the train platform, we say our goodbyes. "Come to London soon," he says.

"Send my regards to mother and Claire," I say. I hold out my hand for our usual handshake.

Dad grabs it, but as he looks into my eyes, he suddenly pulls me closer to him. I embrace him, and I feel the warmth of his neck and the strength of his arms for the first time. He then whispers in my ear, "I won't tell your mother, but I saw the black bottle by your bedside. Everything makes sense now. And you're still my son, no matter what."

He releases me, and without a further word, walks into the first class compartment of the Intercity Express. The black bottle is a bottle of personal lubrication with the picture of a muscular man's backside. I'm out, I'm out, I'm out. I'm out.

I'm out!

11. Alex

This is the worst. I'm shackled to the wall's outlet as I use my phone because when it's unplugged, the battery lasts anywhere from a few minutes to a few hours. There must a problem with the charging, and I've already ordered a new phone, and it should have arrived yesterday, but fuck, the delivery's late. This deserves a two-star rating.

Mom and I have been arguing by text. She wants me to come back to Minneapolis. She wants to discuss things in person, but I text back with furious thumbs pecking the screen. "Why fly back when you won't change your mind." With my Mom, I use full sentences.

She answers, "Please call me."

"I can't even speak to you right now," I write.

"What if I hire someone?" she texts.

"You mean someone to mediate between us?" I write back and take a sip of my beer. Why isn't she answering? I look down at my phone and see my last text message was autocorrected to, "You mean someone to masturbate between us?" The image of a mysterious third man between Mom and me flashes for a brief moment, hands just as furious as my thumbs once were. Hell no.

I call her. When she picks up, I can hear her laughing. "Alex."

"It was that damn autocorrect," I say.

"Some things shouldn't be done over text," she says.

"Or the phone," I concede.

"Does this mean you'll come here and discuss things in person?" she asks.

I don't know why I flew back to Berlin if I was going to return to Minneapolis. "I need to think about this."

"At least we're talking," she says. "After the yelling, we stopped talking—and you flew back without saying good-bye. We were both angry, I know. If you decide to come back, and want to stay at a hotel, it may be good to have some distance until we can talk things through."

"OK. I'll let you know," I say.

"Bye Alex."

"Bye Mom."

Silence. My Dad's last words echo: "You're twenty-nine and have nothing to show for it." I'm in the living room, and Kay's bedroom door is open. Past the bed on the wall, I can see the photos of the places he's been and the degrees he has. Plural.

I take another sip of my beer. What the fuck did Dad know? I have a little more than two years to my music degree, and I'm living in another fucking country. I can speak German. That's something. He was German and couldn't say more than please.

I get a notification that Vicki has just signed into Skype. I video message her. "Hey," I say. It's afternoon and sunny in Minneapolis.

"Hey Alex," she says. "How's the jet lag?"

"The first night was rough," I say. She doesn't seem as pleasant as she normally is. "Is everything OK?"

"Josh has just been a handful today," Vicki says.

Something doesn't seem right. "Is that all?"

Vicki bites her lower lip, then says, "I didn't get my period."

"You said you were on the pill," I say.

"That's your answer?" she snaps. "It's my fault and I lied. I'm a fat single mother who hasn't been with a man in forever so, yeah, I lied."

"You're not fat," I say. I want to say that's she's curvy and I like her curves, but I'm not sure curvy sounds any better to her.

"That's not the point Alex," she says. "I may be pregnant, and if I am, it's yours. I have an appointment tomorrow with the women's health clinic downtown." I think about my conversation earlier with Mom about how some things shouldn't be done over the phone. Or

Skype.

I can see my face in corner of the screen. My face is almost frozen. "What would you do if you are?" I ask.

"I'll keep this one," she answers. "Look, I don't need any help from you. I don't need any hand-outs. I've raised Josh on my own, and although God knows it's been tough, I did it and can do it again."

"Keep this one?" I repeat. Vicki is silent. "What do you mean with that?"

She closes her eyes, and then says, "The summer before you went to off to Georgetown, I found out I was pregnant when you were gone." I had told her I loved her, and I was going to stay in Minneapolis. But I didn't.

"I'm sorry," I say.

"I knew you were going to leave," Vicki says. "I knew your heart wanted to see the world and not be raising a child in Minneapolis. I knew you lusted after something I couldn't give. But I can't stop what I feel, and I keep giving to you." Vicki runs her fingers through her blonde hair and then looks to her left. "I think Josh is waking up," Vicki says. "You want to say hello?"

"Yeah." Josh's father is a guy who entered Vicki's life after me and cheated on her. Josh has his father's eyes, and I'm wondering what it's like to be burdened by a son who reminds you every day of the man you despise.

"Hey Josh," I say. "What did you do today?"

As Josh explains, I also wonder: if Vicki had kept the child, he or she would be older than Josh. Would this child have had my eyes? Would they be blue like my dad's?

"We're going to Skype with Grandpa and Grandma soon," Vicki says. "It's time to say good-bye to Alex."

"Bye Alex," Josh says.

"Bye." I'm angry at myself. I may be that burden.

I'm again alone in the apartment. I wonder why Kay hasn't returned yet but he's an adult and can take care of himself. I put music on, and although my favourite album from Nils Frahm, I still feel restless as fuck. I'm also out of cigarettes so decide to head to the *Späti*.

It's the father working tonight and not the hot son, so I don't linger. Should I go home? I see Vicki and Mom in my head and decide not to. I keep walking.

It's a beautiful night in Berlin. The tree leaves are blooming, and it's warm enough that cafés have put chairs and tables out on the streets, and some customers cover themselves with blankets to enjoy their drinks outside. I can catch snippets of conversation. I remember when I could first do this, I felt empowered—it meant that my German was improving, and I no longer needed to pay attention to understand the language. But the truth was more nuanced—unlike a musical note that I recognize in an instant, some days I understand German better than others.

I peek into the windows of apartments. The ground-floor apartments are the cheapest, so it's not surprising that the insides are full of Ikea furniture and cheap posters on white walls like my apartment. Germans are much better at putting Ikea furniture together than friends back home. Germans actually count all the screws and pieces before beginning assembly and lay them *ordentlich* on the floor in neat piles. There are also Ikea parties where you invite your friends to help put things together and whoever builds the most stable piece wins. Germans actually find this fun.

Why don't I want to go home?

I'm in the very rich part of Prenzlauer Berg with zip code of 10435. The cars here are BMWs, Mercedes, and Audis with a few Porsche for good measure. In my part of Prenzlauer Berg and its less sexy 10437, there are more Volkswagen and French cars. I used to live in this part of the city before my roommate found a real job in Frankfurt and I had to find an apartment with my own name. I used to go to a bar called Zum Schmützigen Hobby where the bathrooms were decorated with old porn magazines. It was a dirty place until neighbors complained about the noise. It forms Prenzlauer Berg's past, like a dance bar NBI. Instead of a dance floor, it's now floor space to sell Apple products. I'm conflicted about this gentrification because although I like to dance, I also like my Iphone accessories.

I also used to go to this place Perle Bar. It opened as a gay bar, but now it's a cocktail bar that's gay-friendly. Big diff. I go inside and don't recognize the bartender, but she smiles and nods when I enter. The bar is narrow with grey walls and grey leather ottomans softened with candlelight. The one gay element is a wall covered in shiny brown scales like a drag queen's dress. I haven't been here since 2010, and it feels like travelling back in time.

"Gin and tonic," I order. She makes the drink and gives it to me. There are large slices of cucumber which aren't just for decoration but add flavor.

As I sit, I notice a man with a lush blond beard and curly blond hair—not only do the curtains match the drapes, but the sofa cushions as well. He's sitting with a straight couple in their fifties. As he drinks and smiles with his companions, I wonder whether he's straight, gay, or bi. That's the only problem with gay-friendly straight bars. That, and the woman's bathroom is actually for women.

A woman walks in that reminds me of Vicki. It's the hair and eyes—Vicki has long blonde hair that she effortlessly pars on the side, and this woman has blue eyes that Vicki has. The German woman joins the bearded guy's table, and says hello with a handshake. Although this woman is taller and slender, and she dresses with more sophistication, she moves stiffly. This German woman doesn't seem to know what to do with her hands or legs so she constantly fidgets from one awkward sitting position to another.

Vicki is different. She knows to place her hand on my chest, to expose her neck to me, her cleavage offered to my lips and tongue. Vicki knows what to do with her legs, to spread them open and welcome me inside. Vicki is confident with her hips riding my own. She's not shy to sweat.

I light my cigarette. I shift in my seat so my erection isn't so obvious.

The bartender comes to me. She says, "I'm sorry but can you please smoke outside?"

At least she's friendly about it. "I used to come here often, and I could smoke then," I say.

"We started serving food," she explains. "Sandwiches." I suddenly remember there was a man with long hair and unkempt facial hair who would come around Perle selling, "Baguettes, baguettes." In the haze of drunk-time, I thought he was saying faggots, faggots.

When the bartender walks away, I reach into my crotch to adjust. I go outside with my drink.

A few drags into this cigarette, the blond beard walks out and stands beside me. "Do you have a light?" he asks. I hand him my lighter which today reads *Dildo King*, black shaft and font in mustard yellow. He smiles. "They have a sale this month."

"Good to know," I say. "That's something I'd never buy from Amazon. Can you imagine the recommendation emails you'd get after?"

He laughs and the beard accentuates the grin. He's shorter than me. I'm 5'11", and he must be 5'7". He looks at me, and asks, "Where are you from?"

It's one of those boring questions that I resent because usually a follow up question is like, "But where are you really from because you look kind of Asian." I hate it when people try to figure me out within two minutes of meeting me.

"America," I say as I anticipate the inevitable.

"I have family in Oregon," he says and switches to English. "I have a trip for this summer. Can I practice my English with you?"

"Absolutely," I say. "Who are you with tonight?"

"Just friends," he answers. "We went to see a movie. Don't ask about it. It was bad. What did you do tonight?"

"Talking to family back in Minneapolis. Then I needed a walk."

"Without family," he says, "I would be lost. I see my parents every Sunday, and my daughter will come next weekend."

For a moment, I want to think about my Dad, but instead, finish my gin and tonic. "Your English is very good," I say.

"Thank you," he says, and finishes his cigarette. "Are you lonely?"

Lonely? That's a big question to ask. I think about my list of Facebook friends, and it's over three hundred. I've moved so often and met so many international people that I can go to Paris tomorrow and have drinks with a friend. These are people that have always been there for a laugh. But when Dad died, who actually came to see me?

"Sorry," he says before I could answer, "I mean, are you by yourself now?"

"Yes," I say. "I've got lots of friends in Berlin."

"Are you gay?" he asks.

That question came out of the blue. "Bisexual. You?"

"Gay," he says. He then touches me on the small of my back. "I'm Karsten and I live across the street. Want to go to my apartment?"

"Yeah. I'm Alex."

He says good bye to his friends, and we literally just cross the street and go upstairs to his building on the third floor. I read the last name as he unlocks his door, "Müller." As soon as the door to his apartment closes, he grabs me and we start to kiss. He pauses and is careful with hanging my jacket. We start taking each other's clothes off in the bedroom, and he's smooth unlike his beard would suggest. His cock is medium, and his head is purplish pink with foreskin that pulls all the way back.

"Are you active or passive?" he says.

"Top," I say.

He reaches to his side table, and hands me a condom. He is on all fours on the bed, and inserts lube up there with his fingers. I rip open the condom, but my cock isn't really hard. It's happened before, especially when late on a bender after countless beers, but I haven't drunk that much today. His ass is round and firm, and his pink asshole is winking to beckon me in, but I'm just holding onto a condom and a flaccid cock.

I had an erection with thoughts of Vicki just a while ago. What's going on with me?

He looks back, and I see his face behind his ass. He gets up and then pushes me on the bed. I'm flat on my back, and he sucks me but I'm not getting hard. He takes the unused condom and rolls it on his cock.

"I'm versatile," he says. He lifts my legs up.

"I don't normally get fucked," I say.

His cock is pressed against my asshole. I need to fart—having my legs up is squeezing my stomach and intestines. There's a wheeze and I know I'm red faced and I want to laugh, but Karsten doesn't say anything, and once the fart is over he pushes himself all the way in.

I've tried to bottom before. Once with Todd when my parents weren't home. He didn't have a monster dick, but it was large and thick, and the pain was excruciating that I never tried again. Lately, I've had fingers up there including my own.

Karsten's dick is much bigger than a finger, but with him all the way in, I feel goosebumps. This tingling that runs all over my body— like the feeling of taking an epic shit, like when I've held it in all morning on a train through India because, you know, and I arrive at the hotel to expunge it all out and my knees become wobbly. Better the hotel than the McDonald's at the train station. Except this is double the intensity and way more pleasurable. Why haven't I given in to the pleasure before?

Karsten begins to fuck, and is jerking my cock as he does so. My cock stiffens. The sweat reflects the bedroom's lights, and I watch his face as he gets pleasure from my body. His brow furrows in concentration, and the veins and the muscles of his neck pulsates as he grunts through closed teeth. In moments, I see it—the shuddering, squeezing of his eyes, the quivering in his arms. His chest is on my own as his breathing slows, and he pulls out.

My cock is still hard and Karsten places his lips around it. Normally, I can't get off from blowjobs—they feel nice, but I have to either jerk myself or fuck to get an orgasm. This time, I can feel the tingle coming just before I climax.

"I'm gonna come," I say.

Karsten lets go just as I spray volleys of cum on my chest—and his face. His eyes are squeezed closed because of white globs attacking him. We're both laughing now, and the closest thing to me is his shirt so I grab it and hand it to him.

"I think I need a drink," he says. He speaks in German. "Beers?"

"Yes." He heads out of the bedroom and I go to the bathroom. As I pee and then clean up, I realize how empty I feel. I'm glad I'm on the toilet because my legs feel weak.

When I emerge from the bathroom, Karsten has the bottles on

the bedside table resting on coasters. His bedroom is painted dark red with white crown moulding. As opposed to cheap machine-made crown moulding in my Minneapolis McMansion, this is handmade from the early 1900s. His walls have a few authentic abstract paintings in white frames. They're authentic because I see the brush work. His apartment is modestly sized, but it simply means he fills each square foot with carefully chosen pieces. The bed's high-end Ikea.

I grab my drink and see a photo of a little girl. "Your daughter?"

"Her name is Tina," he says. "She's seven-years old." The bedroom continues to smell like sex, and Karsten goes to the windows. He turns the handle to tilt mode, and the window falls back slightly for fresh air, like a door ajar except for windows. German windows are amazing.

"How does a gay man get a daughter?" I ask as I kiss Karsten. We clink bottles.

"I was married," Karsten says. "I only knew I was gay when I was thirty-five. The divorce was hard but I have a beautiful daughter."

"She makes you happy?" I ask.

"Very much so," he says.

"A few months ago, Garbage had a concert at Huxley's," I say. "I loved their songs when I was younger, and their songs were about teenage angst and being depressed. After singing, 'I'm only happy when it rains,' Shirley Manson talks about the daughter of one of the guitarists. She talked about how the daughter sings in the new album, and introduced her to the audience. Shirley looked so happy being Auntie Shirley—and I thought, 'Children are the answer.' Even for depressed alternative bands from the nineties."

"Or a divorced gay man," he says.

There's another photo, but one with Karsten, Tina, and another woman. "When you came out, were you afraid you'd lose Tina?"

"I did lose her," Karsten says. "Ulrike took Tina to Köln and I was here alone. It was freedom and I felt like I had a second chance to live life. I partied and fucked my way through Berlin although the first time a guy fucked me I almost fell in love."

"Was it the hormones or was it true love?"

"It was the drugs," Karsten says. "He was also hypersexual and wanted to fuck me morning and night, and it was as though he needed to fuck me just like he needed to breathe. I loved being needed."

I begin to realize that no one needs me.

"But he gave me something and I almost overdosed," Karsten continues. "As I was in the hospital, I was crying and—Ulrike and Tina were there. Ulrike had lost her job and moved back to Berlin, and I realized I needed them to need me. This keeps me safe."

When you're lying naked beside someone, it's not just your genitals that are exposed. "There's no one who needs me."

"Parents?" he asks.

"My Dad passed away a month ago," I say.

"I'm sorry to hear. How about your Mom then?" he says.

"She hasn't been able to talk about anything but Dad's will and money," I say. "We're having a fight right now over it."

"Both of you could be angry over your Dad's death," Karsten says, "and this fighting is easier than dealing with it." I start to shake now, I don't know why I'm shaking, and Karsten embraces me and pulls the bed covers over us.

I then realize I left Minneapolis to come back to Berlin because I didn't want to deal with this. Being here, I could imagine in the back of my mind that he's still alive somehow, and I can't see him because he's far away. He is alive, only very far away.

"My Dad is dead," I say as soft as the final note of a lullaby. I'm the little spoon and I don't know whether Karsten can see me cry. The entirety of the fact hits me. Dad will not be there for my birthday. He will never take me to another ballet performance. He will never hear me sing in a concert hall.

Karsten kisses me on the back of my neck.

I am hard now. His hands brush against my cock, and he feels my cock's full girth. He pulls the covers off us, and after rolling on a new condom, sits his ass onto my hips and slides my cock in. He welcomes me.

"I need you to fuck me," he says.

12. Thomas

The sun is bright this morning. My apartment faces northeast and receives direct light only for some periods of the year. Sunlight filters through leaves, and in this intense light, the leaves are exposed and their veins visible as they sway to the breeze. What are the physical properties that determine a material's transparency? I'll have to research that later. It's beautiful but there's a throbbing in my head. I left my contacts overnight. That should not be done.

I turn around. There's someone beside me. I have never awoken with someone beside me. My heart rate escalates, and my thoughts race. Did he go through my shelves? Did he search through my computer? Did he make a mess in the bathroom?

"Good morning," Kay says in German. He smiles.

"Good morning," I say. Kay kisses me. A peck on the lips, and I'm glad it's not a slobbery kiss with foul morning breath.

"It's hot," he says, and pulls the bed covers off both of us. His torso is traced in lines and shadows where his pecs and abs are, and there is a coating of black hair on his chest. There's an area where his shoulders tuck into his neck, and it looks inviting. I cradle my head into this fold, and all thoughts of contact lenses and strange questions disappear. Lying on the bed, I am not taller than he is. I rest and hear his breathing for moments that seem like forever.

"Any dreams?" he asks.

My nose smells his skin. "No. I never remember them."

"I dream often. And sometimes, I know I'm dreaming. Last night,

I was being chased through a city."

"That would scare me," I say.

"I was scared too, but then I realised I was dreaming. I ran to a green field, and thought, 'I'm just going to fly away.' Whoosh! Up into the clouds. It felt amazing."

"I've read about lucid dreamers," I say. "I wish I could do that."

"Lucid dreamers? Maybe I'm one of them." Kay strokes the back of my neck, and the touch tingles. "I learned that I was gay when I was fourteen through a dream. In it, I lived with a man in a two-storey house with velvet walls in the bedroom the color of burgundy. I felt love and desire all at once. And I could control the dream. I flipped through magazine pages in my dream, found a man, and whoosh! He came to life, and kissed me."

"What did the man look like?" I ask.

Kay stops stroking, and after a pause, "Kind of like you." He shifts to look at my eyes.

"I'm hung over," I finally say. My eyes are dry and I squeeze them tightly to moisten them.

"I'm just a little hung over," Kay says. Is it really a little or is it English understatement? Wait, is that what I think it is? The toe on his right foot—there's dried blood. Not just on his toe, but there's caked blood on the sheets. There's blood on the comforter. Blood.

"Your toe is injured," I say. "You made a mess of the bed." How can he be so rude to bleed on my bed? Blood equals diseases.

His eyes open and his nose twitches. "Shit. Sorry. I must have injured it last night somewhere. It's not the first time I hurt myself when drunk." He touches my forearm. "You're bruised here."

I inspect the purple bruise. I'm also hurt. What am I feeling? That we're both injured makes me less—judgmental, worried, I don't know. "I get you a bandage. Or you can take a shower."

"Shower first," he says. "Towels?"

"In the bathroom," I say. He limps out of bed and into the hallway.

Alone, I sit. A cloud passes by, and without the light, the warmth is gone. I also feel something inside me. Or the lack of it. Kay was inside me last night, and now there is an emptiness. Before I examine further, I see the piles of clothes on the floor. I lay Kay's clothes on the chair. My clothes reek of smoke. Where's my jacket?

This is not in order. The blood on the bed. I pull the sheets off, and head to the kitchen where I have the washing machine. My clothes, the sheets, and a few others from the laundry basket and the six-kilo machine is full. I turn off the hallway light.

Kay is taking a long time. There's pressure on my bladder, and I knock on the door. "How much longer Kay?"

He opens the bathroom, and is towelling his hair dry. "I was looking for the bandages." His foot is wrapped up, and I rush inside after closing the door.

I sit. How dare he open my drawers? This is my apartment and my privacy.

Kay knocks. "Can I make coffee?"

"OK," I yell. At least coffee would be good for my headache.

The shower head has been moved lower. I raise it back to my height with a grumble. Underneath the water, I think about my day. Sunday is for reading. It's also the day when I allow myself cake. I finish showering then take out my contact lenses. My vision is better with glasses.

I walk to the kitchen. Kay is naked, and pours coffee from the Italian espresso pot. The table is set with the cold cuts from last night's meal. "Naked breakfast?" he asks me.

I sit down, and smile when I see eggs. I have never been made breakfast in my apartment before. "What's naked breakfast?"

"It's like regular breakfast," Kay says, "but we don't fry any sausages."

"Is this a Canadian or Chinese thing?" I ask. There's a moment when he looks at me with a raised eyebrow.

"It's a my-clothes-smell-like-smoke thing," he then answers with a smile. "And you look beautiful in the morning."

I put my coffee down, and stare at Kay in the morning light. He sits by the window, and I'm stunned by how sexy his shoulder and neck muscles are. Thick and dense muscle that is not translucent, but each time he moves, shadows mark the striations in his trapezius and deltoids. "You are sexy," I manage to say. "What do you normally have for breakfast?"

"A protein shake, and on weekends, fried eggs with scallions dribbled with soy sauce," Kay says. His breakfasts sound exotic. He slices a roll in half, and after cracking the egg, he spreads the boiled egg over the soft bread. "What's your favourite breakfast?"

"Nutella," I say. "But I don't buy it anymore. It will make me fat." I put a few slices of ham on the other half of the roll.

"I don't have a sweet tooth," he says. "My favourite is dim sum." Before I can ask what it is, he seems to anticipate it. "It's small delicacies steamed in bamboo baskets. Sundays, my family would go to Kum Koon Garden and women would push steaming carts past us. There was curried squid, barbecued pork buns, pork dumplings called Xiu Mai, but the best were Ha Gao, steamed shrimp dumplings in a soft, translucent rice flour wrapping."

I had thought fried eggs with scallions were exotic. "Food is important to you."

"My Mom spends hours in the kitchen," he says. "It's such a Chinese thing for parents to never actually say that they love you, but with the variety of steamy food on the dinner table, I knew that they did."

"My Mom hated the kitchen," I say. And she was always in her own depressed world to say that she loved me. "But my Dad liked coffee and cake in the afternoon."

"I have an idea," Kay says. "How about we do a cultural food tour of Berlin? Chinese lunch, German afternoon break, and we can see what we feel like for dinner."

"Does this mean you want to spend the entire day together?"

"If you have a fresh toothbrush for me," he says.

"I went to Rossman yesterday so I have one," I answer. "It's the hard brush kind."

Kay laughs. Why is he laughing? He gets up from his chair and walks to me. His crotch is eye level, I see the shape of his cock in the fabric, and I want to reach out and suck his dick. But he sits on my lap, and wraps his arms around my neck. "We went through a lot of things yesterday. Do you remember what happened?"

Drinking too much, him finding me, and coming home. The confession. Him fucking me, and how good that felt. I nod.

"We were both bad and hurt," he says. I don't look away from his eyes, and he doesn't either. "I felt safe sleeping beside you. When I woke up feeling your body, I felt happy. I don't know where this will lead, but I know I'm happy and want to spend more time with you."

"I'm happy too," I say. "I don't pay attention to feelings very well."

He kisses me, and despite our morning and coffee breath, I kiss him back. Deeply. "I wasn't aware of my emotions at first. But I learned," he says after the kiss.

"I'm not ready for a relationship," I blurt.

"Neither am I," Kay says. "I only spent the night here—it wasn't our honeymoon or anything."

"OK."

Kay gets off and his crotch is eye level again. "Do you want to take a walk before learning how to eat with chopsticks?"

"Sure, but after the load of laundry is done," I say. I don't want accidents to happen and have my liability insurance premium raised.

"You're so German," Kay says. "But let's wait then. We'll just have to entertain ourselves while we wait." I take him in my mouth, my breath now a mix of cock, coffee, and cold cuts.

13. Kay

Work parties. At their best, I'm drunk on another's dime. At their worst, I'm stuck with people being boring, people I normally get paid to be around. Work parties—all the fun of unpaid work with the threat of something stupid happening while drunk.

The company has rented the VIP section of the Olympic stadium. I see the rows of empty seats, and on the giant TV screen, CoExcel's animated logo loops non-stop like one of our strategy alignment meetings. As a co-worker drabs on about the controversies of the latest Standard Operating Procedure, I try to imagine what this stadium was like in 1936 with the first televised Olympic Games, and a distinctively moustached man welcoming the world before destroying it. Did he stand here? What went through his head when he heard the cheers echo? It's humbling and exhilarating to feel connected through time to one of the most epic moments in human history.

Scratch that. The booze is what I'm feeling. And my feeling is empty.

"I'm going to get another drink," I say in English. It's part of working at an international company in Germany—there's this constant social tally of whether there are more native English speakers than German, and if so, then the lingua franca is English. As soon as the ratio changes, the switch happens. With my exit, the ratio has shifted to Deutsch, and that same co-worker drabs on in German, but more emphatically so.

My work phone clangs against my private phone in my pant

pocket. I wear a grey suit. I take my own phone out while waiting in line and text Thomas that it'll be an hour more. Hopefully I can leave sooner.

Away from the bleachers, there's a renovated section where food and drink stands serve burgers, sausages, and a mysterious dish from the "Asia Kitchen" stand. The social committee convinced the men from the Board to work various stands. The CEO puts grilled sausages in buns and hands them to the common folk with a smile that reminds me of the smiles of politicians. I'm too bloated for more meat.

A man pushes a cart of salads. Dr. Anton Hoffman is the Chief Medical Officer. He's in his sixties with glasses, a full head of white hair, and trim. He looks similar to the other German executives on the board: no one is ever bald, or fat, or a woman. I once met him during a lunch for new hires with fifteen other people. I had asked a thought-provoking question, something about integrating Chinese sites into study programs. I could use a salad.

I approach him, and when he sees me, his eyebrows lift almost past his head. He must remember me from the luncheon and my intelligent question.

"Hello Dr. Hoffman," I say. "I'm Kay Hung from Client Relations Management."

"It's good to see you," he says. "I'm serving salad. It's not very popular."

"You'd think that working in the healthcare industry, people would be healthier," I say.

He shakes his head. "Greens for better cardiovascular health?" He holds a salad in both hands.

"And a slim waistline," I say and take the garden salad. Our hands touch.

Off to the side, someone calls his name. "Have a fun time here Kay Hung from Client Relations Management," he says.

I take a bite of lettuce. "Thanks, and you serve a delicious salad."

His face reddens and he storms off. Did I just do something stupid?

I need another drink, and maybe I'll have another sausage after all for the U-Bahn ride. In less than an hour, I'm back in Prenzlauer Berg. Although it's May, I sit beside a fireplace. There's a French wine bar that pairs the perfect cheeses to it called, "La fromage qui rit" and has a picture of a cheese wedge with googly eyes and a crazy smile. The atmosphere is warm, the wine impeccable, and the cheese delicious— all for Parisian prices, which is why Thomas loves coming here when I'm paying.

I know, I know—it's supposed to be beer after wine, I'm feeling fine. But in Germany, the saying is, "*Bier auf Wein, das lass' sein—Wein auf Bier, das rat' ich dir,*" which means the opposite. Or the same. German is confusing so fuck it. I'll do what I want.

The glasses are empty, and the waiter comes. He's German, and based on his accent, a Berliner. Thomas is in a shirt and dress pants, and he looks nice. He refuses to grow a beard but thinks the beard on me makes me look older and more masculine, and I've interpreted that as a good thing. Thomas doesn't wear his contacts today, so his enlarged blue eyes make him invisible. He's mine, kind of.

"More of the same?" the waiter asks.

Thomas says yes, and starts talking small talk. I notice this about Thomas. When he speaks English, even with only me, his body isn't as fluid, his face the typical stoic stereotype of the serious German. But when he speaks German, like now, he moves more, he smiles more, as if the video stream has finally buffered and I'm not seeing a choppy mess. I wonder if, when I speak German, I am more reserved.

I realize I'm not paying attention to them. I don't know if it's my being tired or the alcohol, but the German words are simply sounds. No meaning whatsoever. That is until the waiter pats Thomas on his chest, and the waiter's palm rests a little too long for my liking.

The one thing I can still do while very drunk is order more booze. "*Entschuldigung, mehr Wein bitte.*" Quit flirting with my non-monogamous boyfriend.

"Georg is from Friedrichshain," Thomas says to me in English, his shoulders suddenly still. Another Georg in this city. "Where my mother's from. He says I should visit authorities to find out what information the state had on my family. The records may be destroyed, but there could be something."

"It could be bad," I say. "Are you ready for it?"

"I'd rather know and be unhappy than blissfully ignorant," he says.

"Speaking like a true scientist," I say and suddenly regret it. Thomas is appealing his expulsion but hasn't heard back yet.

Georg returns. He's tall and slim, and smiles when he gives us more wine. He has dimples that you can't really see because of his beard, but I notice. He also puts down a small tray of crackers and grapes. "What do you do in Berlin?" he asks me in English. I'm so glad they're speaking to me in English and I can still do that completely wasted.

"I work for CoExcel," I say. "I'm in Client Relations Management." Work doesn't define me so I hate talking about it.

"Have you met Anton Hoffman?" he asks. He smiles a crooked smile.

"Yes," I say.

"He's very gay," Georg explains. "His boyfriend is Vietnamese. His boyfriend has a multimillion-euro restaurant on Friedrichstrasse."

"How do you know?" I ask.

"Gay business owners talk," Georg says. He looks at a blond man at the bar, and joins the man.

"Did you know the owners of his place were gay?" I ask Thomas.

"Yes. Georg and David are married. But who is this Anton?" Thomas says.

I explain about the salad incident. "At first, I thought he just recognized me, but now, I think he may have had the hots for my beef stir-fry." I shouldn't have said that. I am not a mysterious dish from the Asia kitchen.

"With thick rice noodles," Thomas says. "That's my favourite." A gulp of red wine. "You're looking up and into the distance. I know that means you're thinking."

I look at Thomas again. "You know I'm no career girl."

"Work to live, not live to work?" he says.

"Work life balance," I say.

"Half-ass your way through it," Thomas adds. "This is why you're never the bottom."

"But," I say, "I have a chance to advance my career. I mean, I never thought I'd ever sleep my way to the top, but here's a chance."

"Moral issues?" he asks.

"There's always those," I say. "I don't know if I'd actually do it."

"If you do," he asks, "I want jewels for being the mistress' mistress." Thomas can't pronounce the last two double Ss properly.

The place is empty now except for Thomas and me as the only patrons. David comes to us, and I'm ready to pull out my wallet when he says, "One more round on the house?" The gay discount. Thomas and I nod.

David and Georg join us around the fireplace. David looks older than Georg, and besides the contrast in hair colour, David is shorter at 172cm, or 5'8". He looks French, and is a real life example of size differences within Europe. Another are clothes sizes—a T-shirt from Zara's is a M in France, but an S in Germany. It's an XS for the US.

"How was business today?" I ask. So even though there are two native German speakers and only one native English speaker, David is the trump card—and we speak in English.

"There was one asshole customer," David says as he looks around to be certain. "He ordered the wrong cheese with the wine even though I recommended him not to, and when the bill came, he didn't pay for the cheese."

"But that's the restaurant business," Georg says and kisses David on the cheek.

One of the responsibilities of being the only native English speaker is I have to moderate the conversation. "Do you miss France then?"

"No," David says. "I'm actually Belgian but of course from the French side."

"Why a wine bar?" asks Thomas.

He rubs his fingers with his thumb—I guess the sign for money is universal. "Prenzlauer Berg yuppies love their wine." He looks at me, and adds, "Sorry."

"No need to say sorry," I say with a smile. "The smoky gay bar down the street that served cheap beer is now a classy Italian place."

"How long have you two been married?" Thomas asks.

"More importantly, how long did you keep fucking after getting married," I add. Maybe moderating the conversation is a privilege.

"A year and a half," David says. He's the one who answers, he's older, and he's the one in charge. "And we're still, can we say, dipping the biscuit?"

"You mean sex, right?" Thomas asks.

They nod.

"But we spice things up," Georg says.

David touches Thomas' hand. "I see," Thomas says and suddenly covers his crotch with both hands, not from being shy. He gropes it. "Where can we do this now?" He looks directly into Georg.

"There's Treibhaus Sauna, a five-minute walk from here," David suggests.

The doors burst open and a straight couple in the twenties enter. Georg stands with all smiles and apologies, but says, "*Es tut mir leid aber wir haben bald Feierabend. Ich bitte Sie um...*" and shuffles them out the door. After slamming the door shut, he turns around, and then presses his entire back against the glass. "We are going now."

At the sauna, I see scores of blue tags dangling from free lockers. This place isn't busy, especially with the new sauna opened in Kreuzberg and the whopping 2600 square meter premises. I pass the bar with glass countertops, and the main area is a chamber with a hot tub in the centre and plastic vines on one side with sky blue paint for walls. Is this hot tub supposed to be in a verdant outdoor garden? Instead I feel like I'm on the set of a low-budget television show with plastic plants.

I immerse myself into the centre of the garden. Bubbles greet my ears. I love hot tubs. They blow warm kisses over my body, and it's as close to paradise as humans can achieve without drugs. Thomas hops in beside me, and his big cock flops in. I love the sight of it. He kisses me on the cheek.

"This feels good, or?" he says and puts his glasses to the side, and smiles at me expectantly.

"Wonderful," I whisper and stroke his cheek.

"There isn't a lot of people," Thomas says. "I thought there would be more."

"Gay life in Prenzlauer Berg is dying," I say.

Georg and David enter the tub together, their penises jiggling as they splash in. We smile and they smile back, and in the waft of steam, we remain silent. We simply relax. There is the occasional moan when one of us adjusts positions, but we let the bubbles do the talking. Then, I could feel myself stiffen as David pokes his big toe into my thigh, and when I do not protest, he plays with my dick with the big toes of booth feet. His eyes widen when he feels my full thickness.

"Suck my cock," I mutter. The bathhouse is quiet and besides us, there is a harmless old man jerking off in the dark.

David swims to me. I lift my hips so my cock is raised above the water, and David bends down until his lips taste my base and his mouth submerges in the bubbles. He sucks like this is the only way to breathe.

David resurfaces, his beard shaggy from the chlorine water. He pushes me back until I sit by the edge of the pool. My cock and balls are above water, and David then sucks with complete gusto. Clothed, David dominates. Naked, he submits.

Thomas, my bottom, is giving Georg a blowjob too.

My cock is hard and I want to fuck. I lift David up, and after a quick fumbling while putting on the condom tucked with my towel, I ease David to sit on my pelvis. He moans, and starts thrusting himself on me. I jerk his cock, and it's tiny, almost like a baby's wrist. There isn't enough lube on the condom, and the friction is uncomfortable. David ejaculates on his stomach, and when he gets off me, I'm soft without coming.

I look at Thomas and Georg. They're doing it doggy, and Thomas rubs his dick on Georg's asshole. Georg, face red and left cheek pressed against the floor's tiles, commands, *"Dein Schwanz ist so groß. Gibs mir!"* Thomas never fucks me. I can't endure that feeling again.

I throw the used condom to the corner, and head to the steam room. David leans back in the Jacuzzi, a grin on his face. There's the flop-flop sound of my slippers in between Georg's beckoning moans.

Once enveloped by the steam, I see nothing. I'm glad. Breathing requires effort, and my body sweats beyond my control. Steam, sweat, and jealousy mix into a puddle at my feet. What right do I have to be jealous? I am the betrayer and whore after all.

The doors open and without question it's Thomas, his bulky silhouette lumbering in. He feels for the plastic moulded seats. He sniffs, then says, "You're here Kay?"

"Here." He slides to sit beside me. "I didn't know you could tell me from just the smell."

"You have a distinctive smell," he says. "Plus a hint of garlic."

"You Germans can always smell when someone's eaten garlic," I say.

"That's true," he admits with a snort. "We don't use garlic in German cooking."

"A life without garlic is no life at all," I say as Thomas puts his hands on mine. We sit there for a moment holding hands.

"I was jealous," I finally say. "When you were with Georg."

"Does this mean you want a monogamous relationship?" he asks.

"I don't know," I say. I don't know if I deserve it. "I still think about the morning when I first lay beside you. It felt tender and intimate, and when the sun shone on your eyes in just the perfect way, I thought, 'Yes, this feeling could be love.'"

"Love?"

"Don't worry, I haven't said the L word yet," I continue. "I certainly wouldn't blurt it out so awkwardly. But it was a beautiful moment. Then, the birds chirped. And as I kissed you, I kept wondering, 'Where are the birds? Where did they come from?'"

Thomas clears his throat. "And where they are going." It wasn't a question but a statement. "I think the same."

"We think the same," I say. "We are boyfriends but open?" Maybe I've earned this.

"Yes," says Thomas. He leans on my shoulder. "I didn't fuck Georg."

I feel a hand on my cock and it isn't Thomas'. My boyfriend must have felt the same thing because he jolts up.

"*Ich bin Erkan*," comes a voice. Through the mist, a lean and muscular shape emerges. His voice is deep, and his hair curly. "*Lasst euch einen blasen?*"

I reach for his head and guide it to my crotch. He laps up my cock before I guide him to Thomas' dick. We each take turns being serviced by Erkan with his head volleying back and forth between our crotches. This time, I want to come.

***

I've come to the restaurant on Friedrichstrasse. There's only one word to describe the art in this place: *fromage*. French cheese is the cheesiest. A gay artist—because only a gay man would think of doing this—has painted the body of a Greek statue using 1970s-inspired purple and green, but instead of an actual penis, he has painted pixelated squares. It's true of another painting where the pixels appear instead of sultry and curvy ass cheeks. This is art conceived from someone who hasn't seen the timeless masterpieces at the Louvre or Albertina, or understands what makes a body beautiful.

I sip my coffee. This is my third time coming here after work, and I wonder if I'm ever coming back. I order the bill when I see Dr. Anton Hoffman enter with an Asian man who wears gold earrings. Anton sees me, and as he walks toward me, I see the fag with earrings squint and purse his lips, serving me bitch face with a side of spicy before he sashays to the bar.

"Good afternoon," Anton says to me. "You're Kay Hung from Client Relations Management, correct?"

"That's right Dr. Hoffman," I say.

I hold out my hand for a handshake, but he gets in closer and hugs me. "Call me Anton. I think we're past handshakes since you've found my dirty little secret."

"You being gay, this extravagant restaurant, or the jealous man pouring himself Champagne at the bar?" I say.

"All of it," he says. "But it also means you're a gay man yourself."

"Since I was fourteen," I say.

The waitress comes by with the bill, but Anton dismisses it with a wave of his hand. "It's six o'clock somewhere in the world. How about we have something a little more stiff?"

"Whisky," I say. "But the twelve-year old variety."

"That is stiff," Anton says but orders the fifteen-year old whisky. "One of CoExcel's corporate values is to over deliver."

We clink glasses. "To over delivering," I say. The drink is smooth in my mouth, but burns going down. When I breathe, the air tingles my esophagus. It feels like fire.

"To advance in the company," Anton says, "you need someone higher up to advocate for you. A mentor to guide you through the unwritten rules of management and corporate life." He starts listing the men and one woman he has helped advance within the company. "I've never had a gay protégé before. Is this what you want from me?"

"Yes, if you'd have me," I say.

"Good," Anton says. "But we need to make one thing clear."

"What's that?"

Anton leans across the table. He's so close, and at this intimate distance, I see his skin—pale and translucent, the veins pulsing blue on his neck. He whispers to my ear, "We can never have sex." My ears tingle from his breath.

"Never," I repeat.

"Good," he says. I smell the stale coffee on his tongue. He slowly leans back, but without warning, squeezes my crotch while looking at the waitress. "More whisky please." This fifteen-year old whisky is good. I don't know if I can go back to drinking anything else.

14. Alex

"There're no seats," Vicki says as she strokes Josh's hair. Why did Mom insist on traveling on a Friday afternoon with Deutsche Bahn? It doesn't matter to her because she's sitting on the train in first class, and since Vicki insisted on paying for the ticket herself, we're cramped with the hordes of *Pendler* spending their weekend with loved ones in another city. For Germans used to living on a tiny continent, fighting for space on the train is no big deal. For Americans from the Midwest whose hallways are bigger than German kitchens, not having space is suffocating. I had insisted on small bags for our trip so we're at least mobile.

"Wait here," I say.

"By the bathrooms?" Vicki says. "We wouldn't have to do this in America!"

"I'll find us seats," I say while trying my best to not counter with, "But in America we wouldn't have high speed trains going over two hundred km per hour", or whatever that is in miles. It's damn fast, and as the foreground trees blow past like a sneeze, the background brick homes whizz past in spurts.

I'm walking down the blue upholstered aisle. Every seat is literally taken. Keep walking—and try not to notice the Germans staring and trying to figure me out. I need to check the next carriage, and as the glass slides open like a Star Trek movie, I see the dining carriage. I see a free table, and I'm almost running back.

"Come quick," I say as I grab Vicki's free hand and we're running through the train in an accelerated tempo.

We're back in the dining car, and I see a woman in her fifties clutching a Louis Vuitton bag walking toward the empty table. I rush and sit down before she does, and she walks past just as Vicki and Josh sit down. Don't make eye contact Alex.

"I'm glad we have a seat," Vicki says then notices the stare of evil. When she walks away, Vicki adds, "She's mad at us, but I noticed her being mean to Chinese tourists earlier so I don't feel guilty." She gives Josh a handheld video game. It's mine but I let him use it on the trip. "Why don't we drive?"

"If you think this is full, the Autobahns are even worse," I answer without adding that my Mom objected to being cramped in a car with all of us. In Germany where everything is measured and reported, the Automotive Association predicted kilometres of congestion on the A24. I was once stuck on an Autobahn with ten kilometres of congestion, and it took forty-five minutes to clear it. It was at an Autobahn intersection, but once cleared, I gunned my rented Renault Clio 160 clicks only to have a mighty Mercedes behind me signalling for me to get out of the left lane. "Josh, what would you like?" I ask.

Josh's hair is getting darker, but still bordering on blond. His blue eyes look away from the game to the laminated menu. "I don't know. Everything's weird here."

"How about a pretzel and *Apfelschorle*?" I say.

"What's that?" he asks.

"It's like bubbly apple juice," I say. He nods and eyes disappear into a world of pipes and mushrooms. "And you Vicki?"

"A Coke. I can get that here right?" Vicki says.

"Yes, yes." I hold my tongue on the third yes. Of course nothing alcoholic. This is Vicki's first time abroad. My first time abroad was in London, and I was overwhelmed by British English. I go to the bar and come back with a beer for me.

"They didn't have any more pretzels but this is a *Laugenstange*," I explain. "It's just shaped differently."

"Everything's different here," Josh says as he looks with wide eyes at the bubbles erupting from the apple juice drink. "Even for lunch, we had mayonnaise instead of ketchup for our fries."

"But the *Currywurst* sausage was tasty, huh?" I ask.

He nods again, and goes back to his game without drinking anything.

"I need another Coke please," Vicki says. "These bottles are tiny."

I'm drinking my beer, and hold out my index finger. When the half litre is done, I get up to go to the bar. There's a line. What was I thinking, bringing Vicki, Josh, and my mother here to Germany? With my Mom, I thought this would be a good way to see that I'm living a responsible life here. With Vicki and Josh—well, I wanted to provide for them and to show them that there's more to the world than Minnesota.

"*Noch mals eine Cola und ein Hefeweizen bitte*," I order. I then see a bag of Gummi bears and order that too. There's a big smile on Josh's face when he eats a red bear. Finally. His smile makes me smile.

"Are you sure you don't want to go to Sweden?" I ask Vicki.

"I only have a cousin there, and she never emailed back," she says. "Who are we seeing in Hamburg?"

"My grandmother's younger sister. In dad's will, there was something he wanted to give her." This will be the first time I meet Bettina.

Vicki finishes her second Coke. "That hits the spot." She looks out the window, and part of me wants to tell her about it. We're still in the East. Even decades later, there are differences between former East and West Germany. Especially in the countryside, there are more grey buildings in the former East and more non-German cars on the streets. She looks at me and smiles. "It's beautiful out there." She gently places her hand on my own. "I know it's not easy with us, but— I'm really thankful." Her eyes sparkle with tears. Her hands are soft. "I'm finally in Europe and it's beautiful."

"It's just the countryside," I say and feel a little miffed that she didn't like Berlin. "But you're welcome." I squeeze her hand.

In half the time it would take to drive, we arrive in Hamburg. Hamburg is Germany's second largest city—beloved by Germans and obscure to anyone outside of Europe. Hamburg, like Berlin, was utterly bombed, but unlike Berlin, actually had money to rebuild with facades like a traditional European city. No dividing wall, no derelict communist buildings, no monument to the murdered Jews of Europe—a beautiful city with lakes, a port, and a river so clean you can swim in it. I think this is why Germans love Hamburg—the country's tortured past is invisible here.

We meet my mother on the platform. "How was your trip?" I ask.

"Lovely," Mom says. "A nice German man spoke English to me and took my drink order. How was your trip?"

"We had a lovely time too," Vicki says. "Josh tried an apple drink and liked it." She holds her son's hand, and Josh is standing as if frozen.

I lead them from the platform to the arrival hall. We're swimming in waves upon waves of people. The sound of the bustle is chaotic at first, but after moments, my ears hear a melody to them.

"There're so many people. It feels like shopping at the mall at Christmas time," Vicki comments. Yes, except the people here aren't wearing sweats.

We decide to go to the hotel and drop off our stuff. Mom wants to stay at the Atlantic, the most expensive hotel in the city which has rooms overlooking Hamburg's lake. I'm trying to load the map on my phone, but for whatever reason, the data connection is slow. Shit, I just remember that once I reach one gigabyte, my speed is throttled, and downloading cock pics from Grindr probably ate big chunks of this month's data allotment.

"My phone's not working," I say.

"What do you mean it's not working?" my mother asks.

"The map's not loading Mom," I say.

"Why didn't you buy a paper map?" she says as she clutches her purse tighter to her body. "Well, ask someone. You're the one who lives in Germany." She has been doing this the entire time—I'm the tour guide, and if things go wrong whether through a fault of my own or not, she bitches at me. If there is something she dislikes about Germany, she also bitches at me as if I'm responsible for it all. God damn it.

I approach a woman, and ask. She is polite, and her German is well enunciated. "Walk straight up this street, and when you see the church, turn left."

"How long will it take?" I ask.

"It will take about ten minutes," she says.

"Thank you," I say and head back to my American family. I tell them how long it'll take—this is the only way to get my Mom to walk without complaining. We walk together in silence to the hotel, the only sound coming from us are the squeaks from Vicki and Mom's luggage. Josh and I have backpacks.

Straight down this street. It sounds easy but this is Europe, and straight doesn't always mean straight since the road may curve along the way. I learned that a long time ago and this street does just that. Church... Where the hell is the church?

I take out my phone. I see a blue dot with an arrow pointing the direction, but no map and just a grey background.

"Are we lost again?" my Mom asks. Why did I take out my phone?

I ignore her and just take a left turn.

"The buildings are beautiful here," Vicki says. "What do you think Josh?"

"It's weird here," he says.

"Alex, are we lost?" Mom repeats.

Keep walking. You'll hit the lake sometime.

"We've been walking for twenty-five minutes," my mother says. "I'm not walking another step until you ask for directions again." I'm fucking mad and I clench my right hand around my phone.

From who Mom? We're on a side street and there's no one. Keep walking, and she'll follow. She won't dare try to find the place herself. Keep walking—look, there's water. The road leads to the Alster, and the view is magnificent.

I realize there are no squeaks. And there hasn't been any in a while.

I turn back and see that Mom, Vicki, and Josh aren't behind me. My phone is still in my hand, and finally the map has loaded. The Atlantic is to my right, and just twenty yards away.

Shit. Why didn't they follow me?

I run up the street. Maybe they headed back to the main street to ask for directions. But when I scan the area, I don't see them. There are boutique shops, bakeries, and fancy restaurants—but no Japanese American mother, nor blonde woman with a kid. Blonde women, yes, but no accompanying seven-year old boy.

I then see a taxi stand. Maybe they took a taxi to the hotel. I walk alone to the hotel. I enter the lobby with dread. If they're not here...

"Hi Alex," Vicki says. "We took a cab, and we saw a nice church along the way." I sigh and hug her tightly.

Mom looks at me with her hands on her hips like an urn. "I'm going to check in, and order room service. I will see you tomorrow morning to visit Bettina."

Josh looks at me. "Can we eat at McDonald's? I saw one at the train station."

I look at Vicki, and she nods. "OK. McDonald's sounds good. We'll make sure to get ketchup with your fries."

***

The next morning, Vicki and Mom are talking about the breakfast spread, and they both enjoyed the selection of yoghurt and bread. Josh even liked the cereal choices. I'm glad we have something to talk about as we drive in a taxi through the city. Mom has a photo album and the pendant on her lap. The pendant belonged to my grandmother, and was one of the few things she took with her from Germany to America. I wonder why my dad wanted to give it back to Bettina, and I wonder if he put this in his will so we would meet.

It's sunny and we are driving along the Elbe river. You always remember your first kiss, but not always the second or third. This is the curse that is Hamburg, Germany's runner-up.

We pass the Reeperbahn. It's Germany's answer to Las Vegas, and the buildings sparkle with a sunshine glitz although there is something classier about this version. The neon signs aren't as gregariously supersized, there are no fake Eiffel Towers, and even the fast-food joints are housed in brick homes. There's a man walking with a bag of Burger King takeout, and he's more concerned with his phone conversation than the row of female prostitutes with their tight jeans and fanny packs. The police station is across the street.

"I heard the Reeperbahn used to be Hamburg's Chinatown," I say. "But in the 1930s, the Chinese sailors recognized the change in political tidings and sailed off. This is why there are no Chinatowns in Germany."

Vicki and Mom look at me for a brief moment, but continue talking about breakfast. I'm the only one interested in Germany's history.

We continue to Altona, on the western part of Hamburg that used to belong to Denmark. We turn from the main road, and arrive at our stop. As we get out, I see a flower shop and rush in to buy lilies.

We ring. The only thing I know is that Bettina married a man named Johannes Schmidt, and she kept the name. "*Hallo?*"

"*Hallo. Hier ist der Alex,*" I say.

She laughs and says, "*Du sprichst Deutsch! Das freut mich. Erdgeschoss, links. Komm rein.*"

The door buzzes. "What did she say?" Mom asks.

"She's happy that I speak German," I answer.

Bettina's door is ajar and she lives on the ground floor. We close the door and Bettina walks into the hallway with a golden retriever by her side, and the dog's tongue dangles out. Josh's eyes go wide.

"Good afternoon Bettina," I say as I walk to her with arms open.

"Good afternoon Alex," she says, and hugs me deeply. We speak German. "This is my dog Kekse, and she is friendly." Bettina looks at Josh. "Do you want to play with Kekse?" The golden retriever looks at Bettina with the mention of her name, and somehow, Josh understands and slowly approaches the dog with his hand out. Kekse licks it, and Josh wraps his arms around the brushed fur.

I hand Bettina the flowers. She takes them, and says, "Come to the garden. I've set up coffee and cake." We walk through the kitchen. "There's also schnapps for us grownups," she adds with a wink.

I translate for Vicki and Mom. The garden is a tiny plot of grass with a giant tree taking up half the space and the neighbors from above can see everything that we do, but it's still beautiful. Bettina has tomato vines at the garden's edge where it's sunny and it gives a semblance of privacy. She has a crystal vase in her hand and places the lilies in them as the centerpiece.

I can tell it's a ritual with Bettina on how she serves. Mom's first, then Vicki, and she is last. She mentions this is her favourite porcelain set, but we shouldn't worry too much about it. "Beautiful things should be used," she says as she points to a small crack on her own cup. My Mom furrows her eyebrows.

"Port with the coffee?" Bettina asks.

"Vicki can't because she's pregnant," I explain. "Mom?" She shakes her head. "I'll have some." Bettina pours some into my coffee.

"My Mom Keiko has photos," I say. They are sitting side by side, and I gesture to Mom to show the photo album. When Mom reaches into her purse, Bettina pours port into Mom's cup.

Mom takes a sip. "This coffee is good," she says and Bettina smiles a big grin.

As Josh throws a tennis ball to play fetch with Kekse, Mom and Bettina start, and I translate for Mom: who's in the photo, where the photo was taken, and when. Bettina asks further questions like, "Did you make the other women jealous with your dress?", "Is that where you had your first dance with Mike?", or "What was it like to see the sun set on the beach?" At first, Mom keeps the answers short, but as she drinks more and more enhanced coffee, the answers get longer and more elaborate.

"Here's our wedding," Mom explains. I translate, *Hochzeit*. "Mike had set up the business, so we didn't have so much money for something big." It wasn't big—no, just a wedding with 200 people at the Hilton.

"People wrote their thank-you cards and told me how beautiful the wedding was," Mom continues, "the service was impeccable, and we served the best Champagne."

"What did you think of the Champagne?" Bettina asks.

"I didn't have any," Mom says as she flips over the photo album page.

Bettina looks at Vicki, then asks, "When was the wedding Keiko?"

"1984," Mom says. I translate.

"What month?" Bettina asks. I translate.

"July," Mom says. I translate.

"When were you born Alex?" Bettina says.

"March 19, 1985." When I do the math, I can feel my own eyes go wide, and I drink the rest of my coffee. I—never thought about it? Why didn't I think about this?

I didn't translate the last part, and Mom hasn't noticed. She casually finishes her coffee.

"More?" Bettina says in English.

Mom nods but then says, "Yeah, but wait… I'll like some schnapps instead."

Bettina gets a tiny schnapps glass with a stem, and pours peach schnapps into it.

"Oh. This is tasty," Mom says and drinks another sip. When she puts the glass down, there's a distinctive ring. The glass is empty. She looks at the album, and huffs, "How did this photo get in there? It's all out of order."

"What photo Mom?" I ask.

"A photo from San Francisco," Mom says. She used use to live on the Inner Sunset before she moved to Minneapolis, and eventually met my Dad.

"Who's this man here?" Bettina asks as she points to a man of Japanese descent with a moustache and wearing a suit. He has an arm on Mom's shoulder.

I don't have to translate since Mom erupts with, "No one." She gets up from the table. "Excuse me. I'm going to the bathroom." Mom walks with a stumble in her gait.

"There's a story there," Bettina whispers to me. "I don't think it's a good one."

We wait for Mom to come back, and during the wait, Bettina speaks to Vicki in German. Bettina points to things and says the German word very slowly. Vicki repeats, and it's cute to see her try to mimic words.

"*Die Tasse*," says Bettina, pointing to the coffee cup.

"Die Tasse?" repeats Vicki. She says each word as a question.

After a while, we still don't see Mom come back so I excuse myself to check on her. I enter Bettina's apartment, and it's bright considering that it's the ground-floor. It's probably because there's a white wall across from her garden windows that reflect light into her place. The furniture is teak from the 1960s, and the lines are clean but with a mild curve like a woman's thigh. There is one wall full of framed photos. The largest is one of Bettina and Johannes on their wedding day. She's beautiful, and Johannes is handsome in thick plastic glasses. There are a lot of pictures of Bettina when she was in her teens, and there is another girl in black hair laughing with her.

Mom sits on the couch, and her head rests to the side. "Mom?"

"I need a rest," she says slowly. "It's hard for me to sleep on a different bed. The coffee wasn't strong enough." I don't tell her the coffee was probably too strong. The schnapps didn't help either. She starts to snore.

Bettina comes in. "Maybe it was a bad idea to give her alcohol, or?"

"She'll be fine," I say. "She can't handle much, but at least she doesn't get red."

I see the pendant popping out of Mom's pocket. I grab it and hand it gingerly to Bettina. "My father wanted you to have this."

Bettina's hands are shaking when she takes it, and it takes her a few attempts to open the pendant. There's a photo in there of a woman, cracked and almost completely faded. "Mama," she says and she trembles. I see tears on her face, and I rush to Bettina to hold her. Her tears drench my shoulder.

After a few moments, she wipes her face with her wrist. "Thank you. I have no photos of my mother, and I forget how beautiful she was." I give her another hug and she hugs me back. "Not only a beautiful woman, but a strong woman."

"Tell me about her," I say. German history includes my family history.

"Are you sure?" she asks.

I nod.

"Her name was Heidrun," Bettina begins. "She was born in Charlottenburg in Berlin. During the war, father was gone in the *Wehrmacht*, not the SS. So she didn't get special treatment, but yet, she always found food for us. Even near the end of the war." I've heard about the hunger in cities when defeat was inevitable. "I was four in 1945, and she feared the Red Army. Somehow, even before the rumours of rape from Red Army soldiers trickled into Berlin, she knew it was better to surrender to the Americans or British."

"What happened?" I ask.

Bettina holds onto my shoulder. "I tell you this because you need to know. This is part of who you are." I nod again. "Mother smuggled us on a truck heading to Hannover. I don't know how she got papers to leave Berlin, or how she convinced the SS soldiers to take her, your grandmother, and me, but Heidrun was beautiful and charming. That's all I can say. I still remember clearly—she was in the front with the soldiers while your grandmother and I were in the back. There were cables to secure cargo, and mama used that to secure us in our seats. She told the SS soldiers it was our first time in a truck. I was so scared and didn't say a word the entire way.

"Suddenly, the truck swerved off the Autobahn, there was a gunshot. I closed my eyes and waited for another. Weren't there two SS soldiers? But I felt a touch on my cheek, and mama said, 'They're gone. We're safe.'

"Her face was bruised and bloody, but she smiled at Hiltrud and me. We got off the road and walked. Her right hand was bloody, and she tried to clean them on the grass. We walked for hours. She once even carried me and I felt the pistol hidden in her shirt. We came upon a farm, and we waited until we saw an old man come out. Mom told us to wait, and I was afraid she was going to shoot the old man. But the old man hugged her, and Mom waved us to come. We stayed on that farm for two weeks before the Americans found us but they treated us well. That wasn't the case with our neighbors back in Berlin."

Bettina walks to the bedroom and I follow her. There's the rhythmic tick of an old clock. She opens a drawer with her jewellery and

I see it. There's no way to miss it—among pearl earrings and gold necklaces, there is a pin of a bronze eagle clutching the corrupted but unmistakable swastika of Nazi Germany.

Bettina sees my eyes. "You still feel its power, don't you?" I want to touch it. I've seen the symbol in television and pathetically tattooed on the white skin of Neo-Nazis from Alabama. This is a whole different thing— in three dimensions, as something I can hold and touch, and all the suffering it represents, it's more powerful than I could have ever imagined. I reach for it. Bettina doesn't stop my hands. As soon as I finally grasp the swastika and feel it, Bettina clutches my hand in both of hers. The metal is cold, and the grooves of the eagle's talons dig into my palm.

"It belonged to your great grandfather," she says. "He was on the Eastern front, and wasn't as fortunate as your great grandmother and me." She strokes my hands so I unclench, and the swastika falls back into the drawer with a loud thump. "We were wrong ... but this is part of who you are Alex. We must never forget."

* * *

"I want to forget this afternoon," Mom says to me hours later and holds onto my arm. We walk to her room at the Atlantic. She shuffles like a Geisha, and I feel like a dutiful son. "I need a nap. I'll be fine for dinner."

"Vicki and I will do some shopping. Want anything?" I ask.

She shakes her head, but then exclaims, "A Hamburg thimble. I've thimbles from all fifty states." I suddenly remember the wooden cabinet in the study, and the thimbles on display with porcelain figurines. If I don't find a thimble, I'll buy a figurine instead.

We reach her room, and she fumbles with the key card. I clasp her hand and guide it smoothly for her. Once inside, I help her with her shoes and jacket. The curtains are drawn open, and the afternoon sun reflects off the lake's waters.

"Do you want the curtains closed?" I ask.

She mumbles something. I get closer, and kneel beside her. "No."

"Mom," I say, "can you tell me about the man in the photo?"

She turns so that her back is facing me. "The asshole. I'd still be in San Francisco if it weren't for Yuma." Her face contorts in discomfort. "Sing me something Alex."

I clear my throat and sing something she'll know—Ave Maria. Her eyes twitch less, and her mouth relaxes. "You sing beautifully." She opens her eyes, and looks at me. "The trust fund is yours. Pursue your passion, my son." I bend down and kiss her on the forehead.

I walk and am conscious of my walk. Passion is a strong word.

Before I leave the room, I hang the "DO NOT DISTURB" sign on the door handle. The sign is written in five languages including Japanese. At that moment, I wish I had an idea what the lines of characters sounded like.

Vicki, Josh, and I head out. We stroll through shops, and she likes to browse, and although I hate shopping, I'm happy seeing her happy.

We're standing by a rack of scarves and I ask Vicki, "What do you think of Bettina?"

"She's really sweet," Vicki says. "Did you notice the wall of photos?"

"Kind of," I answer.

"There were just three people on that wall," Vicki says. "Bettina, the husband, and a dark-haired woman from decades ago."

"You think the dark-haired woman was Bettina's lover?" I ask.

She puts her hand on my shoulder. "I can tell these things."

I see a scarf and say, "Want this scarf? I'll buy it for you as a souvenir."

Vicki shakes her head. "No need."

We continue out of the store, and walk along a busy street when I see a small church with its roof gone. I want to see it, and we walk up the stairs to cross an overhead pedestrian bridge. Josh is giddy when we realize the bridge has an escalator that only turns on when someone is using it.

"Cool!" he says. "How does it know we want to go up?"

"There must be infrared sensors at the top and bottom," I guess.

Of all the hours spent strolling through Hamburg's city center, this is the only dilapidated building. In Berlin, you don't have to look very hard to see decay.

"This church must have been bombed in the war," I realize, "and left like this as a reminder."

Josh starts exploring the space on his own. Vicki grabs my hand, and we start walking in silence. This was a protestant church, and the cross remains hanging, but it's simple, and it takes on an eerie feel when exposed to the elements. Only in a ruined church does a sunny afternoon feel eerie. Although there is the dull hum of traffic, the acoustics here still resound and our footsteps echo within the hall.

I see tears in Vicki's eyes. "What's wrong?" I ask. I stroke her cheek and she blushes.

"If it weren't for you," she says, "I wouldn't be here. Not just here, but Europe. Josh wouldn't be here to learn this. This is beautiful and amazing. But why did you pay for us to be here?"

"I remember how much you wanted to see Europe in sophomore year," I say.

"I'm grateful, but you know Josh will be talking about this forever. He'll talk about Berlin and Germany, and will always think about you. But you're not his father." She lets go of my hand. "Is this trip some way for us to be part of your life? Is it some weird way for you to practice being daddy? You can't just do this with one trip. If you're going to be part of our lives, you need to be all in. There's no in between."

I'm silent. A bird's chirp echoes in the hall, and then Josh yells, "Alex, what's this?"

We walk toward Josh. There's a bronze statue of a boy sitting on top of a pile of rocks, his body hunched over, his face in his hands as if he were crying. I read the plaque, and look at Josh. His eyes are wide, and he knows that this isn't "weird" like mayonnaise with fries, but something more profound.

The bronze boy is crying on top of a pile of bricks from the walls of a concentration camp. This boy is crying—I don't know if the boy is Jewish and is sad because he lost family, or if the boy is German and he's sorry for what his parents did.

"I feel sad," Josh says.

"I feel sad too," I say. "This is —" but Vicki shakes her head. I'm not his father. It's not my job to explain something so difficult. That death in Germany is a shared emotional experience.

Vicki wraps her arm around Josh's shoulder. She's the mother and she has to explain World War II to a seven-year old. I want to say, "This is what happens when people blindly follow without thinking." Vicki says something about bad things happening to Jewish people in Europe during a very bad war.

We are the only ones here. In Hamburg, there are monuments to the tragedy that happened, but it requires further digging. I think about the hordes of tourists doing their shopping at the posh avenue of Mönckeberg, and the late-night revelry basked in the neon signs of Große Freiheit. This is one way to cope with the ghosts of the past. Pretend it doesn't exist. In a similar spirit, we can reinvent the past, like how a German can move to America and his history is forgotten, if not always forgiven.

Then, there is Berlin. Right beside the iconic symbol of Germany, the Brandenburger Tor, there is a field of grey pillars that reach high into the sky and you feel lost in them. The monument does not sugar coat the past. It's called *the Memorial to the murdered Jews of Europe*. Every tourist to Berlin sees it, walks through it, and experiences it in various ways. Children giggle while playing tag and running through it. Some gays take selfies to put on their Grindr profiles. But others walk through and feel succumbed by something deeper. One year, an artist gathered fallen red leaves during autumn, and gently laid them between the grey pillars like a stream of blood. This is another way to cope, and when I saw the red leaves blown by the wind, I felt tears.

My father with German ancestry is dead. Vicki and our child are alive and here. As much as I'd like to forget, my past holds on to haunt me, if not forgiven. All this time in Germany, I've been experiencing the history here like it was someone else's. But it is mine, and I need to decide my future with my history in mind.

15. Kay

In the sun, Germans are happy. When the sky is blue, Berliners lounge outdoors like it were an art form, broad smiles on their faces. It's Wednesday during the first week of June, and not only does the sun shine, it's 28C and I'm tempted to wear shorts into the office. But Anton would not approve so I continue to wear my grey suit that reflects the sunlight.

The yellow joy has spread to Thomas. He texts me. "Juhu! Sunbathing in the park. Reports say Saturday could be sunny. If yes, want to go to Müggelsee?"

There's no air conditioning in my office, and as my sweaty thumbs text back, droplets smear the screen. "Yes. I need to cool down." I add Saturday's sunbathing as an appointment into my calendar, and code it yellow with the words, "Strategic Self-Development." Anton has read-and-write access to my Outlook and adds one-on-one meetings on the weekend.

June's calendar is already full with meetings colour-coded as per Anton's instructions. With senior management support, things move quickly within the company. I was enrolled in fast-track management programs developed by HR. I passed with flying colours, and Anton invited me to the new project dubbed "CoExcel 2020" where the company would take a more prominent role in developing study protocols with strategic pharmaceutical companies in return for greater milestone payments. No one ever defines what strategic means.

I receive an email from Anton. "Make sure you comment on these aspects during the kick-off meeting next week." I know to read his emails as soon as I receive them. As I scan the points, I feel like I'm stating the obvious. Greater revenue and profitability while burdening greater risk— and we can mitigate the risk by more intensive site visits. Except more pharma companies are entering rare diseases where no one has tried to enrol patients in Phase III clinical studies, so the rate of patient recruitment can be fast like in Cystic Fibrosis because everyone who has it knows they have it, or it can be completely hidden and misdiagnosed for years like Chronic Thromboembolic Pulmonary Hypertension. It seems like we're burdening greater unknown risk.

A reminder pops up on the computer screen: another fuchsia strategy alignment meeting for "CoExcel 2020." Why are we going through the slides again although there's no new information? Didn't we decide on an action plan last time? I tighten my tie. At least there's air conditioning in the conference room.

In the climate-controlled conference room, yesterday resembles today, and tomorrow will feel exactly the same at a cool 20C within the shadow of shuttered windows. Otherwise it's too bright to see the PowerPoint presentation. The hours drag as we micromanage lines on a budget. Another meeting over and I return to my office. It's hot inside my room. It's Friday. Today is Friday.

My private phone vibrates. Thomas texts, "Saturday's forecast is rain :("

My fingers tap on my desk. I stare at my calendar with the colour blocks filled for the next two months, but for the rest of today, it's an island of beige. No more meetings but I'm supposed to send Anton an updated strategy slide deck by the end of business. There are ninety-three slides in the deck. I know he hasn't read all the slides because I accidentally put in a misleading number in one chart but received no comments on it.

I call Thomas. "Are you lounging in the park again?"

"With my favourite book," he says.

"Can you go home and bring two towels? Let's go to Müggelsee while we can."

"But aren't you in a suit?" he asks.

"Yes, and that's why we're going to the FKK section," I say. FKK stands for *Freikörperkultur*, and is the nude part of the beach.

Thomas is silent but then says, "OK. I'll meet you at *Hauptbahnhof*."

I update the one figure and jazz up the wording in the executive summary slides. I'm a high-flyer and no longer a low-level nobody, so I feel confident when I use the word strategic. I email the slide deck to myself. At the end of business, whenever that is, I'll forward this version to Anton and see whether he notices. It's time to enjoy an island of beige by going to the beach.

From the main train station, we take the RE1069 to the lake. I roll up my pants, and walk on the beach barefoot. Thomas and I are still in the clothed section, and it's loud and bustling with children and their heterosexual parents wearing multicoloured bathing suits. Near the end of the beach, there is a wooden wall with a "FKK" sign and a narrow passageway through. The unofficial gay section is deep within the nude flesh.

The cries of children fade away, and we're greeted by the sight of glistening skin in various shades of German pink, beige, and peach. Whereas the main area is rampant with people running, throwing balls to impress, or otherwise being douche bags, here people lie relaxed without a care. The crowd is older and marked by gravity's relentless pull on breasts, ass, and balls. But it's honest. There's no hiding behind brand names. There's no bravado to prove you're more of a man. There's nothing more equalizing than being naked.

Thomas and I stop at a free spot close to the water. "Are you ready?" I ask.

"After Snax," he answers, "I'm ready for anything." So am I.

Thomas wears his contacts. He pulls of his T-shirt, and in one swift motion, his shorts and underwear are off. He starts putting on sunscreen.

My turn. I have my gym bag with me, and place the jacket in there. Everything else comes off, and I feel the breeze blow against my balls. It's FKK freedom.

"Don't forget your genitals," I say as Thomas covers his thighs in cream. "You don't want those parts to burn."

Thomas smiles. His penis now glistens, and he hands me the bottle.

"Shall we play the penis game?" I whisper as we lay on our towels. "I've counted five already."

"Does it include mine?" Thomas asks.

"Six then," I say.

"Eight," he says. "I'm taller and can see more."

A gay couple builds a sand castle. One is a skinny, olive-skinned man with a thick flaccid penis and a black beard. Number Seven. The other is a beefy, big-boned pale man with ginger stubble and a modestly sized Number Eight. I assume they're a couple because who else would make sand castles on the beach together? They're hard at work making a European style castle with a domed roof.

I also like playing the game, "Who's on top?" I know people wonder that about Thomas and me.

The beefy ginger then bends over to work on the roof and I have full view of his ass. "He's the bottom," I whisper to Thomas.

He furrows his brows. "How do you know?"

I get close so no one else hears us gossiping. "The ginger has an ass dent." I've seen it with porn stars that bottom. Their ass cheeks get so pushed apart that there's a triangular divot with a very exposed asshole.

"I better not bend over then," Thomas says with a smile.

I'm transfixed by the sand castle, but more so by the crowd of Germans that form around the castle. Number Nine through Twelve, including a few boobs for good measure, discuss the merits of the height of the roof, the need for a column here and there, and whether the windows are straight. German constructive feedback consists of, "It's not in order here." Try making your own sand castle and only then can you say something, I want to say.

Number Thirteen is a long wrinkled one of a man in his sixties. His stomach is flat, and his legs are thin with skin instead of hamstrings. When I look further up, past a chest with white hair, I see the face of someone resembling Anton. But it can't be him because he doesn't have glasses, and also, why would Anton be here? Doesn't he make shitloads of money, and when he wants to relax on the beach, can't he fly off to the Cote D'Azur and not the mundane lake accessible by train?

"There's an old man waving at you," Thomas says.

It is Anton. Do I have to say hello to him naked? I've purposely not gone to the company gym so I can avoid awkward hellos with naked coworkers. But I rise, and walk toward him. I am calm with my strides so my flaccid penis does not jump at him.

"It's a good day not to be in the office," Anton says. His arms open for a hug.

"Great minds think alike," I add and hug him back. I pivot my hips back so our genitals don't touch.

But Anton goes all the way in. "*Zwei Dumme, ein Gedanke,*" he says while pressing my back into him, and our cocks touch. "Two idiots, one thought," he whispers to my ear. He pauses like he's expecting me to admit to something. I know the game he's playing but why make me work on a Friday afternoon if you're going to be on the beach?

"Did you see the sand castle?" I ask and break the embrace.

"I did from my living room," he says.

"You live here?"

He points to a white house across the inlet adjacent to the sandy beach. "It's a retreat home. I live in Schöneberg during the week. But I saw the castle and swam here to investigate. I'm still a scientist at heart."

"That's a beautiful home," I say. The white house has a domed roof like the sand castle.

"Want to come by?" he offers. "I always like to show my protégés this home. Normally, this is later in the process when you've worked yourself to exhaustion and think you can't go on any further. But this is what you can have when you climb the corporate ladder."

I'm intrigued. "OK. I'll walk along the inlet and meet you at the house."

"It's faster to swim," he says.

I pause. I bite my lower lip. "I can't swim."

He shakes his head. "What do you mean you can't swim?" he says. His is as shocked as if I had said that I don't drink alcohol.

"I can swim a few strokes," I say to somehow defend myself. "The frog. But I usually get tired very quickly."

"You won't get far in the company if you tire like this," Anton says. "You're struggling against the water. There's a rhythm to the water, and your arms and legs have to move in unison with this rhythm." He takes my hand and leads me into the water. The beach leads to a shallow part of the lake that only slowly grows deeper. I can feel the coolness on my calves, then knees, then thighs. At my stomach, goosebumps erupt.

"It's cold," I stammer.

Anton dives in and when he emerges from the water, he says, "Once you're in, it's not."

I look back to Thomas. He's watching me but he has said that when he wears contacts, his vision isn't as good so I don't know how much he sees. I turn back to Anton and dive in. Within the water, I scream. Bubbles swirl around me, and I see a fish swim by my feet. For a moment, I hear only muffled water.

My head resurfaces but it's true—once neck deep, the water is warm enough.

Anton commands, "Swim to me." He's three metres away but still within the shallow part of the lake.

Stroke, stroke, and I stop. My feet touch the bottom. I'm exhausted and struggling to breathe.

"Your hands need to twist back to better push the water away," he says and walks another three metres. "Try again."

I do, and I reach this time. I'm happy. I'm doing it.

But Anton sees it differently. "Your feet need to kick back and out," he says. "Try again."

He walks six metres away. I swim five, and when tired, my feet touch the bottom. It's littered with the smooth shells of mussels and swaying tendrils of wild celery. We continue this for more than an hour. I've lost track of time. Anton looks at me patiently, but keeps urging me to swim further.

"You just swam thirty metres," he says. He's German so of course he knows how much thirty metres is. "That's enough to swim across the narrowest part of the inlet. You're ready."

Ready? He grabs my hand, and we walk past the beach. He swims halfway across the inlet. "Swim to me," he commands.

It's different here. I can tell he's treading water while looking at me. It means the bottom is deeper than 180cm. "I've done my life-guard certification. Kay, swim to me." Swimming like this is like doing a trapeze act without a net. Babies drown in water only a few centimetres deep. I can't tread water. I can't swim. "I'm only going to say this one more time," Anton says. "Swim to me."

I dive. I swim. I see him and the white house. My arms and legs are in sync, and I can feel the water give way to me. There's an undulation, a rise and fall, and I find the rhythmic sweet spot to tread water at the crest of this undulation. My muscles are tired, but I'm close. I keep my head above water to breathe. The sun shines on Anton and the white house. I keep swimming. Just keep swimming. Swim, swim, swim.

Then a wave comes just as I breathe in and I choke on water. I'm losing air, my muscles can't go on. I can't go on. I can't swim. I'm going to sink. The water is around me as I plunge and fall within the lake's depths. It envelopes me. I just feel cold.

Then hands and arms. I'm held between Anton's arms and chest, and he swims to the shore with me in tow. When I feel the bottom of the lake with my feet, Anton lets go. I scramble to the shore. I turn back and see him walking out of the water.

Did I trust Anton to save me, or was I stupid for diving in?

"You tried," Anton says. "And you followed my instructions. That's a good protégé." He continues to his white house while cupping his genitals in his hands. "You deserve a drink," he says when all I see is his backside.

He enters inside. I follow, but wonder, why was he hiding his penis?

"Help yourself to a beer," Anton says. "I need to go to the toilet."

Inside Anton's white house, one word comes to mind: opulence. This is what I see here. I've seen my share of European castles and the baroque interiors within, and this is no different. The living room has a fireplace and ornate upholstered chairs to either side. There's a painting of a man in hunting clothes atop the mantle. An intricate rug covers the hardwood floor. The walls are painted pastel blue.

I head to the kitchen. The shelves are white and modern, and the appliances are polished stainless steel. I'm envious. I want this.

I head to the fridge and am expecting shelves stocked to the brim. But as the cold air greets me, all I see are wine bottles. There are no fresh vegetables or meat that can spoil. And I realize the truth of weekend retreat homes—good food cannot be had here. Good food requires a kitchen full of ingredients, and these ingredients would spoil and their stench would contaminate a home that is barely lived in.

I then notice a shelf. This is where the butter would be stored, but instead, I see a poppers bottle in its bright yellow and red package. He is a gay man. But what are these unlabelled bottles with pipette tops?

I hear footsteps. I close the fridge.

"I couldn't see the beers," I say.

"*Scheiße*," he says. "I left them in the car. Why not have a glass of wine?"

I turn around. Anton is wearing white shorts. I can't tell the brand, but I know they're expensive—and with that simple act, the egalitarian nature of nudity is destroyed.

"I should go. Thomas is probably wondering where I am," I say.

"Thomas is your boyfriend?" Anton breaths in and his chest puffs out.

"He is," I say. Thomas is a poor student, but he's my boyfriend.

"He's a big guy," Anton says.

I look through the windows and see Thomas by the sandcastle. "I'll walk along the inlet to get back to the beach. I'll see you Monday morning Anton."

"You'll send me the updated presentation by the end of business?" he says.

"Yes." Without a further word, I leave.

I walk the long way around the inlet. When I am finally back on one of Thomas' towels, his head lifts from his book. "How was it?" he asks me.

"I swam thirty metres," I say and Thomas' face is happy for me until I add, "and almost drowned."

Thomas grabs me, holds me, and kisses me all at once. "Do you want to go home?"

"No," I say. "It wasn't so dramatic. I'll simply stay in the shallow part of the lake."

"I'm up to twenty-three," Thomas says after a while. "When you're ready, I'd like to go to the water with you."

"OK," I say. "If the weather is beautiful next weekend, want to come back here?"

"Yes," he says.

I then rest my head on the towel. I don't need a white house on the water. I'd rather nap on the beach with my other free-body-culture enthusiasts. A breeze blows across my cock and chest. I hear the waves lap against the sand. Thomas holds my hand. I want this feeling to last forever but know that by end of business, I need to email that slide deck.

16. Timothy

Of course there's a bloody questionnaire, and the questions force me to confront the unpleasantness of how much of a slut I've been. There's a question about how many sexual partners I've had in the last year. The last option is ">10". Is that not simply a good month?

I stumble my way through these questions in German. Context certainly helps—*Geschlechtsverkehr, Oralverkehr,* and *Analverkehr* must mean sex in its various forms, but doesn't *Verkehr* also mean traffic? Does this mean that if I'm late to a business meeting because I encountered bad traffic, I shouldn't do a literal translation into *Schlechtenverkehr?*

I do, however, resort to dict.leo.org on my phone to enter such marvellous words as *Erguss* (noun, outpour but also bruise), *abspritzen* (verb related to *Erguss*), and *spucken* (instead of swallowing it like a lady). Rimming is *Rimming* in German.

The male receptionist calls numbers. He repeats the number once, then twice, and on the second time, he looks directly at me; he was the one who gave out the numbers, his eyebrows rise, and he nods to a room on the left. I'm such a twat. German rearranges numbers so one hundred twenty-three becomes one hundred three and twenty, so my mind envisages "1320." My head implodes with the overwhelming digits.

I rise in a huff and rush to the private room for my consultation. I close the door behind me. A tall and skinny man sits in a black chair, but his smile puts me at ease. He says something, and I'm having a bad German day so I understand none of it.

"Shall I speak in English?" he offers.

"Thank you," I say. "I drank a little more than I should have last night." I omit the drugs.

"Your questionnaire please," he requests. I hand the clipboard to him. He reads the responses, and then asks, "So it was just the one time with a guy where you bottomed without a condom?"

"Yes," I say. That's the one I can remember. "Three months ago." Was I safe with the twins?

"I recommend you take the HIV rapid test, but also the syphilis test." I agree, and I'm charged for the tests at cost. As I hand him money, he explains that being the receptive partner without a condom is a higher risk activity, but even if the partner is infected, it doesn't always result in an infection.

"But if the insertive partner is recently infected," he further explains, "his viral load is higher and the risk of infection is greatest." I thank him again, especially for speaking in English, and go to another room. I wait for the doctor to call my number.

I understand the number this time, and the doctor is a woman with rimless glasses and a brown pony tail. She sprays alcohol on my inner forearm, and the cold feels refreshing. She says something, and makes a fist with her hand so I do the same. I look away when she punctures my skin, and I grimace. This is why I can't be part of the BDSM scene. Pain bloody hurts.

"The syphilis tests takes longer," she explains.

I'm back in the waiting room, or dread room. In any other situation, gays cruise one another and give lingering glances. Here, no one makes eye contact and faces are unmoving. They regret the past or fear the future while waiting for the results—and whether they can live their lives like they always have, or whether it's time for a serious look in the mirror. It's not long before I can't stand anymore of this and head outside for a fag. The cigarette leads to turning on my phone, which then leads me to cruise Gayromeo. I've the Uncut version on my Android, and being unapproved by Google, I'm ogling dick pics until my cig is down to the butt. I love how Germans are unabashed with nudity. I throw the butt off to the side, and notice there's a man in a hoodie talking on the phone in Turkish. I can't see his face, and I'm curious, but not now, I tell myself.

I head back inside, and hear someone call a number. That's my number, isn't it? I follow to another room, and with the door closed, I notice it's not the tall and skinny man who smiles. It's a short and bald man who looks at the clipboard.

He says something and I only understand, "I'm sorry but the results…" This bald man looks up, and his eyes open wide, then he furrows his brows. "Your number?"

I envision the numbers. "*Ein hundert drei und zwanzig*," I stutter in German.

"*Ein hundert zwei und dreisig!*"he barks at me. Shit. Twat. Idiot. I scurry out of the room, and sit in a corner hidden by a coat rack.

I peek through a hanging jacket. The man in the hoodie enters the room, and when he pulls his hoodie back, I gasp. It's Orhan, the Turkish delight I picked up over a feigned mutual liking of vodka Red Bull, the one who fucked me raw.

The short and bald man enters the room, and calls "132" out. Orhan gets up, and the bald man asks for the slip of paper with the number this time. They both enter a private room.

My hands shake.

I fumble to the bathroom. I feel it coming. I clutch the sides of the sink as I wretch. I wretch and vomit until nothing comes out, yet my stomach squeezes my guts even further. The pain is intense. I want to scream, but instead, only a barely audible breath escapes like a deflating balloon.

I turn on the faucet once the pain subsides. I rinse my face and slowly ascend to peer into the mirror. It's fluorescent bathroom lighting, and I see the bags under my eyes. Actually, not just bags but the flesh underneath my eyes puff in distended shades of purple. There are remnants of lunch dripping down my right cheek.

I don't bother waiting.

It's a blur until I'm again outside. It drizzles, and the smell of rain in the city reminds me of an autumn London afternoon, but this is summer in Berlin and I haven't my trusty umbrella. Nor a place to go. I sleep in a disdainful flat, and no work demands my presence. I find shelter under the awning of a bakery, and watch as the drizzle becomes rain. The sight of rain and people walking take on a hypnotic quality. I mouth the letters "HIV" like a mantra.

I'm unsure how long I've been staring transfixed, but the craving for a cigarette pulls me out. I reach into my breast pocket and find one last fag. I inhale, and hold my breath as if I were a petulant child threatening his mother over a denied bonbon.

I need another cig. There's a convenience kiosk on the other side of the street, and I rush from under the awning to cross. Just as I clear the curb, a lorry drives past, one massive tyre treading on the puddle that I had deftly skipped over, and drenches my back with a splash.

"Piss off!" I scream to the driver, but all I see is the rear of the black lorry.

Drenched, I buy a pack of fucking cigarettes nevertheless. I pull out my wallet, a handmade leather accessory with handsome stitching, and remember the shop in Soho.

Fuck this. I may be diseased, but this isn't the 1980s and HIV is not a death sentence. I step out, and with the first drag and its associated buzz, I realise—I've got money. The first payment from selling the company assets have gone through. I may end up buying the stocks that my dad recommended, but for the moment, I am flush with cash.

I needn't wallow in this, whatever I'm feeling. I could check into the Adlon if I were so inclined. I could freshen up with an invigorating shower, then head downstairs to the hotel restaurant and order red wine with a juicy steak grilled medium-rare. I could go to the bar and wash the meal with a snifter of brandy. Maybe strike up a conversation with a businessman and discuss matters of import.

Except I'd find that dull. I'm a prissy faggot who, despite it all, craves cock.

I see a cab and flag it down. "Der Boiler," I say. I'll shower there.

Der Boiler is advertised in the monthly gay magazine as having 2600 square meters, and when I first saw the ad, I was tickled how German the ad was, as if I was supposed to know how big the place was just from a number. But this place isn't big. It's enormous and encompasses three levels.

I'm naked and wet. I'm under the hot shower, and scrubbing myself clean. I feel the street's grime and dirtiness wash from me, and at least skin deep, I'm clean.

I dry myself, and wrap the towel around my hips. I look down at my legs. I may have a skinny boy's upper body, but my legs are shapely from jogging, even if that jogging is intermittent. I take off the towel and fold it in half before wrapping it around my waist again. Wrapping an unfolded towel is so last year.

I'm on the uppermost level with lockers and showers. I walk down a flight of stairs, and this is the café area. Like some kind of surreal movie, topless men in towels sit around café tables drinking coffee and beer. I need something and head to the bar for a shot.

"Jägermeister?" the bartender asks.

Sure. It's served in a large glass with an ice cube and a slice of lemon. I gulp it down.

I walk down another flight of stairs. I'm in the cellar now, and it is well lit. The light shines from above and the sides, and reflect off the polished metallic finishes. This gives the place an out-of-this-world atmosphere like I'm in a science-fiction spacecraft.

I'm surprised how busy it is for Friday afternoon. Maybe it's the rush of closeted married men before they have to go home to their wives and children?

I first observe. I'm about to sit down on a bench when I notice another bar. Observation is a task best done with a beverage. I return to the bench and watch, careful not to spill the beer in its plastic cup. The alcohol is exquisite in numbing any doubt, fears, and the nagging voice wanting me to take a good look at myself in the mirror.

There's an L shaped Jacuzzi in front, and perhaps the biggest Jacuzzi I've witnessed. Although there are only two people in it currently, I'm certain it can accommodate fifteen. A man in his late fifties walks past me, and heads to a door adjacent to the hot tub. He takes off his towel and hangs it to the side, exposing his hairy but firm ass. He enters the darkness. The glass door must lead to a steam room.

My beer's finished. A sporty guy who looks Mediterranean, maybe Portuguese, walks past. His shoulders are wide and taper down to a waist that'd be the envy of runway models. He slides off his towel, and I'm not surprised that his ass is firm and supple, and in the light, his cheeks glisten. He hops into the hot tub, and I decide to hop in as well.

I wade in the water to sit against the wall with a full view of the bathhouse, but more importantly, directly across with a full view of the Portuguese coast line, and I'm like a pirate ship anchored offshore and waiting to invade. His face is wide with large, dark eyes and a firm jaw made firmer by a beard. His nose is big, and my imagination runs wild with the idea that his cock must be as big. As boys and men descend the stairs to trickle in, I contemplate what a "Come hither" look would resemble.

The hot tub suddenly stops. It must be set to a timer, and because Lisbon is located closest to the red button on the wall, he gets up and walks toward it. In that brief moment, I glimpse his penis and I'm disappointed. Call me a size queen if you must, but I want to be fucked—not stung. Hoist anchors! This butt pirate is setting sails for other seas. I avert my gaze and rest my eyes on the stairwell.

A hairless German walks in, followed by an Asian twink. The twink has flip flops on, and I surmise this means he's prepared. A bear walks in, hairy belly overflowing his towel. As boredom sets in and I'm about to go to the sauna, the most masculine man lumbers down the stairs.

He must be even taller than Thomas, but dark hair cropped short contrasting with his very pale skin. He is muscular, although not in the veiny-steroid bodybuilder type of way but almost gorilla-like in the slabs of beef that are his hairy pecs, biceps, and thighs. His moves are slow as he lumbers to the hot tub. When he unfurls his towel, I glimpse his cock. It's almost as thick as his wrist, and dangles midway down his thigh. What is it like to be this man, and never have to question your masculinity? To enter a room and know that your simple presence demands respect? As the giant approaches the tub, two men in his path recoil to give way. The man settles against the wall, and his face is stoic with eyes unflinching. Why don't his eyes move? Is he so bored of the half-naked men that he decides to stare straight ahead into a mundane wall?

My boredom sets in and I want to leave, but wait until an unsuspecting twenty something with a nerd body walks out from the steam room and into the hot tub. It's all about timing darling, and when I leave now, my body doesn't look so prissy in comparison to the bored and boring giant.

I grab a towel, which may or may not be my own, and head to the sauna.

I sit bare-cheeked on the wood with the towel covering my thighs and genitals, but a German man pokes me in the shoulder and says something. Towel, sit, what does that all mean? He then points to his ass sitting on the towel. This is Germany, so of course it's more important to protect the wood than one's decency. I'm a good foreigner and do as I'm instructed, but I scan the walls for some sign explaining the rules. There is none, so how was I supposed to have known?

The dry heat feels wonderful. There's a sauna theory that one is supposed to go from hot to cooler, but I'm here to relax and do what I feel like. I close my eyes and focus on the heat entering my lungs, the cotton towel on my bum, and how my sweat trickles down my skin. I hear the door open, and there's a speech in German. I open my eyes, and there's a man with a big nose holding a bucket and ladle with a towel covering his dick. I know now that a big nose does not correlate with other particular body parts.

I can't understand him, but he says the word *Aufgüsse* many times. He spoons some liquid from the bucket, and then pours it on the stove. The water sizzles, and then the smell of raspberries permeates the room. He grabs a towel and spins it in the air like a helicopter, the scents circulate, and the smell intensifies. When the aromas dissipate, he says something. Another bucket, another ladle, and a whiff of tangerines wafts up my nose.

The Asian twink with flip flops then enters the sauna. Instead of sitting down, he stands. Even with the towel wrapped around him, I can tell his ass is supple like a mango. I wonder if it'd be just as juicy.

Is that actually a good thing? My bum is more like a dry crumpet.

The big-nose German says something. I don't understand, and the twink's wide eyes show he doesn't either. But his eyes move everywhere. When he speaks, he speaks slowly, his vowels extended and bordering on melodic, like how a Thai lady boy would speak. I even understand this German. "I only want to stand in the heat for a bit," he says.

The response has words "welcome but sit." Another few words, and there's a chuckle from the crowd. The twink looks back, and I'm uncertain whether he looks at me or the man behind me, but I shrug my shoulders. Without a further word, the twink opens the glass door and walks out.

What a contrast. I think back to the giant specimen of masculinity, and how space was made for him. For this lady boy, he struggled and was even laughed at.

But just as the big-nose man spins his towel, I see the lady boy return from the far corner. He looks directly into us, the ones who mocked him, with fierce eyes and a pout on his lips. I feel as though I can read his mind, and he's saying, "I'm a model bitches." He puts one hand on his hips, then like a runway in Milan, Paris, or more likely, Bangkok, he sashays past us, serving revenge with each fabulous sway of his booty. The helicopter stops, and it's a few minutes before the big-nose German swirls his towel again.

When one guy leaves, I wait a few seconds and leave as well. I'm heading back to the main room with the bar and hot tub, but as I am to cross the room, I see Morgan. That twat. That frenemy. Everyone in central London knew he enjoyed bum action, even my mother, but my prissiness was like Rambo compared to his flamboyant wrists. If he sees me here, he'll certainly blab to all our social circles.

The steam room. I dart inside when Morgan turns his head to the bar.

My nostrils flare in the steam. It smells clean but metallic and electrified like steam from one of those irons found at the dry cleaner. As I creep deeper, the smell of cleanliness is replaced by something more pungent, the air fouled or perfumed by the sweat from the scores of men who've wandered through here. In the darkness, each step resounds, and we are simply silhouettes for men to touch.

I breathe through my mouth, and taste the air. My cock stiffens in the anticipation for sex. Once my eyes adjust, the room's vast layout stretches before me. I am not in a tiny room but a vast chamber with maze like walls in ceramic tiles. It's not a steam room; it's a steam labyrinth.

I relish the warmth of the tiles as I meander.

There are two strategies to this, I realise—one can either wander and hunt, or wait to ensnare. Wolf or spider. I lack the patience so decide to be a wolf. Down a path, a pale man stands and waits. His form is tall and lithe with limbs that are more bone than flesh. He smells bland. I continue my hunt, turn a corner, and stalk my next prey. He's bulkier and darker, but shorter than I am. I am the wolf. When I sniff, there's a hint of spiciness. I salivate in anticipation, but when I near him, so near that I smell remnants of cumin and sandal-wood from his cologne, he retreats. I only see a hint of his cock as he gallops away, a member so fat and long that I see it dangle down his thigh from behind.

I bare my teeth to growl, but stop at a hiss. There's more prey, I remind myself.

I turn around and follow another path. Intense heat emanates from the heater basking the shadows in pale orange light. Two bodies are engaged in the pungency of sex. A boy is on his knees and sucks the cock of very tall and muscular specimen of a man, and as I approach, the boy rises, leans against the wall, and presents his backside. This is how the spider weaves her web. The tall man spits on his cock. It's so thick that when the man aims, his fist doesn't fully wrap around the base. The boy moans with a lady-like lilt to his whimpers.

In a span of a few thrusts, more bodies have converged. This is the third strategy—to swarm like hornets. Hands grope everywhere, and one hand grabs the back of my head and forces me down. I'll let you think that you're the top, but I am the wolf. My knees feel the hard tiles, and I taste the cock before I gag on it. It tastes like cumin. He withdraws and teases my cheek with his spiced meat.

"Fuck me," I growl.

There's a little perch built into the wall, and I lean against it. He fingers me. I want to shout at him that I'm no amateur bottom. Just give me that cock. I breathe heavily in anticipation, and my tongue licks the sharp underside of my fangs. The head of his cock nudges in, and I tremble. My arms and knees quiver, and he rams deeper. The heater flares bright orange, and the heat is overwhelming. The heat overwhelms. Liquid warmth, not steaming heat, trickles down my lip and splatters onto the tile.

Blood. Even in the darkness, I see its colour.

I don't feel pleasure. Pain and intense pressure builds in my head to the point that I feel the distended veins throb on my forehead. "Stop!" I growl. My rage shocks everyone into stillness. I stumble over naked men, and when I see a door, I lurch toward it.

Light greets me. But this isn't the room with the hot tub. There must be two doors to the steam labyrinth. I grab a random towel and walk. Walk, keep walking. This is the cruising area with cubicles painted black. A door to one of the cubicles is open, and when I close the door, I slump onto the leather mattress and sob while holding my nose closed. My tears wallow in drying blood.

How could I deny something had happened? Pretend to live my life care free?

There's a paper tissue dispenser nailed to the wall, and once my nose no longer bleeds, I grab a few sheets. The powdery mess scrapes my upper lip, and I dispose of it in the rubbish bin where a used and limp condom rests at the bottom.

I walk out. I have never lived care free. From childhood, there were the pressures of living in a Goodall household. There were A Levels, then Oxford, and business school in London. There was burnout from an internship at Barclay's.

I return to the hot tub, and it's fully occupied, but I manage to find a spot beside a Spanish bear. I stare at the bubbling water and try to push all thoughts out.

I then see Morgan exit from the steam room, and there is a frantic moment when I seriously consider dunking my head into the hot water to hide. But then that would be submerging my head into dick soup, and I'll add pink eye to my list of conditions.

Morgan sees me, and with a smile, steps toward the hot tub. The Spanish bear leaves. Perfect timing.

"Timothy, darling, what a pleasant surprise to see you here," Morgan says as he sits beside me. At least I'm successful in not seeing his naked body.

"What a surprise indeed Morgan," I say. "Bored of London?"

"Not as bored as you, it seems," he says. "A weekend getaway. I haven't seen you in forever."

"I moved to Berlin to set up a new web start-up," I say.

"Different location but it's still the same Timothy I know," he says. "I'm still clocking insane hours at BTM Group, but as a senior consultant now."

"Congratulations are in order I believe," I say. "I'd offer to buy you a flute of sparkling wine at the bar, but they only serve beer here."

"Let's not. For now, I'd rather lay in bubbles as opposed to drinking them." He leans back and closes his eyes, and for the briefest of moments, my gaze lowers to see his rather average cock swimming in one of the jets. My cock is more average than monstrous, but it is larger than Morgan's. A consolation prize. "When was the last time we saw each other, darling?" he continues.

"Pritchard's cocktail event," I say.

"That's right," he says. "When you were chatting up a storm with that Italian fellow and I pulled him away to ask for his opinion on the new production of Madame Butterfly." I was so close to getting him to leave for a private drink with me. He was way beyond my league, and his English wasn't good so he was happy that someone was talking with him. It turned out one of Morgan's friends studied Italian, and I did not see him the rest of the evening.

It's time to be honest. "You cock blocked me that night," I say.

"If I had known darling," Morgan explains. "I would have left you to your devices. Why did you keep being gay such a secret?"

"You've met my parents," I say. Now that father hinted he knew, I don't know why I don't come clean to mother. Oh yes. She's a controlling woman who once said that all gays and their buggery should be rounded up on an island. I wanted to say that would be my idea of the perfect holiday, but bit my lip instead.

"Understandable," Morgan says. "Jennifer Watson came out as someone who likes to lick the minge, and it shocked her family to no end." Here's Morgan discussing the affairs of others again. "Do you remember how we'd gather and play Dungeons and Dragons in your attic? Jennifer loved playing the barbarian. How we didn't have an inkling she was a lesbian is beyond me." I loved D&D. As opposed to the outside world, here was one that I could understand simply by reading. Understand and fantasize, the fantasy of more than a wolf—a dragon. I hosted an epic campaign of Pyriss the red dragon and his assault on mining towns until the King's army brought him down in a glorious blaze.

"I'd appreciate your discretion in being mum on meeting me here today," I say as casually as possible.

"Of course darling. Discretion assured." He opens his eyes, then cranes his head to whisper in my ear. "Speaking of discretion, I noticed caked blood in one of your nostrils. It's quite unsightly."

"Excuse me." I rise and pivot ever so slightly to ensure Morgan gets a view of my longer dick. I grab a towel and then head to the WC.

The mirror. I stare only briefly before getting soap and washing the crud from my nostril. The water still runs when I look up again, this time with purpose. I'm getting older. Not only are there bags, but the skin under my chin sags ever so slightly like a chicken. I'm getting older and I need to return to get my test results to be certain. I then notice a cluster of grey hairs on the side of my temples. Not just one, but a cluster. I'm getting older, uglier, and I'm HIV positive.

Fuck this. I smash my palm into my reflection, and a crack forms diagonally through my face.

There's the buzz of Boiler's door as I return outside. In the bath house, the rooms with no windows obscure time, and it's already evening. The rain has stopped, and it's almost warm. My jacket remains wet from the afternoon, and I feel marked as I leave the courtyard to enter the main boulevard of Mehringdamm.

I walk. I know where I am. There's the chatter from the Lonely Planet victims waiting an hour to buy the supposedly best Döner in the city. There's the competing noise of the other line to Curry36, Berlin's supposedly best place to grab a Currywurst. The smell of meat and grease is wretched.

One step after the other. It's not much further. I'm fatigued and wonder whether I should return home, but as I turn a corner, I've arrived. This is Orhan's street.

I clench my fists. His house is the only new building from the 1980s, an eyesore in an otherwise picturesque tree-lined street. My eyes narrow with renewed purpose, and I am deliberate with my steps.

There's the door buzzer. Now that I'm here, I'm not sure what I want. Just to talk? To talk. Which one was his name? There is only one Turkish sounding name, Ozturk, and I buzz. No answer. I buzz again. I want to talk to you, you bloody asshole.

The doors suddenly open and a young couple leave the building. They are drunk and so in love that they are oblivious to me, and I sneak inside. Which floor was he on? I read the names on the door. Ozturk, fourth floor left. I'm winded by the time I reach this floor, and breathe deeply as I knock. No answer.

I'm tired. I sit on the steps that lead to a dark attic. The timer for the light kicks in, and the stairwell is dark now except for little orange LEDs marking the light switch, and they look like eyes. My fists almost unclench. What am I doing here?

There's a click sound, and the lights come back on. I wait like a spider. I hear a man walk up the stairs, and I peek down the stairwell to see a man in a hoodie with grocery bags. It's Orhan, it must be. I clench my fists again, and I'm holding my breath when he reaches the fourth floor.

There's the sound of keys. I have only a moment—and in this moment, I'm consumed by impulse. I rush and tackle this man in the hoodie, and grab his legs as my chest barrels into him. His scream is high-pitched, and there's a chaotic rustle of groceries falling, and a thump as an orange smacks against the wall.

I mount him. My hand is on his neck, pushing him to the ground. The light from the hallway is enough to see his body.

"Orhan," I grumble. "You piece of shit." I want to spit on him.

Another gasp. "Orhan? *Nein! Nein!*" He says something else.

I flip him around. The face. "You're not Orhan."

"No English," this man says. His hands shake as they feebly defend his face. He breathes in short bursts, and between the fingers, I see his eyes and the whites all around his irises. "I'm Yusuf. Orhan, Orhan is, he is …" This man struggles with the last word and I don't think it's because he doesn't know the word in English. "Boyfriend," he finally finishes.

Of course Orhan is a cheating boyfriend. I point to myself. "*Orhan hat mich gefickt.*" I see the tears in his eyes. "He gave me AIDS." I feel something wet on my backside. I rise, and I realise the wetness is from Yusuf pissing himself. The hallway light clicks off. I rush out, and hold onto the railings as I descend downstairs to flee in the dark.

17. Kay

"I forgot something," Alex says to me and heads back up the stairs. I'm on the ground floor in the hallway with mailboxes, and dressed like an Indonesian monk wrapped in a sarong hand-painted like tree bark—souvenirs from my last business trip to Jakarta. I flew Tuesday and returned this Saturday morning. This is one benefit of a jet-set lifestyle at CoExcel. I've flown business class, complete with welcome Champagne to Seoul, Cairo, Istanbul, and now, Jakarta.

I wear the Javanese sarong for Christopher Street Day, or what Pride is called in Germany, and named after the street where the Stonewall riots happened. CSD is a free-for-all rainbow parade like Canada's Pride events, but people along the route drink in broad daylight, so it's rowdier.

I hesitate. I've never dressed so different. Men dress up for Berlin's CSD; from a man naked on the streets with rainbow dildos glued to his back; or a lanky body in a green rubber suit with gas mask, urinal moulded to his torso, and drain connected via a long and black hose back to his mask like a perpetual urine machine; to drag queens galore, CSD is a multi-coloured multi-gendered festival. I touch my exposed pec. A shirtless Javanese monk is tame in comparison. I've a man purse since sarongs have no pockets.

CSD happens forty minutes away, and there's no privacy in public transport. Shirtless and with a skirt, I'll have to walk to the U-Bahn as parents take their children for their Saturday shopping. And I'll also have to deal with my mistake, my mistake with Thomas.

Alex returns. He wears a tank top and jeans. His brown eyes stare as he pats me on the shoulder. As roommates and friends, I know how much he wishes for blue eyes. "You look amazing, your holiness," he says. Alex opens the building's door, and light streaks past my sandals. I think of Timothy and the strength he had to wear drag on the streets when it wasn't CSD. I step out with purse swinging beside me.

The U2 snakes its way from the North East of Berlin through its centre. There are ghost stations where no one exits or enters the train. I imagine these stations in the 1920s bustling with Berlin's finest, and not eerily quiet like it is now. I take out my phone to text Thomas. Should I say I'm sorry? But as we emerge from the underground to overlook a park, I simply text, "We're at the first wagon of the train."

The train arrives at Stadtmitte. Thomas enters the U-Bahn compartment in his two-metre glory, his head almost touching the roof of the cabin. He wears rainbow suspenders with his jeans and white shirt. "Hi Kay."

"Hello Thomas," I say. We don't hug.

"Hey Thomas," Alex says with a hug. "I'm underdressed." Thomas nods but says nothing. I listen to the chatter from others dressed with more colour than me.

When we arrive in Schöneberg, Thomas walks ahead of us. "What's the deal with you two?" Alex asks.

"You know how I was in Jakarta for work this week?" Alex looks at my sarong and nods emphatically. "When I landed this morning, I was jet-lagged and still drunk from flying business class. I called Thomas and may have accidentally blurted out that I loved him."

"Shit," Alex says. "I usually just piss my pants when drunk from an intercontinental flight." It didn't help that I was looking at a sexy picture Thomas had sent me with his new phone. Sex isn't love, I know, but I'm not sure if Thomas knows. He stops to watch the parade from a gap in the wall of people. We're close to a *Späti* and can quench our thirst with beer—legally.

Alex texts Timothy our location. "Data's slow," he says, and taps the phone. "Finally."

I think about the floats during Winnipeg's Pride parade. We were happy when more than two thousand people showed up to our dozens of floats. The floats didn't have much money, but time and effort compensated. One float was a garden-themed truck decked in plastic ivy, dancing drag queen painted green, and accompanied by her matching poodle dyed with Kool-Aid. The floats during Pride in Montreal gleamed from commercial sponsorship—except for the topless pre-op transsexual who danced with hands bound to a cross. Those boobs were definitely post-op. I saw the parade in Paris with high hopes, but the floats looked like they didn't have money, time, nor effort—the drag queens could barely afford rent let alone co-ordinated outfits. Pride parades around the world have love, money, neither, or everything.

Berlin, poor but sexy Berlin, has everything. Corporate sponsors with flashy floats, check. Non-profit organisations with charm, check. Drag queens dressed for fashion and not function, check. Gay clubs with shirtless muscle Marys pumping house music, check. Topless dykes on bikes, check.

"Thank God it's not raining," Alex says. A beautiful woman with jiggling breasts struts past. "I'm going to find a place to piss." Men disappear into a parking lot while grabbing their crotches.

I can talk to Thomas now. "I like your rainbow suspenders. What do you think of my outfit?" I say.

"It's good," he says without looking.

"Can we talk about earlier?" I ask.

"I'm not ready to," Thomas says.

"There is a time and place to say such things," I barge ahead, "and over the phone after a long-haul flight is neither the time nor the place. The jet lag must have had something to do with it." I also have to tell him about the offer of a PhD position from my meeting a university professor on sabbatical.

"I said I'm not ready," Thomas grumbles. We watch in silence as a porn actor walks past, his muscles and cock best described as big. Simply big. When he walks away, I see the patch of acne on his back. Some things need help to get big.

Alex takes his sweet time, and the awkwardness with Thomas

makes me feel like it's a high school dance. Then, Timothy appears. He wears Lederhosen like it's September and we're in Munich. Not drag but leather. There's even a biological/cis woman beside him, and she's dressed in a Dirndl.

"Berlin is alive with the sound of music," I say as they approach.

"That's Austria, not Germany, darling," Timothy says, "This is Anna, and she's Dutch." It doesn't surprise me because she's one eighty, or 5'11".

"We're paying homage to this wonderful country," she says, "and I already had this in my closet from last year's Oktoberfest." The Dutch can be extremely practical. Her blue eyes grow wide when she looks at me. "You're paying homage to Indonesia. Have you always had this in your closet?" Also leave it to the Dutch to have flawless English.

"I'm Kay and it's a recent acquisition to my collection," I answer. "Kudos to your knowledge of Asia."

"Well, just Indonesia," she says.

"This is —" I begin to say while gesturing to Thomas.

"I'm Thomas," the Hanoverian finishes with a firm handshake.

Alex returns with three bottles of beer in his hand. "Finally Timothy." Another round of greetings and introductions. "I would have bought you two a beer if I had known you were here."

"No need," Timothy says. He takes out a flask from his pocket. "Cheers."

"Cheers," we boys say in collective agreement. Anna eyes my beer with pouty lips.

I hand Anna my bottle and warn, "You're welcome to it but only if you're willing to accept herpes into your life."

She hands the bottle back to me empty. "Herpes sisters!" she exclaims.

Techno music blares past, and the beats are jarring with sunlight and not the flashing lights of a club, like seeing a woman in a cocktail dress buy juice and eggs at the supermarket. Anna loves it though, and dances with movements that only a woman with child-bearing hips could pull off.

"Shall we follow this float?" Alex asks.

"It's not the Schwuz float, is it?" Timothy frets. "Our relationship is complicated currently."

"Greifbar," I answer. "One of the last bastions of gay smut in Prenzlauer Berg."

"It only exists because it's outside the Ring Bahn," Alex adds. "Gentrification stops at Schönhauser Allee station."

"Let's follow and dance then," Timothy says.

"*Endlich*," Thomas grumbles.

Dancing and walking are not normally compatible activities. Dancing is a free-flowing expression of feeling through limbs, and is a rhythmic chaos that can lead left, right, or nowhere. Walking, on the other hand, is a deliberate move from Point A to Point B. But we are going so slowly on the parade route that grandmothers in their strollers can overtake us, so it's less walk and more dance.

I see a *Späti* coming up, and announce, "It's my round lady and gentlemen." By the time I return with more beers, the caravan has moved only ten metres.

CSD begins in Schöneberg, the heart and prostate of historic gay Berlin. In the 1920s, hundreds of gay bars like that featured in the movie *Cabaret* jostled for patrons on Motzstrasse. The route then hugs the Siegessäule, the golden angel atop a six-story high spiral adorned with bullet holes from the Second World War. This is where West Berlin gays cruised before the wall fell because the free world stopped here. The climax of the parade erupts at Brandenburger Tor. The massive gate adorned by a chariot on top is the emblem of a united Germany. Nazi troops marched through these gates, and now, it hosts a stage for fags to dance.

After four rounds, two genre changes in music, and countless pee excursions later, we arrive at united Germany's emblem. Anna sips her second beer, and I think she's not drinking so much because of the uncertain bathroom situation. Anna is almost running when she sees the rows of Port-A-Potties.

"How did you come across such a sassy lady?" I ask Timothy.

"She's my neighbour," he says.

Thomas stands beside me. The beauty of the music was that we didn't have to talk. It's CSD and I'm feeling bold, so I touch Thomas on the small of his back. This is something he enjoys when we're on the couch, but he suddenly says, "I'm hungry. There's a sausage stand over there."

"I'll join you," Alex says. I can see Alex feast his eyes on one of the bearded men handling the sausages.

"It's my turn for rounds," Timothy says. "Would you mind waiting for Anna?"

"Not at all," I say. "We are herpes sisters after all." With a grin, Timothy departs.

Anna comes back before the others. She sighs. "Margaret Cho was right."

"About what?"

"That if gay men hook up, they'll leave you so fast." Her blue eyes look right into me. They're actually blue-green.

"They're on food and beverage service," I say. "They'll be back." I hope. I don't mention the gay code that just because you arrive at a party together doesn't mean you leave together. "How do you know about the goodness that is Madame Cho?"

"I spent a year in Vancouver improving my English," she says. "I lived in the West End, and my roommate ensured I got a thorough education."

"I've never been to Vancouver," I say. "What else did you learn?"

"A lot," she says as she touches my shoulder. Her smile seems as broad as the Rockies. "Not only did I eat amazing dim sum and pho, but more importantly, about myself. Like how I fit in the world." She then says after her eyes open wide in realization, "You are Canadian, right?"

"Yes. How did you know?" I say.

"I've met enough nice Canadians to know you come in all shapes and sizes, and you didn't jump to assumptions about me being Dutch and Amsterdam coffee shops. Plus your accent." That, eh?

"Well, your height speaks for itself," I say. "I met a very short Dutch man at a business meeting at Schiphol airport. During lunch, the waiter spoke to him in English and he had to say that he spoke

Dutch. I wondered whether other Dutch assume he's not Dutch because of his height."

"Probably," Anna says.

Alex and Timothy return, but not Thomas. Corralling gay men is like trying to corral cats. "He met a Russian guy," Alex says. "He said he'll call us to find us." Is the Russian guy Yuri?

"Let's dance and wait for him then," I say.

The eight-lane boulevard that is the Strasse der 17. Juni is packed with vendors, DJ booths, and people. A queer party is held in the same spot as Nazi propaganda marches of decades ago. History is not without a sense of irony.

We head to one DJ area, and dance. A guy dances with Mardi Gras beads hanging from his neck, and as he bounces, colours swirl and catch the light. A bigger gal in pink pants dances, and without a sports bra, her boobs move to a different rhythm than her hips. A gaggle of gay men surround her, all with blonde hair, some of it natural.

A few more songs, and I scream through the music, "I'll be back."

I need to piss, and I flow through the crowd like a shallow stream over a bed of crags. Why am I thinking of water? I first head to the portable toilets, but the line of mostly women is way too long. The street intersects a park, so I delve deeper into the bushes to find a semi- private place to piss. I pass a lesbian couple making out. The music is fainter and I find an isolated spot. With my sarong, I unfurl it and wrap it around my neck with my purse. I pull down my underwear, and spread my legs wide so the urine doesn't puddle around my sandals.

I waddle to a dry area and wrap the sarong around me again, and it's less and less tight, like trying to reroll a fallen paper towel roll. Being drunk doesn't help.

I walk back, but stop when I hear a muffled whimper. My curiosity is piqued, and I head to the noise. There's just the chirping of birds now, but as I peak through a patch of leaves, I see the side-view a very tall man in rainbow suspenders fucking a guy bent over, the top's hand pressed against the bottom's mouth. The tall man's face is obscured by leaves, but I know who he is. I know we're not monogamous, but Thomas fucks a man untainted by rape. This bottom doesn't freeze up and hyperventilate with lingering fear. He moans from pleasure.

I rush back to the wall of sound on the eight-lane party street. "We don't need to worry about Thomas," I say to Alex.

"No call?" he asks.

"No need. He's occupied with a guy in the bushes." I deserve this.

"Good for him," Timothy says at first, then looking at me, "How forgetful. You two are an item. Sorry."

"There's the alternative CSD in Kreuzberg," Alex says. For those who want a more punk techno atmosphere.

"That sounds exciting," Anna mentions.

No disagreement means we're off. We make our way through Brandenburger Tor, past the Hotel Adlon where Michael Jackson dangled his baby from the balcony, and past the Russian embassy housed in the biggest building on the most expensive street because the Red Army suffered the most in the war. In Berlin, each building has a story, even if it's as humble as simply surviving intact through May 1945. We find a cab and hop in.

I'm sitting on the back middle seat. I straddle the ridge with open legs despite my sarong. Timothy is to my left and Anna to my right. Germany, Indonesia, Germany. Alex rides shotgun. Clouds appear as we pass Friedrichstrasse.

"Are you mad at Thomas?" Anna asks me.

"Yes," I answer. Anger is easier to admit than telling the truth.

"I would be too," she says while rubbing my shoulder and bicep.

We arrive in Kreuzberg. The crowd of people are fewer, but dressed with more piercings and tattoos. Anna and I get out, there's a rumble from the skies, and within seconds it pours. Anna grabs my hand and we rush to a café. Everyone seems to have the same idea. We rub shoulders with hordes of others who escape the downpour. The air is stale with the smell of dank clothes and wet skin.

"Berlin weather can turn on you in an instant," Anna says as she tries to comb through wet hair with her fingers. We wait for Alex and Timothy, but minutes pass and we don't see them. Like cats.

"How about a coffee?" I offer. Anna nods and smiles. I work my way to the counter and order. I'm about to pay and reach for my man purse—where's my man purse? Not again. This time no credit cards because I left them at home, but my house keys and phone were in there. "Anna?" She hears me and I motion her to come. "Can you pay?"

She reaches into a pocket on her Dirndl and pays. "What happened?"

"I don't know where my bag went," I say. "This is consequence of form before function."

"Where did you last remember having it?" she says.

We get our coffees and stand to the side. "When I went to pee. I think I also had it in the cab though. Maybe it slid off."

"And maybe Timothy has it," Anna adds.

"Can you call him?" I ask.

Anna reaches into another pocket, and pulls out her phone. "Shit," she says. "I have one of these crappy discount plans, and it's usually fine, but when I go to concerts or events with a lot of people, I can never dial out or even text."

I sigh and close my eyes. Anna hugs me. I can smell what shampoo she uses, and whatever brand it is, it's nice. With my free arm, I hug her back.

"I feel better," I say and open my eyes.

"Timothy and Alex are around somewhere," she says. "The rain stopped. Let's try to find those boys." She takes my hand and we head out of the café. It's only been minutes in the sun, but the DJ booths have restarted and crowds already fill the wet dance floor. Berliners seize every possible moment to celebrate.

We grab beers and we rush from one dance area to another, all the while with Anna holding my hand. Techno to house to techno again, yet no sign of Alex or Timothy. It's dark now. The crowds have thinned. Perhaps Anna's phone will work this time. "Can you try again?" I ask.

We lean against a wall. Her thumbs tap dance on the screen, and within moments, her phone beeps. "They have your bag. They're heading back to Timothy's place. Should I tell them we'd meet them there?"

"OK." Relief floods me. Anna smiles, and hugs me again. Her hand holds my hand as we head underground to take the U-Bahn. I've never been to Timothy's apartment. We knock on his door, but there's no answer.

Anna is on her phone. "Hey Timothy. OK. See you in a bit then." She looks at me. "They're still in transit. Do you want to come in for a drink while we wait?"

Anna opens her door. It's decorated with wood-veneer furniture and a twin bed. She has personalized a wall with photos, and a Hello Kitty blanket covers the bed. A woman lives here.

"Shoes off?" I ask.

"Yes please." She heads to the kitchen and I look at the photos. "Red wine?" she asks.

"Sure." I hate mixing my drinks, but mixing is better than no alcohol at all. I scan the photos. "How old are you?"

"Young enough to tell the truth," Anna answers. "Twenty-three."

For a woman who is only twenty-three, she has been to a lot of places. There's a photo of her in front of the Eiffel Tower, Big Ben, and the Colosseum. For EU Citizens travelling within Europe, it's like when a guy from Toronto travels to New York or Boston. Do Europeans see these monuments with the same awe that North Americans do?

Anna also has a lot of photos with people, all of them different. She's a social butterfly. The exception is her with an Asian man in multiple photos, a man that looks like me. I'm always skeptical when someone, Asian or not, says they know someone who resembles me because when the photo evidence presents itself, I'm rolling my eyes inside. But this man looks like me. There's a photo of her standing in front of a totem pole in a redwood forest, probably Vancouver, and my doppelganger wraps his arms around Anna's waist. There's also one of them standing in front of a mountain lake, one photo of them with eyes poking through ski masks, and one of them at a Chinese restaurant with empty bamboo steamers on a white plastic tablecloth.

She comes back with red wine in cheap white wine glasses. "*Prost*," I say.

"*Prost*," she says.

"Who's this guy?" I point to the photo in front of a mountain lake.

"He's Eugene," she says. "He's a cardiac surgeon at Vancouver General."

"We look similar," I admit.

"I may have noticed the resemblance," she admits. "But he doesn't have your beard."

"Is there a story behind this photo?"

"We did this long weekend trip to the Okanagan valley to do wine tasting, and Eugene found this hotel right on the lake in Summerland. We had breakfast on the patio while the sun rose over the mountain. I had never seen something so beautiful."

Surgeon and romantic. "Eugene seems like a special guy," I say.

"He is. He doesn't speak any Cantonese, but studied French. I know—why would a Chinese Canadian study French? He said that when he was young, he stayed up late one night and watched *Decline of an American Empire* and concluded French was sexy." She docks her phone to a speaker charger combo. A few swipes and we're listening to an acoustic French Canadian mix. "Don't worry. Celine Dion isn't part of this." A sip of her drink. "This is my favourite one, Rive Sud."

I listen and try to understand but I only took French up to Grade 7, and learned words like *métro, prochaine station*, and *billet*. As a kid growing up in Winnipeg with no subway system, I kept thinking, why am I learning this and what is this magical system of underground transport?

"Was he your first?" I place the glass to my lips and drink.

"First boyfriend, love, or first time I had sex?" She then places her hand in front of her mouth in mock shock.

I almost breathe out red wine. "Boyfriend?"

"Yes to the first two," Anna says, smiles, then gives me a peck on the cheek. "I'm not ashamed to talk about sex."

"So when was your first time?" I ask.

"You first," she says.

"My first time was with a guy named Chris. In a bit of foreshadowing, he was of German descent. I met him at a gay youth group when I was sixteen and he was nineteen. Neither of us had cars and we both lived at home, so we took late night walks in parks. It was June, I remember, because few mosquitoes were out. When no one was around, he took my hand. I kissed him. My heart was racing. We hid behind a tree. Like what were we thinking? That a tree would hide us? But we gave each other handjobs, and I was embarrassed because it only took maybe ten strokes before I came. Chris took a little longer, and when I took the bus back home, I could smell the cum on my hand."

"My first time," Anna says, "was with a guy Renilt when I was sixteen. Except I didn't want to." She doesn't continue.

I feel goosebumps on my forearm. "How did you feel after?"

"Ashamed, dirty, worthless." She finishes her wine. "Like every bad thing that happened to me, I had it coming because I was marked with what happened. But I went online to chat groups and that helped. Talking about it, even anonymously, helped. It wasn't my fault. But it wasn't until I was in Vancouver that I even considered being alone with another guy. Then Eugene came and showed me such beauty, and when we drove to Summerland, I said he could put his hand on my thigh."

I touch her hand. I'm breathing heavily, and I'm crying. I feel like when I was fifteen and coming out for the first time. "I was raped," I manage to say. Anna sets her glass aside, and embraces me. The warmth of her body and the smell of her hair is sweet comfort. "You're the third person I've mentioned this to."

"It was recent?" she asks.

I nod.

"It's not your fault," she says. Coming from Anna, the words ring true. She breaks the embrace, and I see her eyes are teary. "Does Thomas know?"

"I told him, but he doesn't know what it feels like," I answer. I close my eyes and try to think of nothing. But I keep seeing Thomas fucking in the bushes, and the feeling of anger tinged by hurt fills my being.

I open my eyes. I see Anna and her beauty, and the tenderness in her eyes. I lean into her, and she doesn't lean away. I want her comfort, and I kiss her. She kisses me back. I'm kissing a girl. There are clanking sounds as the empty wine glasses drop onto the floor, but plastic doesn't shatter.

Anna's hands reach for my crotch. Pulling off my sarong is like pulling off Velcro. I'm just in my boxer briefs. How do I navigate a dress? Is there a zipper in the back? My hands fumble with her back, and through some miracle, I manage to find the head of the zipper and pull. Anna's Dirndl splays around her like a peeled banana, or maybe flower petals, and my next hurdle to heterosexuality is her bra. I'm new to this. I feel like a teenager. Or a virgin, and with a woman, I am.

There's a pause, and Anna senses my ineptitude. She straightens her back, and twirls her head as she unfastens whatever powerful contraption it is that contains her bosoms. Her hair swirls around her cleavage, and she pushes her elbows together to let her bra fall off her arms.

Here are Anna's breasts. They're not small. I cautiously approach them. Her nipples are larger than any man's nipples I've been with. I cup them, feel their weight, marvel at how they jiggle. I think about how in the past, I've cupped pecs and they were always firm. These mounds are softer than anything I've felt.

We kiss again, and while our lips are still locked, we tango to the bed. Before falling onto the mattress, I pull off her panties and she pulls off my underwear. I'm kissing a girl and she is completely naked in front of me. I ignore that I'm naked in front of her, and my penis is as soft as her body.

Anna straddles me and rubs her hips against my own. For a moment, I wonder what our babies would be like. The child would probably be coloured like vanilla caramel ice cream. Would the boy have my chin and Anna's long limbs? Would the girl have my eyes and Anna's lips?

I'm intellectualizing this. Anna continues to grind but I feel no carnal need to touch her. My soft and flaccid is proof that I am indeed a fag.

She dismounts, and lays on her side with her back toward me. We're silent, just like real teenagers trying to have sex for the first time. I don't want to say anything because I'm tired, drunk, and my attempt at heterosexuality is a disaster.

I roll to my side. Maybe I should go. I'll just rest my eyes for five minutes.

I dream of flowers. I'm running through a field of tulips, the yellow, red, and violet contrasting with the lush green field. Suddenly, this giant tulip beast rises from the ground, and just as it begins to chase me, I awake to a knock on the door.

My eyes open wide in a rush. We've slept with the lights on, and when I glance at Anna, she's still in slumber. I put on my boxer briefs, and walk to the door.

"Oh," Timothy gasps. "It's you Kay. This isn't your apartment."

"Hello yourself," I whisper. "Anna's sleeping. Weren't you supposed to be here earlier? And do you have my bag?"

"Alex has it," Timothy says. "He had a little accident. He's fine now, but he was running down a flight of stairs when someone bumped into him and he fell. His mouth was a bloody mess. Why would you run down a flight of stairs drunk? Because you're drunk. We just left the emergency ward. Alex should be at your place."

"Can you call him to ask him to wait up for me?" Timothy nods, and as he calls, I go back into my den of shame to collect my things. I see a notepad on Anna's desk. "Dear Anna, sisters should only do each other's hair," I write then wrap the sarong around my waist. I'm careful to wrap it tight, and it looks almost respectable.

I turn off the lights, and blow Anna a kiss to say goodbye. The door clicks and echoes in the empty hallway.

"What happened?" Timothy asks.

"I'll tell you another time, but it's a CSD to remember," I say.

Timothy scratches his arm. "My CSD is one I'd like to forget. Considering how drunk I am, that won't be hard."

"Can I borrow cab fare?" I ask.

Timothy reaches into his pockets. "I've only three Euros in change darling." He holds the gold coins in his palm like he's feeding birds.

My fingers peck at each coin. I lent you cab fare and this is how you pay me back. I walk into the elevator after a grumpy goodbye, and Timothy enters his apartment. At least I can take the subway back since it runs twenty-four hours on weekends. I'm a big girl and I can take the subway.

The light's out when I walk to the U-Bahn. Dawn breaks, and the sun reflects off the disco ball of the TV Tower. CSD is over. CSD is over and I'm returning home in my CSD clothes after "sex" with a woman. I don't appreciate the irony that only in Berlin does a gay man celebrate Pride by having "sex" with a woman. I descend down the stairs to take the train home.

18. Thomas

"A bratwurst with mustard, please," I say.

As the woman behind the counter hands me my food, she says, "Cute rainbow suspenders." I was not going to wear them, but Kay urged me.

"Thanks," I say and give her money. I hear someone order the same with a Russian accent. I turn and recognize him immediately. "Good day Yuri," I say in German. I want to sound powerful.

But he answers in English. "Happy CSD Thomas!" he screams. He smiles and hugs me. I stand motionless. Did he forget what he did to me, or what I did to him? Or is he on something? "How are you?" he says.

"I could be better," I answer. I learned to say this from Kay.

"That's a shame," Yuri says. Why hasn't the woman given Yuri his sausage yet? "Just look at all the beautiful people. It's a day to be happy." He finally gets his sausage, and I want to say good-bye when Yuri opens his enormous mouth. He clamps down, and squirts mustard on my shirt. Yellow mustard on my white shirt.

"Look what you did," I growl at him. "You clumsy piece of..."

"I'm sorry, I'm sorry!" Yuri says. He uses his napkin to wipe my shirt, but there is mustard on it too, so he ends up making the stain larger. I push him out of the way, and walk toward the toilets. There may be sinks where I can wash up.

I see a half circle of portable toilets, and in the center, a sink. Yuri's queeny voice repeats his apologies. He's followed me, dammit.

I pull off my shirt and let water run over the stain and add some soap. "You're sorry for this, but not sorry for ruining my PhD prospects. You're a fucking hypocrite."

"That's different," Yuri says. I see him eye my exposed stomach. "I just wanted you to not get grant. You weren't supposed to assault me in front of entire lab."

"Like this?" With my wet hand, I grab his neck. I hold him still. I think, fear me, Yuri. I want your eyes to go wide. I want you to sweat. I want you to gurgle from choking. I want you to suffer.

But his eyes don't go wide. He doesn't choke. He has a white tank top with white swim trunks on, and the swim trunks are so tight and cut short that his fluffy balls hang out below. His bare cock head peeks out over the top of his waistband, and it's obviously hard.

Yuri's breath quickens. "Please."

"You disgust me," I spit.

He drops to the ground, but clings to my leg. "Please, Thomas. I want your milk." I want to shake him off me, but he continues. "I'm sorry. I didn't mean for you to be removed." Are those genuine tears? "I have friend, well, former boyfriend. He's university professor at University of Zurich. I can write to him, explain situation and that I forgive you. Maybe he can be supervisor for your PhD there."

"In Switzerland?" Yuri nods and nuzzles his nose in my crotch. A crowd of people linger, and watch the show. One man in leather wearing a black collar around his neck has dropped to his hands and knees like a dog.

I pull Yuri up and walk away. He follows. Some of the people boo. Further into the thicket, there is just the sound of our footfalls and the chirp of birds. Yuri massages my cock through my jeans. He unzips me, and pulls out my engorged cock. "That is so big." He bends over with a gaping mouth, but I turn him around. I pull his shorts down to his knees. From my pocket, I pull out a condom. I press my cock right against his asshole.

"Wait," Yuri says through his breaths. He reaches into his shoe and pulls out an opaque bottle with a yellow wrapper. He uncaps it and inhales deeply. The smell of nitrates wafts to my nose. Yuri's asshole is more relaxed now, and I push in deeper with little resistance. I know I have a massive cock, and either he's a slut and used to being fucked, or the poppers help. Or both.

When I'm all the way in, he lets out a loud groan. Shut up, I think. I cover his mouth with my hand before starting to fuck him. I thrust, I pound. I fuck with growing force. There is no tenderness in this fuck. There's no love either, and I can now tell the difference. I'm fucking this slutty faggot with anger and spite. Yuri bites on my finger and I fuck him harder.

I breathe through flared nostrils like a bull. I keep fucking but I'm nowhere close to orgasm. I pull out and force Yuri to his knees. The condom is dirty with brown, and I pull it off. I want to come on his face. Yuri pleads to for me to give it to him. I'm jerking off and trying to focus on my pleasure, but I'm distracted by irrelevant details—the sweat on Yuri's face, the sound of the leaves in the breeze, the lingering smell of poppers and ass.

I'm disgusted and my cock is no longer hard.

I zip up, and without a word, leave. I stumble through the bushes toward the Strasse der 17. Juni. My shirt still has the mustard stain, now even messier with caked soap scum.

Where is Kay? The others? They're not where I last saw them. I try to call Kay but there's no service. There are thousands and thousands of people here. Shit.

The crowds part as I walk through. After a few minutes of looking, I give up. I walk to the U-Bahn station, and pass the glass windows of the Russian embassy. I see my reflection—me without glasses, a mustard stain, the rainbow suspenders. Disgusting. I rip off the suspenders and throw them in the trash before heading underground, home, then underground again.

I reemerge to take the 16h10 intercity train to Hannover. There are a few other passengers, and I try to read a few journal articles on my laptop but slam the computer closed. How can Kay leave me? When the train arrives two hours later, I walk to the grocery store. I buy sausages and cheese, and as I wait in line, I hear only German in an accent as clean as my own. No Turkish, no English.

Mother lives in List, the most beautiful part of Hannover, although some say Südstadt with its man-made lake is more picturesque. The houses in List survived the war, and my Mom lives in a house built in 1915 with a garden in front. She moved after the divorce to a two-room apartment.

I look up to her apartment on the second floor, and see her looking out the living room window. Her hair was once bright blonde, but now is gray. Even from here, I can tell she's not looking at anything in particular but focused more on what is in her mind. Voices and whispers.

I ring the bell, but there's no answer. I don't expect one. I take out the brass key and open the door. There's no elevator, so I walk up the stairs. When I unlock the door to her apartment, I notice the name has been changed from "Urning" to "Schulz."

"Mother, I'm here." I close the door and drop my bag in the hallway. "I bought sausages for tonight's bread." I head to the kitchen. There is only milk and yoghurt in the fridge. I lay the sausage and cheese on a shelf and leave the bread on the counter. There are coffee cups stained brown and wine glasses spotted purple standing in the sink. On the table rests a mixing bowl with an opened bag of flour and a carton of organic milk. Beads of condensation coalesce on the surface of the carton.

While walking to the living room, it dawns on me. It's supposed to be the mother who visits the student to stock his fridge with food, not this way around.

"Hello Thomas," she says as she turns her head. She sits at the bay window. My mother is 191cm tall, and she fills the entire bay window with her body. She tries to smile, and there are no wrinkles around her eyes.

"Hello, Mother," I say.

"It's raining in Berlin." The TV is on but muted. On the screen, there's an animation of clouds and angled lines.

"It was sunny this morning."

"It's not going to rain here," she says. "When you called to come over, I was going to make a cake and thought we could take a walk. I wanted to go shopping, but I couldn't. See? I even got dressed." She wears a red dress with sleeves that cover her wrists. I remember her going to church in it.

She stands. She walks toward me, and when she hugs me, I smell her and hug her back. It feels good. This is my mother, and the only love I know. "I'm sorry, Thomas. I was happy when you called, but I'm sorry I couldn't bake you your cake."

"I saw," I say.

"There were no more eggs, and I thought about how I have no more eggs, how you and Nelson are all I have, and how I've failed you."

"You haven't failed me, Mom," I say. I hug her again. "I wouldn't have eaten the cake anyway."

She manages a smile. "You're no longer the boy who would read in the kitchen while I baked so you could lick the spoon."

"Mom, I noticed the name on the door. You changed it back to Schulz."

She breaks the embrace, but holds me by the arms. "Your father did not tell you?" She squeezes my biceps while looking at me then shakes her head. "Of course, he didn't tell you. He got remarried. It was three months ago, but he finally called last week to tell me. It no longer made sense to keep your father's name." This probably triggered this latest bout of sadness, I think.

It has been four years since I last saw my father. He did love her. He stayed with her for years despite the trips to the hospital—first when she took too many pills, and then when she slit her wrist. He was there, and he held her hand each time. But while I was at the University of Heidelberg, and she drove her car into oncoming traffic with my thirteen-year-old brother Nelson in the front seat, Dad said it was too much. She said it was an accident, but he knew it wasn't. I knew it wasn't. He filed for divorce and moved with Nelson to Essen, where my grandparents live. Maybe it was Dad's love for Nelson that made him leave.

It has been two years since I saw Nelson although we speak over the phone. While I'm tall and blond, Nelson is normal height and dark-haired, like my father.

"I'll call Nelson later."

"Do you want something to drink? Coffee?" She looks at her watch. "Wine?" I nod. She goes into the kitchen, and returns with a glass. She pours from the open bottle by the window, and we sit on the sofa. "*Prost*," I say.

"*Prost*," she says. Her eyes look weary.

"Do I have to worry about you, Mom?" I ask.

"No. I'm taking my medication. This time it should pass." I've dealt with her bouts of depression enough times to know when something is serious, and she trusts me enough to confide when things are indeed bad. She looks at me. "Should I be worried about you?"

"The appeal was not successful," I say. "I'm not sure what to do." The meaning of this statement is like a hammer hitting my head. For once in my life, I don't know what to do. There are two things that people have told me since I was a teenager—that I was tall, and that I was determined. I also knew they talked about my weight, but that was never directly to me. To go to university and get my degree, then get my doctorate—I was driven to do it all. Losing weight, that was the hardest, but I succeeded there, too.

Now, I don't know.

"Mom, I don't know what to do, and it scares me." I lay on her lap and cry.

She strokes my hair. "My little Thomas," she says. "When you were young, you never cried much. You always seemed happy to live in your own world. The few times you did cry, it was easy for Mother to fix. I bandaged you, cooked something sweet, and kissed you until you felt better. This time is different, and it's not so easy for your mother to fix. But I know this feeling."

"You do?" She strokes my cheek. Only a few people have caressed my face this tenderly. My mother, my father. Kay.

"Yes. When I was twenty-two, studying medicine at the Charité, Professor Doctor Wissmann wanted me to accompany him on a talk in West Berlin. He asked me to join him. The presentation was a study about women's health and a propaganda opportunity for East Germany, and since I was the only female medical student, that was the official reason I would accompany him."

"But the unofficial reason?"

"He knew I was unhappy living in Friedrichshain. He knew about my sadness—he had seen so many of his friends in the DDR take their own lives. So, he applied for a day trip to West Berlin, and I was approved to go with him only two hours before the talk. He never said that I should escape, but only said that in the West, there were new treatments being developed for depression. I was still in my lab coat when we crossed the border with a briefcase of paper with fake data. He gave the talk, I presented some data, and then we were on our way back. We were still on the West Berlin side, and I wondered whether I could flee. I saw the East Berlin guards, and knew I couldn't go back. I started to walk away, back to the West. But then Professor Doctor Wissmann grabbed my hand, and screamed, 'You must return' before whispering, 'Hit me.' I pushed him to the ground and ran. He was a much smaller man than me."

I'm shocked, as Mother has never wanted to talk about this before. "What happened next?" I ask.

"The West Berlin guards didn't chase me. I immediately went to an immigration office. This was 1982, and the only family I had in West Germany was in Hannover, Aunt Carolina. I was given thirty Deutschmarks and an airplane ticket to Hannover. It was the first time I flew. While waiting, I tried to imagine a life in Hannover but couldn't. I felt like you do now."

"When did you feel better?"

"It's the fear of the unknown. I didn't know how Aunt Carolina would treat me, whether living with her was temporary or permanent, what to do for money, and whether I could continue my studies. I didn't know whether being from the East would mark me forever. I also didn't know if my bouts of depression would go away."

"Did they?"

"With knowledge, the fear was gone. The sadness, and the mark of being from the East—these things stayed."

I thought about my knowns and unknowns. I know that I want to be a scientist and finish my PhD. But the unknowns—money, university programs, these things I'd have to research. I need to write down my priorities, and figure out how to find the information I was missing. I may need to pursue a PhD outside of Germany. I wonder whether Yuri can be trusted with promises.

There was also the unknown of Kay.

"If I study outside of Germany, what would you think?" I ask. Switzerland is only an hour's flight away, but it isn't part of the EU.

"I wrote a letter to your grandmother the day I arrived at Aunt Carolina's," she explains. "I was sorry to leave her, but this was a chance for a better life. She wrote back, and wrote that she would never forgive me for abandoning her. I think her life was made miserable by the Stasi after." Mother never went to grandmother's funeral in Berlin, even though it was years after the wall had fallen. "Thomas, if you need to go, say goodbye, but I will be proud of you."

I rise from her lap and she kisses me on the forehead. "I love you, Mom."

"I love you, Thomas," she whispers. "I know you brought bread and sausage for tonight's dinner, but how about we go to the Italian restaurant around the corner? My treat."

"You are dressed for going out," I say.

"Help me pick up a pair of shoes then," she says. We rummage through her closet to find a pair of red high heels. We head to the restaurant.

Hours later, we return, Mom is giggling and holding her heels in her hand. "These shoes were a terrible idea. I can't believe I let you convince me to wear them." I keep silent on how she insisted on the bottle of wine at dinner and then that we go to the beer hall after. We shared a table with men from St. Petersburg, and Mom spoke school Russian with them. They loved it, and bought us rounds of vodka and beer.

I drank none of it. I had consumed all my calories during dinner, so I had the unfortunate situation of being the only sober person around a table of drunks. But Mom was happy.

"Shit," she says. "I forgot to make your bed." She clutches the doorway while looking forlornly at the living room sofa.

"I can make it," I say. "I'll find the sheets."

I lead Mom to her bed and help her out of her dress. She stands in her bra and panties. I see the scars on her wrists. I help her with her bra, and she kicks off her panties before I put the cover over her. I am her son and am tucking her into bed.

"How are things with you and Kay?"

I want to say that he abandoned me, but I say instead, "He told me he loved me, and I don't know if I love him."

"Do you?"

"I honestly don't know."

Mom laughs. "If you watched more romantic movies, maybe you'd know." Then, "Your father loved me," she says.

"He was devoted to you."

"I thought I loved him," she continues. "No. I thought I would love him. He was an engineer and came from a good family. Whatever you decide to do, make sure it is for love."

"I will. Good night, Mom." I get up and turn off the light.

"Good night, my little one."

In the morning, we have the sausages and bread before I head to the train station to return to Berlin. As the train pulls out, I wave goodbye to my mother from the window seat. She waves, and I watch until she becomes too small and distant to see.

Mom lives alone, and dad—I haven't seen since Nelson's birthday party. This is what happens when two people don't love each other, even if there are children that they love. I don't want that.

I text Kay. "I don't know what happened Saturday, but can we meet tonight?"

I wait for a response. The problem with taking ICE trains is that you sometimes travel too fast to send or receive messages. The train slows down in Wolfsburg and Kay messages back. "Unexpected meeting with my boss this evening in Schöneberg. Can we meet at Heile Welt around 21-ish?"

Canadians and their imprecision. I'll probably be waiting but I text back, "OK." It's better that we meet in a public place.

I spend the afternoon in my apartment reading. I don't want to eat anything in my fridge. Since I'll be close to Nollendorfplatz, I decide to eat at the Korean restaurant Ixthys. The restaurant has handwritten bible quotes on the wall, as well as pearls of wisdom interspersed between a menu of bibimbap and japchae. Kay told me that if you ask about a quote, one of the cute women will take the time to talk to you about Jesus. I order bibimbap instead. This is one aspect of me that will forever change after Kay—my appreciation of and desire for Asian food. No longer will I be satisfied with the *Imbiss* menus of Thai/Vietnamese/Sushi all-in-one, excelling at none.

I stir the rice in the stone bowl as the egg and carrots sizzle on top. I feel a tap on my shoulder.

"Hey Thomas, I knew it was you," someone says. I turn around to see Alex, smiling. I say hello. "Great minds think alike," he says. He asks me what happened at CSD.

"I was with the Russian guy," I say, "and when I came back to join you and Kay, you were all gone. That was very friendly of you." I know my sarcasm in English does not translate so well, but he seemed to understand.

"Kay saw you having," he says, then whispers the next word like he was saying it in church, "sex." Then louder, "After that, he said we shouldn't wait for you."

Kay saw that? How could he have? Even if he did, we have an open relationship, so what does it matter?

Alex orders glass noodles and eats them with a fork and spoon. I find it funny because I'm the one eating with chopsticks. "He was kind of upset about it," Alex continues. "But I'm not one to butt into a friend's relationship."

"I talk to him later," I say.

"At Heile Welt, right? I'm going too. I can't believe Kay has to work on a Sunday, but he's a big shot at CoExcel now."

"How was your CSD?" I ask. I want him to talk so I can eat.

"I chipped a tooth," he says while pulling his lip open to show a chip on one of his top teeth. "It was a drunken mishap, but in the end, a little booboo isn't going to stop me from eating something spicy."

When we finish, it is 20h35. We pay and walk up Eisenacher

Strasse. It feels like summer. Alex wants a *Laufbier*, but I say we don't have too far to walk. We reach the intersection with Motzstrasse when I see a guy in a red plaid jacket run past. There's no bus nearby, so why is he running? Then a second man runs, also wearing a red jacket, and a bag clutched in his hand. There's something familiar with that bag… a second later, I turn the corner and see Kay face down on the ground. Blood leaks from his nose.

"Kay?" Alex gasps.

It is only a flash, but then it's clear to me—the two men robbed Kay. I chase after them. If you're robbing someone, why would you wear red? I can clearly see them. I scream, "Stop them! They're robbers!" But no one does anything.

I run and am glad that I have done a lot of cardio to lose weight. The men turn left on Nollendorfstraße. The street is poorly lit, but I see the man in the red jacket. I feel the adrenaline rush through me.

I take out my phone and call the police. "Good evening. My name is Thomas Urning. I just saw a robbery and am following the robbers. We are on Nollendorfstraße."

"What do they look like?" the emergency dispatch asks. A woman.

"There are two men with dark hair. One is 170, the other 175 maybe. One has a red jacket on, and the other one has a red plaid jacket," I say.

"Understood. Where exactly?" she says.

Shit. "They just turned into a courtyard." I look at the number. "It's Nollendorfstraße 25." This place is a large complex of businesses and homes, and there's a map by the entrance—it shows two exits. This was probably their getaway plan, and there's no way I can follow them. My phone is slick because sweat drenches the screen.

A German man in his forties walks out. "Good evening," he says.

"Did you see two men walk into the courtyard?" I ask. The woman on the phone says the police will come.

"Yes," he says.

"Do you know whether they left through the other exit?" I ask.

"They can't. I just locked it. I'm the building's caretaker."

"The police should come soon," I say to the woman. "The second exit to the courtyard is locked. The robbers are trapped inside."

"The police are on their way," she explains. "Please wait outside."

A third man of Middle Eastern descent is beside me now. "Did you find the robbers?"

"They're trapped inside this courtyard," I explain. "Who are you?"

"I was on the street and saw it," he explains in broken German. "One of them started talking and when your friend was distracted, the other guy came from the side and pushed your friend to the ground. They took the bag and started running."

In my mind, I see Kay on the ground, and I clench my fists. How many minutes has it been?

"When are the police coming?" asks the German man.

"Not soon enough," I say. I walk inside. These pieces of shit hurt my friend! The courtyard is dark, filled with parked cars, and it reeks of gasoline and grease. One of the businesses here is an auto repair garage. "You assholes are trapped!" I scream. My voice bounces off the walls. "The guy you robbed was my friend." I can feel every muscle in my body flex and tense. Kay isn't just my friend. "Show yourself!" I demand.

I hear a scraping sound. "I'm here." The man in red plaid pulls himself out from underneath a station wagon. With just those two words, I can tell he is not German. He holds his hands up.

"Where's the other guy?" I stare down at him like a beetle.

"I'm here alone," he says.

I stand in the middle of the courtyard. Here, without shadows or corners from which to launch a surprise attack, I have the advantage with my brute strength and height. I feel my breath blow through my flared nostrils. I want to beat this man. I want to hurt him.

"Where's the bag you stole?" I say.

"Hidden. Let me go and I tell you." His eyes are large and spaced wide for his face, and in another situation, he'd look like a boy starting puberty, with a hint of a moustache. But innocent boys do not rob. Innocent boys do not assault.

I take one step closer and he tries to step back, but the car's bumper juts into his thigh. "Tell me," I say.

His eyes go wide and he nods. I hear shuffling behind me, and without hesitation, I pivot, so the wide-eye boy and the shuffling are to my left and right. His partner has appeared, and in his hand he holds an empty glass bottle that catches the dim light.

I am not afraid but angry. When the red-jacketed man comes close, he realizes his mistake, and I raise my leg and kick him. I aim for his chest, but my foot lands on his face instead. There's a crunch, a groan, and the echo of the bottle landing in the darkness.

The man in plaid tries to run, but I push him to the ground as he rushes past me. He falls on his back, and I mount him. I could punch him, I could make him bleed.

"You hurt him," I grunt. My voice is ragged, more spit than sound. I grab his neck and squeeze with one hand. "You hurt the man I love." The words come out, finally, in anger. This pathetic boy who can barely speak German gurgles saliva in a futile attempt to breathe. I want to squeeze harder, so hard that he goes from gurgling to purple to pop.

But I stop. "Where's the bag?" He points to a corner with a garbage bin before he clutches his own neck to massage it.

As I walk, I hear the police scream, *"Halt! Polizei!"*

I freeze and put my hands in the air. A fat police officer comes toward me. In flawless German, I explain. "I called you. These two attacked my friend, and when I confronted them, the one in red attacked me with a bottle. I kicked him in self-defense."

"You should have just waited on the street," the police officer says.

"I see a smashed bottle here," says a female voice.

"We're going to have to take you in and get this sorted out," he says.

My phone rings, and the police officer nods. "Urning," I say.

"Hey. It's Alex. We're at the hospital. Kay wants to talk to you."

It's like fizz from sekt when I hear Kay's voice. "Hey, Thomas."

"Hey, Kay. I love you."

A moment of silence, and I can feel my atom's apple as I swallow. "I love you, too," Kay says.

"How hurt are you?"

"My nose and a cut on my cheek," he says. "It should heal but maybe I'll have a sexy scar after. Or a crooked nose."

"Even with a crooked nose I'd love you."

I hear Alex's voice. "Crooked noses are a new Wednesday night at Lab!"

"When I was on the ground, my first thought was, Thomas will find me. Even though we were supposed to meet at the bar, I knew that you'd find me. And you did." Kay's voice changes tone. "I met a professor of psychiatry this week. He is interested in your work, and encourages you to apply to continue your PhD. At the University of British Columbia."

"Moving to Canada?" I say. I don't say what this implies. After spending all this time with Canadians, Britons, and Americans, I know that saying the unpleasant isn't just rude, it can also make it true.

"Vancouver, yes," he says. "But it would mean good-bye." Kay is becoming more German. "I should go. Good-bye, at least for now."

"Good-bye." I put my phone back into my pocket. "Can I grab my friend's bag before we go to the police station?" The officer doesn't object, and I walk to the corner. Despite all the years in Europe, Kay uses his University of Manitoba backpack. I pick it up and dust the dirt off before walking out of the courtyard to the police wagon.

19. Timothy

It's finally the end after a long day, and I can be myself. A little nub on the right trouser leg of my Lederhosen has rubbed me raw the entire day. This CSD has been a blunder, with no sex to speak of. *Would you have been able Timothy, or would your nose have ruptured infected blood?*

I empty my pockets, and lay the box of cigarettes on the desk among piles of unopened letters. Two are opened, the envelopes ragged from my finger sawing through the edge. One is from the investment firm filled with bland international English that glosses over the horror of reading negative numbers. The second is from the *Finanzamt*. It's not just in German, but in lawyer-speak German, and I can still comprehend the numbers, five digits owing while my stocks are only worth three.

Failure. You're a failure, an abject failure.

I slide off the braces from the Lederhosen, and in my impatience, tear one strap completely off. Fuck. What does it matter? Shirt, pants—everything off. I stand naked. A breeze blows in through the tipped-open window, and as I see myself reflect in the glass, chill air tickles me. My skin tingles as if ants are crawling over my body, a path of goosebumps forming from my calves to inner thigh. Fuck no.

I rush to the shower. The hot water burns away the tingles. Droplets, one, two, three, ten, ten hundred, ten thousand and tens of thousands of droplets echo in the tiny shower stall.

I emerge with a towel, folded in half, draped around me. I blink once, twice, then a third time at the sight of the pack of cigs moving on the desk, as if crawling. I hear the subdued scratches from scores of cockroaches with pincers, antennae, and hairy legs. I scream and flap my limp hands around.

Bloody. Fucking. Hell. I'm infested. Is it surprising? Your flat is filthy.

Bloody hell, bloody hell, bloody hell. Those bugs must have touched the floor. I jump on the bed, and the white towel falls from my hips.

What do I do? What do I do? *What do you do?*

I need to leave, even if I'm aching with exhaustion. On tippy toes, I prance to the wardrobe and pull out some clothes. Once dressed, I hesitate by the desk. Did the cigarettes stop moving? I grab my wallet and keys. I wince as I reach for the smokes, but stop midway. What if one of those things clings to the cellophane, and once inside my pocket, crawls to my groin and nibbles on whatever flesh it can? I'll just buy a new pack.

Just sleep, let the critters crawl. It does not matter. You're already infested.

Is that a red welt on my arm?

I rush out. I knock on Anna's door. No answer. "Open the door, please!" I beg. "It's dire! My flat is teeming with bugs. Please open this door." *What if her flat is just as infested?*

I stop knocking. Her place is as terrible. The only safe place is outside. The lift's doors open. But the light flickers, maybe from the fluttering of moths. Screw this. I'm taking the stairs.

Outdoors, I hear birds. Birds, sweet birds. There's nothing to disparage about birds. Their song is peaceful, and the air is refreshing. I breathe in as deeply as possible—and cough. I need a fag.

I've developed a relationship with the owner of the *Späti* around the corner. He's a friendly and polite Berliner, from the east. He's also patient with me and my halting German. When I turn the corner, however, his shop is dark, and I feel foolish when I pull on the door but it does not give.

He knows about you, Timothy. He knows you're a Nancy boy, and doesn't want to serve the likes of you. He knows you've buggered one man too many, and he doesn't want to catch what you've caught. And he can still smell the piss from when you assaulted Orhan's boyfriend, that sweet innocent man who was just returning home with groceries.

"No one knows," I mutter. "No one."

I walk to the next street with aching feet. One *Späti* is open. The outside is run down, and inside, I am not disappointed. The space is cramped with aisles wide enough for only one person to browse. Suddenly, there's music—Karaoke music with nineties era synthesizers creating a rendition of a song remotely familiar.

It isn't. The cashier is an Asian woman with black hair in a bowl cut, and she sits by the till while staring at a compact telly mounted to a wall. She sings in a language I can't recognise. I grab my favourite pack of fags and without missing a beat, she rings me up and points to the price on display while continuing to blare out her ballad in full gusto. This is why *Spätis* are different from Tesco's convenience stores—they are independently owned, with all the personality this entails. I'd hate to see this Karaoke-loving woman forced to wear a generic blue smock if Germany GmbH takes over.

I pay and when I peek at the screen, I see words scrolling by in Vietnamese, Roman letters attacked with a swarm of lines, squiggles, and dots—like bugs. Bloody bugs. My head tingles as if goosebumps are forming on my cerebrum. I run out.

Fuck this. I walk to a major thoroughfare and wait for a taxi. *They won't serve your kind here.*

A beige Mercedes stops. "Hotel Adlon," I say. Execute Plan B.

As I enter the hotel lobby, the place is packed. It must be brunch time, and in a sinful city like Berlin, Sundays are reserved for the worship of a cold-cuts buffet. I walk to the receptionist, and she smiles.

"A room please," I say in English, feeling completely at ease now that I am in an international environment where the lingua franca is my own. I ever so subtly remove my Platinum card. It will expire in two weeks, but I'm focusing on the now.

"We can have your room ready at three," she says.

"Are any rooms free now?" I inquire as I scratch my forearm.

"I'm sorry Mr Goodall, but we are fully booked," she says, but adds, "If you want to enjoy our brunch, I can send over a complimentary glass of Champagne." I wonder whether I should execute Plan C and call Alex to spend a few nights there.

If they know, they'll never want you.

I grab my card and walk to the brunch area. "They can't know."

The chairs are plush, and when a man dressed in black and white attends to me, I order, "Champagne." None of this sekt bullocks.

The crowd of well-dressed tourists and Berlin elites chat, and after a few sips, all I focus on is the mass of varying colours and a hum of unrecognisable words. I relish the crowds, I need the crowds, how they look, how they sound. Blue, green, the day is sunny, I know what you mean, white shorts.

"Timothy?" A short man in dark green shorts and a darker purple polo waddles toward me. It's Morgan. Why in God's fucked-up hell is Morgan in Berlin again? He looks like a court jester in those garish monstrosity of colours, doesn't he?

I remain sitting when he embraces me. "Morgan."

"Please don't tell me the ever-affable Timothy is dining for one," Morgan says. "I'm here with my gay besties for Christopher Street Day." A little softer. "We may even frequent a certain establishment to relax, but I've kept mum, and hence my promise."

Morgan grabs my hand and lifts me from my chair. I manage to hold onto my Champagne flute and shuffle along. "Timothy, have you met Jordan and Nikos? Boys, Timothy lives in Berlin now and he could give us a few pointers."

"How do we get into Berghain?" Jordan asks. Do I know Nikos from somewhere? Is he giving me a wink? Jordan frowns. "It seems like it's a privileged secret."

How long have I been silent? Morgan grips my arm. "Are you OK, Timothy?"

Then I catch the sight of two police officers in the lobby. My brain ruptures in tingles. *They've found you. You attacked that man, and they've found you.*

I rise. Morgan utters something through his shocked face, but I don't bother to listen. No one is following me—yet. I walk past crystal glasses atop white tablecloths, down the wood-paneled hallway, through the hotel and past tables with freshly cut lilies. There is a rear way out somewhere. A hotel like this must have another way out.

A door. With all force, I push it open, and suddenly my ears ring with the blaring of an alarm. I've barged my way through an emergency door.

They'll hear you. They'll find you.

I run. Tiergarten is nearby. I'll lose them in the woods with chirping birds. Run, run, run Nancy boy. Why did I wear these shoes? I run and am surrounded by trees. There are no birds here, only silence. I listen for the inevitable sound of men chasing me, but all I hear is the wind in the leaves.

"I should go home."

They're watching your flat.

"No, London."

You can't fly without your passport.

Is that a noise? A crack of a twig? I run again. I pant and my legs hurt but I keep running. I then see an S-Bahn station. I look behind me and see no one. They haven't found me yet! I run up to the train platform where a train awaits, and its doors are almost closing, but I dive inside just in time.

They'll find you on this train.

"No, no, no." I look up, and see the next stations on the LED display. I need to get off. But where? Warschauer Straße. Berghain is there. I watch people enter and exit the train. "Berghain, Berghain," I whisper. We pass Alexanderplatz and its giant TV tower. Even in daylight, the disco ball glitters.

Warschauer Straße. When the train pulls in, I run out. I run up the stairs while trying to avoid hordes of tourists speaking in Spanish. There was a wooded path. I remember that from Snax. I hear the wind in the leaves.

They won't let you in with what you're wearing.

I look down. Why did I choose to wear something respectable, like slacks and a jumper? It's summer. I pull off the jumper, but I'm wearing a button-down shirt underneath. I rip that off. Now just a tank top.

"Are you happy?" The wind in the trees says yes.

It's Sunday afternoon and there is still a line to enter the club. I wait, and my feet tap the ground. *You won't get in. No one likes you.*

In minutes, I'm at the front. The doorman on Sunday isn't the same large giant of a man as on Saturday. He has a beard and smiles through it. But he looks at me, and his smile disappears. I know he's about to turn me away when I see a tall man walk up to him.

"*Hallöchen Karl,*" the man says. This man is 6'2" with large hands. They faux kiss.

"*Allein heute?*" the doorman asks.

The tall man is about to answer, then spots me. "Timothy?"

"Yes?" I say.

"It's Heidi," he says. Without her make up, I didn't recognise the drag queen Heidi Klo. "I'm Jaochim today." He looks at the doorman and says, "He's with me."

Just before entering the cavern that is Berghain, I look back to see two men in police uniforms at the back of the line. They won't get in and ascend to techno heaven. I'm safe in this world of dancing and drugs, and I disappear into the dark.

20. All

Alex

I'm about to come when a video call pops up on my screen. My mom. Fuck, did I forget to close Skype? I'm sitting at my desk, and even though Mom wouldn't be able to see anything, I pull up my underwear first then click on the green button. My chest heaves as if I've been running.

A moment later and her face appears on the screen. "Hi Alex."

"Hi Mom," I say. I try to slow my breathing.

"Are you OK? Your face looks red," she says.

"I've been practicing," I explain.

"Oh yes. I wanted to call to wish you good luck on your performance tonight." This is big. She has never talked to me before a performance. That's usually my dad's job. I'll be performing with some actors tonight, and of course it's bad luck to wish me good luck, but I don't tell my mom that. It's the thought that counts. "Thanks, Mom."

"I'm glad you're doing what you love," she says. "Next time you visit, will you do a performance for us?"

"OK, Mom," I say. I hear a moaning sound, perhaps two men. That porn site must have autoplayed another video.

"What's that noise?" she asks.

"It's my roommate."

"Your roommate is gay?" she asks.

"Mom, I need to continue preparing."

"OK. Bye Alex."

"Bye." And I log off.

I have a preparation routine. I jerk off, otherwise I'll be too tense on stage. The last thing I want is to sport an awkward boner while singing my aria.

I return to the porn site. The previous video doesn't seem spunk-worthy anymore. I find a video of two guys with a woman, and the woman fucks the brute with a strap on while the twink licks the brute's cock. OK. I've fast-forwarded to the good parts.

Just as I am pulling my pants down, there's a knock on the door. "Hey Alex," Kay says.

"Busy!" I say.

"I know, but I'm going to leave and wanted to double check—when should Thomas and I arrive at Kit Kat Club?" he asks.

"Nine," I answer. "Fuck off please."

"One more thing. Should we wait for you after the performance or will you be mingling with your musician friends?"

"Mingling!" I say.

Silence. I listen to the audio with earphones this time. Fuck, that's hot. Take it in your man pussy. Take it. "I'm coming!" he says in Eastern European-accented English. Shit, where did my tissue go? I can't stop, I don't want to stop—the pleasure of my orgasm consumes me, it's powerful, it shoots like a cannon, and I jizz all over my face.

Kay

I ride the elevator in Thomas' building. I have a bottle of Champagne, and although I bought it from a discount grocery for less than twenty euros, it's still called Champagne with all the protection and snobbery of EU labelling law. It's definitely not Canadian champagne and the headache that implies.

I also have a bouquet of lilies. Thomas' apartment is full of green, but because his apartment receives little light, he can only grow hearty ferns. This little bit of colour should be good to celebrate into his birthday.

When I exit the elevator, his door is already ajar.

"Hey Thomas," I say as I walk in and instinctively take off my shoes. I hear him in the bathroom, and after leaving things in the kitchen, I turn to stare at Thomas wearing nothing but a towel and shaving cream. He smiles when he sees me in the mirror. I walk toward him, and he lets the razor soak in the sink as I kiss him on the small of his back. My lips part from his skin and leave a garden of goosebumps.

"Do I really have to go?" he says while resuming his shave.

"It's not every day we get to support Alex in his singing," I begin. "Plus, you said you wanted to celebrate into your birthday." It's bad luck to celebrate a birthday early, but being consistent with German accuracy, if one drinks the night before and well past midnight, it's not technically celebrating the birthday early.

"Isn't Kit Kat Club a straight sex club?" he says.

"Except after the show, it'll be gay," I say. Thomas finishes shaving, then kisses me. I want to kiss him like a herpes infection—for life— but in a few minutes, I fart. "I'm wearing really tight jeans," I say and I can tell I'm blushing from the mirror.

He exits the bathroom while saying, "Or did you have some cheese earlier?" He winks and closes the bathroom door. The day after cheese and the sauna, I had more than stomach cramps. Biological business, then I go to the living room. Thomas has the flowers in a vase, and two flutes of Champagne ready. He's dressed in jeans and a football jersey.

"To still being in your 20s," I say. We clink glasses. "What's your fetish?"

"I have soccer shorts underneath," he says. "You look—boring. Just a button shirt?"

"Leather," I say. I pull down the collar and show a leather harness. I don't mention how difficult it was to get into my jeans with a leather thong on.

"I received an email from UBC," Thomas says as we sit on the couch. He told me about Switzerland, and we agreed to pursue both options until a concrete offer surfaces. I know he's excited about Vancouver because he drones on about the process in excruciating detail.

I'm trying to focus on what he's saying, but my crotch is so uncomfortable. There's something about a face-to-face visit, but I suddenly get up, and unbutton my fly. "I didn't know talking about post-graduate admissions turned you on," he says.

"It's the leather thong I wore to match the harness," I say. "It itches."

"It's worth it." Thomas looks at me with these eyes that I know means sex.

I turn around and pull my pants further down, although it stops mid-thigh because the jeans are too narrow. "Like what you see?" There's no answer, but I do feel Thomas' nose nudge against my crack, and he sniffs. The air passing over my skin and asshole tingles. "You want this, Thomas?"

His "Yes" is muffled by my ass cheeks.

"Happy birthday my love," I say.

His tongue lashes out and drenches my asshole in spit. This thong leaves my ass wide open, and Thomas means business. Eating ass must be the perfect meal for a man watching his diet. All the taste but zero calories.

Love means giving all of oneself to another so in that spirit, I've been practicing. At the friendly neighbourhood sex shop (i.e., online), I bought dildos of ever increasing length and girth, and inserted them on my own, small then big then bigger. Within the safety of this relationship, I don't have to worry about the power dynamics of sex. Sex means pleasure. Pleasure is something I want to give to Thomas—a man I love, a man who loves me.

Thomaschen was the name of the biggest dildo, and I found I could accommodate him better if I was bent over. "Give it to me," I say to the real Thomas, and wait expectantly. He disappears into the bedroom and when he comes back, I'm bent over the couch and wink at him.

I close my eyes. Darkness. There's the sound of crisp plastic ripped open. Then, Thomas huffs and says, "The condom's too tight." I turn around with open eyes to see him, and his own eyes crinkle. His cheeks are flushed with embarrassment, but there's also this huge grin like he's saying, "Big dick problems." I kiss him, and he then turns around and bends over. "This is my birthday wish," he says.

I take a moment to appreciate Thomas' beefy, blonde, and bubbly bum before going to the bedroom and taking a fresh condom.

When I return to the living room, Thomas' back is on the floor with his legs spread eagle. This is the mechanics of when David fucks Goliath. The thong has a zipper for easy access. I push my cock into him, and his shoulders, neck, and face surge with blood.

I thrust and his hands jerk. He moans, and I thrust. We sweat. Our eyes never break contact. I thrust, I thrust, I breath, I thrust.

There's a door bell ringing. What the fuck? I keep thrusting and ignore it, but then there's kicking. "Kay! Thomas! I know you're in there! Open the fucking door!" I see Thomas' eyes go wide in recognition of Timothy's frantic voice.

"Coming!" I scream. The wrong kind of coming. Fuck. Fuck!

Thomas and I get dressed. I grab the evidence of sex and throw them in the trash as Thomas opens the door.

"I'm a bloody mess," Timothy says as he barges in. "What time is it?"

"It's twenty hours," Thomas responds. Shit, we need to be at Kit Kat soon.

I stare at Timothy. He wasn't exaggerating. His hair and clothes are drenched, his hair covered in a Baroque blond wig. I hear rain from outside but he also reeks of sweat and urine. He was being literal—underneath his fingernails I see dirt and brownish crud of what, blood? Where is the English gentleman that I once knew?

"What's happened?" I ask and hold my breath.

"Horrible week," he says, then with a smile pulled right from a West End show, "Investor meetings, darling. What horrors we put ourselves through to get cash into our business, am I right?"

"You want to shower?" Thomas says.

"May I? That'd be lovely." Timothy hobbles to the bathroom, and screams through a closed door, "May I borrow some clothes?"

Thomas shrugs his shoulders as he points to himself and where Timothy's head would be on his chest.

"You mean Thomas' clothes?" I ask.

"I'd be swimming in his trousers, I know," he says and I hear the sound of the shower. "But I'm going to change into my birthday suit once inside Kit Kat, so it really doesn't matter."

Thomas goes into his bedroom and pulls out an old pair of sweats and a dingy T-shirt that reads, "World Cup 2006." He leaves it by the bathroom door with a towel.

Thomas and I head to the living room. "Is he all right?" Thomas asks.

"I don't think so," I say.

The bathroom door creaks ajar. "Brilliant!" Timothy exclaims before he slams the door shut. A few breaths in silence, then the door bursts open. Timothy sashays into the living room like it's a Paris runway. He ripped the sleeves off the T-shirt, and has cinched it high on the side to expose his belly button. The waist of the sweats has been tightened so much that the thighs seem to bulge outward like he has hourglass hips. Yet, somehow it works. "This is incredible, Thomas. World Cup 2006. You've retained things from almost a decade ago. There's nothing in my flat of mine older than six months." For a moment, I hope perhaps Timothy's thinking clearly.

Timothy then eyes the Champagne. "Bubbles!" He grabs the bottle and scans the label. "Champagne and not sekt? How decadent!" He drinks directly from it. He chugs it and some of it dribbles down the side to his shirt.

"Timothy," I call to him. He places the empty bottle back on the table and sits between Thomas and me on the couch. "Are you OK?"

"Never been better," he says, and I imagine the West End audiences applauding his performance. "Ecstatic even."

"I'm worried about you," I say, placing my hand gingerly on his thigh. "I don't think we should go out. Maybe we should stay here."

"Or go to a hospital," Thomas suggests. I know he was being supportive, but the furor that ignites in Timothy's eyes makes me cower.

"I. Am. Not. Sick," he spits out, each word slow and drawn out, the final consonants landing on my ear like blood drops landing on white sheets. A sudden smile and Timothy says, "It's Alex's big performance. We need to go and show him how much we love him."

I grip Timothy's leg, tenderness gone. "Please. Let's stay in."

Timothy's hand lands on top of mine. His fingers clench my wrist. "I will go and no one will stop me." He squeezes and his knuckles go white. He hasn't washed his hands fully and I still see traces of blood. I look into his eyes, and notice how wide his pupils are.

Only a brief moment passes, but I say, "OK."

Timothy hops up and twirls with a flourish. "We're taking a cab. You're paying." There's a tingling in my mouth, and I realize I've bitten my tongue.

We wait underneath the shelter of the apartment awning for the cab. Whereas the smell of rain in the countryside is earthy, the raindrops here splatter on to the cobblestone and churn up the smell of urine mixed with heat in Berlin's party districts. Public urination is a side effect of public drunkenness. But this night is different. Through the sound of rain and swooshing of tires on the wet road, through the sidewalk odour, I taste the metal from the cut in my mouth.

The taxi arrives, and we three hop in. Thomas takes shotgun, and Timothy and I are sitting in the back.

"I wonder how many will come considering the rain," I say.

"As cavity-inducing we fags may be," Timothy says, "we're not made of sugar. We can afford to be a little damp." He looks out the window. "Berlin is beautiful in that shabby chic kind of way, isn't it?" He doesn't wait for an answer. "But it wasn't always like that. It was a wealthy metropolis. Schöneberg was once like its namesake, beautiful, and not the rubbish pile of fleshpots and sleazy sex it has become today. Berlin did terrible things, had terrible things happen to it, and through the rubble, Berlin crawled free. But I wonder, would we love Berlin so much if it hadn't been bombed to smithereens and endured this tortured past?"

This time, he waits for an answer. "I wouldn't," I admit.

"Neither would I," he says as he examines the crud on his nails.

"But Berlin persevered," I add. "Whatever blood Berlin had on its hands, the city accepted its fate and endured to be reborn. Berliners now lust life each and every single day."

Timothy looks at me with calm. "One must die before being reborn." The taxi stops, and Timothy rushes out. I pay the taxi driver despite Thomas sitting shotgun. I feel my heart racing and rush to follow Timothy, but he's walked past the long queue and is already inside.

Kit Kat Club is named for the burlesque club featured in the movie *Cabaret*. It has moved a few times before settling in a nondescript neighbourhood between real Mitte and gritty Kreuzberg. Every Berliner knows about Kit Kat and the swimming pool hidden within, even if most Berliners would not dare go inside. As we stand by the entrance, a projector beams an image some five stories high on the white wall of an opposing building. An emaciated man lays dying, his chest exposed and ribs caved in, and an angel crouches beside him, her wings folded and her face hidden within her lap. The image changes, but only the skin of the fallen, morphing from flesh to skeleton to electric circuit. This is not a manufactured club for wannabees wearing bling to throw cash around. It's a club of more than burlesque. Kit Kat is a magical place where consent is given to explore dreams of sex, lust, and a bit of kink.

"We're on the guest list," I say as I try to cut in line with Thomas. I speak in German, and although I make it halfway through the line, a bald leather daddy with a red beard sticks out his hand.

"No," he says. "A guy just did that, and I'm not being fooled twice."

Thomas pats the hand away. "We're on the guest list," he says. The rest of the line makes room for us.

The bouncer has to look up to see Thomas eye to eye, and he suddenly puffs up his chest like a blowfish. "What are you wearing?" the bouncer asks after a croak.

"Sportswear," Thomas answers, and as he points to me, "Leather."

The bouncer nods, then steps aside. A shirtless woman greets us, her breasts so much more corpulent than I've experienced. She checks our names and lets us through.

Kit Kat is a complex of chambers opening to chambers. Like the neighbourhood, it starts nondescript enough. We first enter the area with coat check and benches, and there is chaos as men undress and change into fetish wear for the evening. There are wicker sofas like those in Mediterranean hotels or the VIP lounge of clubs anywhere. But I know there's more. Through white lace curtains, I see the swimming pool in an outdoor garden decorated in teak like a tropical garden in Bali.

Before entering paradise, I need to change. I stand in black leather, the harness resembling an H across my torso, the thong a V that opens to my thighs. I hang my street clothes neatly on a hanger. A man with a moustache exchanges my clothes for a coat check number sealed in a little plastic bag. The last thing he wants to deal with is a slip of paper soaked in an unknown liquid.

Thomas drops off his clothes—how handsome he is. He has a football jersey on, but his broad shoulders and slabs for pecs show through. He wears knee-high socks with shorts that are ultra-short and ultra-tight, so his thighs look even more massive than normal. I grin a crooked grin—just a short while ago, he opened his legs for me.

"Let's look for Timothy," I say after my eyes have fully feasted on Thomas.

"He shouldn't be too hard to recognize," Thomas says. "He said he'd be naked."

We enter a chamber with red leather chairs arranged in a circle. There's a painting on the wall with a bearded man in the center who looks like Jesus. It could be a copy of *The Last Supper,* but instead of eating and discussing religion, everyone's having sex.

I scan the crowd as I try to order beers. Still no naked Englishman. I have a leather wristband with a zippered pocket, and pull out some cash. The harness is new, the leather's stiff, and the tight strap restricts how fluid I can move. We hear the band start to play. "The show is about to start," I say. "Maybe we can find Timothy there."

We pass through double doors to the next chamber. There's confetti on the ground, and with the black lights, it glows like a trail of fairy dust. A lush red carpet is spread in front of the stage, and pillows are strewn around. We have entered a deeper chamber of magic, the walls painted with elves, fauns, and other mystical half-human, half-animal creatures. All are naked and some smile mischievously. It's not that they're bad, it's that they're up to no good.

We're at the album-release party of a band that combines techno and classical music. Alex is one of the back-up singers until his own penultimate number just before the closing piece. Thomas and I find some stools to sit on, and we wait. More men, and women, trickle in. I see Alex walk on stage with the others, all dressed in white tank tops and slacks. I wave at my roommate, and when he sees me, he raises his eyebrows in salute.

Timothy, if he is naked as he had planned, is nowhere to be seen.

Darkness. The stage appears with dim light. A man and a woman, both in sweats and hoodies sit around a table with booze, a big bong crusted brown, and a bank card on top of a glass plate. I feel like I'm inside a basement apartment. When the music starts, the couple imbibes and snorts in unison to the rhythm of the techno. It's only later that the violinist and cellist play—and of course, accompanied by an outfit change from hoodie to leather jacket.

Video montage, further inexplicable wardrobe changes, and a spilled bottle of vodka later, it is Alex's turn to go on stage. The man and the woman have fallen to the floor, chests heaving in exaggerated breaths, and Alex makes his grand appearance with gentle steps like he's a geisha. Dressed in white, is Alex supposed to be an angel? He sings in Italian, and his voice resounds in the club. The words hold no meaning for me, but I imagine Alex sings for their redemption. There's a pause where Alex is silent and the chests stop heaving. Alex bellows one last note in an overarching crescendo—the man and woman begin to breathe again, and they struggle to rise. When the note is over, the man falls back down, his chest exposed and ribs caved in. The standing woman pivots to the side and shows her belly, now swollen.

The final number is a group piece, and I'm glad when it's over. They take their bows, and I cheer extra loud when Alex himself bows. The audience keeps clapping, so they go back on stage for another bow. I'm getting impatient. My beer is empty. Thomas' eyes are weary. He hates anything that smacks of pretentious art.

"Should we wait for Alex?" Thomas asks. I shake my head.

We jump off our stools, follow the fairy dust, and walk through another pair of double doors. Kit Kat's final chamber. It's darker here. The creatures guarding the walls are no longer mystical woodland creatures up to no good. Here, evil is embodied in skeletons that dance with demons under the watchful eye of a metallic dragon, its metal snout gleaming.

"Why is this room called the dragon room?" Thomas asks as we approach the bar. A burst of flame shoots from the dragon's snout. A real flame that dances with a life of its own.

"That's why," I answer.

We clink beer bottles and say, "*Prost!*" People are streaming to this dance floor. "What do you think of the show?" I ask Thomas. He sits on a stool.

"There's more to life than drugs, booze, and self-destruction," he says. I kiss him on the cheek, and he smiles.

A naked man emerges from the basement like a lizard from underneath rocks. It's Timothy. I call his name, but the music is too loud. Thomas and I walk to him, and Timothy's back is toward us. I tap his shoulder, and when he turns around, his balls swoosh like a tail.

"Where did you disappear to?" I ask.

"My downstairs lair," he says. I stare into Timothy's eyes. They're brown flecked with blue.

"I didn't see you at the performance," I say.

"I don't understand this art stuff," Thomas says.

"Alex sang well," I add. "Do you want something to drink?"

"Red Bull to fuel my fire," he answers. I'm relieved that it isn't alcohol. We head back to the bar. I order two beers and a Red Bull.

"Vodka Red Bull!" Timothy roars. His eyes look at me as if daring to stop him. I know to never block what Timothy wants.

We drink in silence and then Thomas says, "I'm getting tired. Can you hold my beer while I go to the bathroom?"

He hands the beer to Timothy and disappears.

"We may have to leave soon," I say.

"Tragic. Departing is such sweet sorrow," he says.

"Come back with us, we'll take a cab," I say.

"No." He sniffs. "There are still armies of men to ravage." He reaches into his boot for something. He turns his back to me, and sets his glass on the perch against the wall.

"What are you doing?" I ask.

"Magic," he says.

My voice growls. "What are you doing?" I demand. I grab Timothy by the shoulders and turn him around. He has a pipette in his finger and thumb, and its opening dips inside the beer bottle. "Are you spiking Thomas' beer?"

"The magic of Liquid E," Timothy explains.

"That's wrong, fucking wrong," I say and try to whack the pipette out of Timothy's hand. He jerks away.

"How dare you assault me now," he says. "Last time, you flew on a second wind."

"Last time? You spiked my drink? When?" I say.

"Ages ago, at the Sharon Stonewall party," he explains. In my drunken state, my mind stumbles with the thought of what happened that night. Sharon's, Snax, and then sex—not sex, rape.

"You did that to me?" My voice grows loud with rage. "You know what happened to me that night?"

"Magic through alchemy," Timothy says. He grins a crooked grin.

"You motherfucker!" I shout. I invade his space and his cock dangles a centimeter away from my leather jock. "I got raped. Fucking raped! If I had gone home, none of it would have happened."

Timothy tilts his head like he's looking at a child or dog. He bursts out laughing. He laughs at my pain, he laughs and snickers like the men who saw me that night. He mocks me so I shove him. The beer and pipette crash onto the floor.

Thomas returns, and all he sees is us looking at each other. Not staring, not glaring. He doesn't understand that the expressions on our faces mean something more. He doesn't recognize the anger. "Strange thing happened to me in the bathroom," Thomas says. "A guy wanted me to push down on the faucet so he could wash his dick because the guy he fucked wasn't clean. I said, 'You didn't use a condom?' and he said he did, but why would you need to wash your dick if you had?" Thomas looks around. "Where's my beer?"

"We need to go," I say. Thomas looks puzzled. "Timothy was going to put GHB in your drink."

Thomas and I start to head to the exit, but Timothy shouts, "You weak-willed shall miss something truly glorious!"

There's a long line for the coat check, but Thomas and I are the only ones wanting to leave. I'm angry, I know it. I stare at the man in front of me. He wears rugby shorts and his thighs are meaty and succulent. In my anger, I bare my fangs. I want to devour his flesh—hair, muscle, and throbbing veins. I want to fuck my anger away.

Thomas' familiar hand grips my shoulder. "Timothy is really sick and needs our help," he says. Thomas, young, clean-shaven, and blond. The anger dissipates and I hug him.

"You're right, let's go find Timothy," I say.

We walk away from the exit, back within the chambers of Kit Kat, and the red plush chairs ooze with people as the crowd continues to swell. "We should split up," Thomas says. "When you find him, call me. I'll set my phone to vibrate. I'll check here, and you check the dragon room."

I change my phone to vibrate. I stuff it back in my boot. "OK."

Thomas heads to the bathroom, and I head back to where we left Timothy. He had come through a door in the back. I head there, a stairwell with a low ceiling. The basement's walls are black. Only black. No mystical creatures or magic.

I head back to the room with demons and dragons. I dance through the crowd. I stare at the skeletons and demons. They're not dancing. They're fucking in a massive orgy. Death and debauchery fuck in a massive orgy. HIV lives here.

At the back, I see stairs. Men climb and disappear up the steps. Do these stairs ascend to redemption?

I climb. With each step, I feel more of my skin. I feel the air prickling the hairs of my forearm. I feel the weight of my boots. I feel leather encasing my cock. I feel constraint of the harness on my chest. Above all else, I feel the lack of a body against mine.

I reach the top of the stairs. Everything's dark. It's not redemption. It's only a mezzanine the size of a classroom, a half-level co-cooned on the front and right in balcony guardrails and netting. It's just a balcony that overlooks the dance floor, except in the center is a large bed made of black pleather, and bank seating surrounds it like the walls are about to engulf the bed.

I inhale deeply the musk of men and the humid sweat of men engaged in sex with men. We're more than twenty, more than fifty. We feed from the energy of sex of others. We're more than ourselves, a creature all its own, a creature craving flesh. Faceless limbs groping for other limbs, mouths gaping open for a taste of cock, any cock. My own cock strains in search of a mouth, any mouth.

I'm here to find Timothy. He may be here.

I'm swallowed by the crowd as I step in, and feel a sweaty chest against my back. The harness scrapes into the chest of others. I see the solid silhouette of a beefy bald man furiously jerking his extra-large cock. I delve deeper and my harness scrapes further. Hands grope my chest. Deeper. More scraping. Fuck this harness. I push to the exterior railings. I have space and release buckle after buckle. The dance floor is below me, and I discard the leather to the corner. I return to the orgy that is the creature. I am engulfed by bodies and swim through flesh to the bed.

A young man wears only shorts, and they glitter briefly in the dim light before he pulls them down to his knees. He impales himself on the cock of another man and rides it bare cheeked. The ceiling here is low, and when I walk on the bed, I touch it like I'm a Greek statue holding up a roof. I use it as support for men who stream on either side of me.

A hand grips my cock, and before I can object, warmth envelops me like silk. I'm at the edge of the bed. It's so warm and intense, my breath syncs with the mouth's sucking. I release the ceiling to try to force this mouth all the way down, but a man sitting on the bench rises. He pushes me aside as he passes, and I need to swat the mouth away to balance myself. I land on the bank bench by the wall.

Legs from dozens of men strut pass me to the rhythm of techno. Sitting on the bench, my legs rest in a valley, and my eyes are at cock level to the men on the bed. A bear with a thick cock mostly hidden by pelvic fat shoves his dick into my face. I look away only to be smacked on the lips by a long cut cock from a bearded Arabic man. The man beside me, a tall and smooth German guy with lengthy limbs and an even lengthier penis, strokes his member while his legs are spread eagle.

I love Thomas. I'm here to find Timothy.

The bearded Arabic man gets on his knees in the valley before me. He's thinner, and if it wasn't for his beard, he'd be a twink. He nuzzles his nose against my crotch, and looks up at me. In this darkness, his blue eyes shine in contrast to his skin and hair. Maybe I misjudged him. I unzip the thong, and he grins. He grins before going down on my cock. Warmth, pleasurable warmth.

I turn around and the spread-eagled man has left. Seconds pass before a bald muscle man plops himself beside me, lifts the leg of his shorts, and exposes his uncut dick. His thighs are thick with muscle. I dig in with fangs exposed and become only a mouth for his pleasure. Or so he thinks.

I venture a finger into his ass. My finger wiggles two knuckles deep, and this bull of a man doesn't object. This time, I'm in control. I fuck him by giving him my middle finger while my mouth holds him in place. His hips grind, either to my mouth or finger or both, but he has submitted to my pleasure. As the blue-eyed man continues to work on my cock, I feel the telltale pulses of a bull's cock ready to orgasm. I pull my mouth away, and continue jerking with my other hand. He comes and comes, and his silence belies the twitching intensity of his orgasm. I take out my finger and he leaves without a word. I feel something clump against my nail and know what it is, but I'm afraid to look.

The blue-eyed man stops sucking my cock to comment in English, "That was rude." He speaks with a British accent. "The least he could do was say thank you."

"I know," I say. "Basic anonymous sex etiquette." He smiles. "You were giving a top-notch blow job by the way."

He says something, and it must be "Thanks" but the sound is muffled by my cock impaling his throat.

"I'm close," I moan. This is another one of those rules of anonymous sex etiquette. But this man doubles down, and fuck, it'd feel good to squirt in his mouth. I breath in quick bursts like I'm suffocating, all my muscles flex and tense, and just as my balls burst into this man's eager mouth and tongue, there's a loud, girly shriek from my right, a gut-wrenching, blood-curdling scream that is forever connected with my selfish climax.

Timothy

Tonight is about the perfect orgasm. Not the quick-draw orgasm in one's undergarments, tinged with fear before Mother barges in. Nor the orgasm that's just a satisfying release from a bad work week, with a "You're close and you'll do" kind of man from Grindr. No, tonight's orgasm is about something sublime, like experiencing a starlit night in the Alps over Lake Geneva. It's an orgasm that curls the toes, electrifies the skin, with spasms beginning from balls to gut to dendrites connecting my cerebrum. An orgasm to end all orgasms.

I failed to achieve even an erection with the man from this morning. He lied about his name and the size of his dick. I hid my rage over his phallic fallacy. As I rode his disappointing cock, at the moment when he was most vulnerable, I seized the moment by seizing his neck. I squeezed and squeezed, his eyes wide as if popping out of his sockets. But I relented, and in that moment, he achieved climax, his face reddened so much it bordered on violet. He uttered "*Geil*" without realising his nose bled all over my hand. I showed it to him, and he rushed to the sink to wash.

I dressed and left. My penis was flaccid the entire encounter.

The afternoon was not remotely orgasm-inducing. I went back to Heidi's. She was practising for another performance, and paid me little heed. My only memory of that afternoon was her commanding me to practise with her rococo wig. Did I promise to do something for her the following week? How naughty of me. When I was in her dressing room, I went to the drawer where she kept her stash. It looked ample and delicious, and my mouth began to salivate.

"What are you doing?" Heidi said to me. "Are you robbing me after I let you stay here?"

It was owed to me. Berlin owes me, after all I've endured here.

Heidi lunged at me but had been drinking that afternoon. Her lunge was sloppy, and I stepped aside, and her lumbering body couldn't stop in time. She crashed into the dressing drawer. I stared at her twitching body, the shards of glass around her like rose petals. Her wig had fallen off. Heidi resembled a pathetic, half-dressed mannequin from a Neukölln fashion store.

As I was to leave, it started to rain. A wig is as good as any umbrella, so I picked it up. It smelled like perfume and sweat. I saw Heidi's landline phone, and with my hands through my shirt, I dialed 999 and left the phone off the hook.

I hurried to Alex's and ran into him at the entrance of the U-Bahn. He told me the whereabouts of the happy couple before meeting his performing friends, and I debated whether to intrude, but fuck it. The wig certainly helped me keep a seat to myself on the underground and the repetitive rumbling as the train travelled over tracks.

Rumbling. Now. Shit. I lost track of time. Alex's show at the main stage of Kit Kat.

One last line, and my nostrils flare from the burn, like a dragon's snout. But how beautiful is this feeling, as if glorious fire were coursing through me.

The basement DJ stares at me with something of a look, and I can't figure out what it is so I grab my flaccid penis and jiggle it at him with a snarl, like I'm wagging a tail.

As I ascend the stairs, I imagine my arms are draped in leathery wings, and I crawl from the depths of my lair to the expanse of the dale, and its ignorant village folk will cower before the power of a dragon who dances to techno.

Who dares call me? Who dares call the wrath of Pyriss, the mighty red dragon? These ignorant peasants will scream and dance when terror rains upon them with a four-beat tempo. I feel something, and swivel my scaled belly toward the affronting touch.

"Where did you disappear to?" It is Kay the knight, and he is accompanied by his ogre Thomas with the massive club.

"My downstairs lair." In my lair, where the gold is white. He peers deeply into my dragon eyes, searching for something.

"I didn't see you at the performance." Is this knight ready to duel? A dance duel where I'll thrash my tail to the music.

The ogre speaks. "I don't understand this art stuff."

"Alex sang well," the knight says. "Do you want something to drink?"

Dragons do not drink water. "Red Bull to fuel my fire." We slither to the dale's lake, and I hiss to the bar wrench, "Vodka Red Bull!" I drink and relish the flavours on my tongue.

The ogre speaks further. "I'm getting tired. Can you hold my beer while I go to the bathroom?" How dare the ogre hand me his wineskin as if I were his indentured servant?

"We may have to leave soon."

"Tragic. Departing is such sweet sorrow." You dare leave before the duel? Coward!

"Come back with us, we'll take a cab."

I hear the clang of spears and shields in the distance. "No." I sniff and smell musk. "There are still armies of men to ravage." Perhaps if the ogre is revitalized, then his trusty knight companion would remain. What can achieve this? Magic.

"What are you doing?"

Must I explain the ways of the dragons? "The magic of Liquid E." Kay the knight barks words, and sparks ignite in his eyes. Yes, let that fire burn. We may have a duel yet.

"That's fucking wrong," he says, and tries to slice my claw from the wineskin.

"How dare you assault me now," I hiss. "Last time, you flew on a second wind."

"Last time? You spiked my drink? When?" Conflagration. The village blazes in the night.

"Ages ago, at the Sharon Stonewall party."

"You did that to me? You know what happened to me that night?"

The knight's legs brace for impact, and he readies his sword.

"Magic through alchemy." I grin a vicious, searing grin.

"You motherfucker! I got raped. Fucking raped! If I had gone home, none of it would have happened." His words arch like a long sword but his attack is feeble. I stare at him in wonder. I once respected this knight's skill. How sad. Perhaps he's no knight at all, but an ass. My grin morphs into laughter, and when dragons laugh, mountains shake.

He crashes into me. I relish the feeling. Thomas returns and says something insignificant. They grab their possessions and are about to depart. The duel cannot end like this. "You weak-willed shall miss something truly glorious!"

The ogre and the ass gallop away toward the horizon.

Dragons are demigods, and we need not beg. Drums strike, and my hind legs smash into the earth with each beat. The drums reverberate like church bells, and I imagine the church parish warning the folk of the next village of my impending attack. I hiss like fire spews from my lungs.

I look up. Off in the distance and above the dale, they've amassed an army. The King's army with plated men wielding spears. Savage men to ravage the beast. I crawl to the stairs, and with one final gulp, I fly. I know how these stories end. Halfway up the ascent, I stop. Why does Pyriss the red dragon leave the safety of his lair? Does he truly think that one creature, no matter how powerful, no matter how majestic, no matter how, can destroy without consequence? How does he profit? Is he so vain or self-conscious that he needs to hear screams to validate his worth?

The pungent smell of sex emanates from the mezzanine. I sniff and it intoxicates me, and the answer comes. Pyriss hears screams as he bears down on warm and wet man meat—that is the moment he feels most alive, like a perfect orgasm.

Into the cocoon, I go. I pass a bald bull of a man and continue my slithering. I crawl on to the leather bed. The rhythm of legs and crotches induces me into a cock-hungry trance. On my knees, I beg for cock. I reach out, slowly and tentatively, expectant. But my pale nakedness excites a man with skin so dark it blends with the shadows. My eyes focus on the whites of his nails as he grabs my willing head. He feeds me. I taste him and smell him. I feel his girth. It fills my mouth and strains my jaw, but my tongue laps nevertheless, and I taste veins.

I don't know whether he finishes in me or whether I'm an appetizer before the next course. I suck on countless cocks, and although countless, each cock is unique. There's one with a hefty head but skinny shaft. There's one pierced with a Prince Albert, and the metal bangs against my fangs. There's one who tastes silky, but he bats me away with his hand.

I reach for one more cock. This man has tanned skin and fine blonde hairs over thighs shaped from squats and sprinting. His cock is long and thin. The foreskin retracts only past his piss slit. My mouth deep throats his shaft while my hands squeeze his ass, feeling the heft of his glutes flex and unflex as he fucks my face.

Hands prod my backside. A man fingers me, and I withdraw from the slender cock long enough to command, "Fuck me." He invades my body with his dick, something so thick it rams in me like a cannon. It's too thick, I can't take it, he rips my body in two. But I can't protest because the cock in my mouth won't relent, he's close, I know. He pushes down to his hilt, balls slapping against my chin, and he comes. I gag on his orgasm. I want his juice in my mouth, not my throat. I want to taste it, but he won't let me.

I see the blond legs withdraw, and I inhale deeply like I'm drowning in air. The man behind me with the wrist-sized cock drills his way into me, but I kick him and slither away from the excruciating pain.

I know tears exist in my eyes.

I try to stand and walk away. My legs are weak, and I sway like something fragile. The bald muscle bull of a man pushes me out of the way as he walks past. I sway too much, and break. I try to reach out, but I fall off the mattress onto the valley between bed and bench. There's beer or piss or whatever on the floor, and my hands and knees submerge into this liquid ooze.

I feel defeated and only look at the floor.

A hand strokes my cheek. Do I dare look up? The caresses are gentle. My head lifts to see him, and see his face. He looks like me. He's pale with dark curly hair. Although his jaw is only a semblance of a jaw, his neck is thicker than mine, and his body is broader.

"*Bist du OK?*" he asks.

"*Ja, danke.*" He holds his hand and I clasp it. He lifts me up. He leads me to a corner where I sit down. In German, "I'm Timothy."

"I'm Steffen," he says. He smiles. I feel smitten. I reach for his crotch, but he grabs my hand. "I'm going downstairs to dance. When you're ready, come look for me. I'll buy you a drink." He kisses me on the forehead. I watch Steffen navigate his way through the orgy. Maybe it isn't about the perfect orgasm. Maybe it's all about tenderness.

My muscles ache, but I do want that drink. I reach into my right boot, and grab the plastic bag with white powder. Just a hit to reinvigorate me. I place a wet pinky into the bag, and lay a copious line on my left fist. Just a hit. I sniff, and don't smell sex. My nostrils burn, but it's glorious.

A drink. That'd be wonderful. Steffen has seen me at my worst, and I need not hide behind pretense.

But I smell it again. Sex, glorious sex. There's a swarthy couple in front, close but out of hand's reach, and the skinny man fucks the built one from behind. I stroke my cock. I just want to watch. I can allow myself this indulgence. I stroke, and the phantoms of tonight's cocks haunt me. My mouth, my ass. One more line. It comes, my orgasm. It's intense. It's gut-wrenching and I'm dizzy. My entire body spasms. It's not perfect but it's so bloody close that even my teeth chatter.

Are the drums suddenly loud? Thump, thump, silence. Everything's on fire. I only see red.

Thomas

There's a scream as I walk on to the dance floor with demons on the wall, demons that are fucking. The scream comes from upstairs. I look up as a tiny black bottle falls down. The bottle lands on my forehead and its contents spill over my face. My glasses protect my eyes, but the liquid spills into my nose. It burns. I feel lightheaded, and I choke while trying to wipe the rest with my inner elbow. I stumble to the bathroom.

It's poppers. How rude that someone threw it from the balcony.

I push through the line for the toilet stall. The water is refreshing. When I stare at my reflection to make sure everything is clean, I feel my pocket vibrate.

"Urning," I say.

"Thomas?" Kay's voice is rushed. "Shit. How could I forget. What's the number for the ambulance?"

"112," I answer.

"Can you come to the mezzanine area? Now, right now."

"OK."

The man who I helped earlier with his dirty dick gives me a grin. "Can you help me again?"

"No." I walk past him, shoulders brushing against his.

Past the dancing crowd and up the stairs. Everyone is still, and I don't know why, but I have the feeling like I'm a mother walking in on her son and best friend's "movie" night. At a corner, various naked men have the flashlight function of their phones on. I see Kay and I climb on the bed and crawl to him because I'm too tall for the ceiling.

Kay's eyes are staring at an unknown man. This man wears a wrestling singlet with an open ass, and he pumps down on something, someone. It's Timothy lying flat on the bed, his eyes focused on the ceiling, cheeks caved in. God, no.

"We need to get Timothy out for the ambulance," I say. "You doing the CPR, follow us." He doesn't respond, so I repeat in German.

"I saw him fall over," he says, looking at Timothy as though it were a mirror. "How could I not scream? It scared everyone."

"I will lift him," I say. "Follow us."

He then nods, and I slide my arms under Timothy's back and thighs. I lift, and walk in the valley between bed and bank benches, and my hair grazes the ceiling. A path clears for us, except for a couple still fucking.

"*Los!*" They don't respond so I twist to the side to protect Timothy and barge into them. They crash onto the bed. As we pass, Kay explains the situation. When we are down the stairs, Kay walks ahead to clear a path. The music still plays, but no one dances.

"Thomas, where is your coat check ticket?" Kay asks me. Shit. That's right. My apartment keys are zipped in my jacket pocket, and I don't know if we will make it back before the place closes.

"In my right shoe," I answer. I stop and Kay bends to dig in. He then runs ahead.

I look at the man who was giving CPR. "Once we're at the entrance, I'll lay Timothy on the ground so you can continue CPR until the ambulance comes. Is that clear?"

"Yes," he says.

There are still people waiting to enter, but the bouncers seem to know what's happening. I lay Timothy on the ground, his eyes staring at the ceiling. The man pushes down on Timothy's chest for a few seconds and the blue lights of the ambulance appear. A stretcher arrives.

One of the paramedics asks me, "How do you know him?"

"He's our friend," I answer.

"OK, come with us." There are shocked stares from the line up as we strut past. I look back to see the man in the red singlet stare at us with the golden ambient light of Kit Kat radiating behind him.

Inside the ambulance, as the woman administers the defibrillator and we drive through Berlin with sirens on, I wrap my arm around Kay. He mumbles repeatedly, "I'm sorry. He was there. I could have stopped him. I'm so sorry."

We wait in the emergency room, but we don't wait long. When the doctor walks toward us, I know what this means, and I see Kay knows as well. Kay drops the bundle of clothes, grimaces, and shouts his tears. I hold him. I feel him shaking. This is the first time I've experienced death. Timothy was alive, not an hour ago. He's not dead. He's not dead! How can someone so young die? But the look in the doctor's face tells me the truth. I cry, and the pain is the most intense feeling I've ever had in my life. It's now Kay who holds me.

Alex

Karsten hugs me because it's windy on the rooftop terrace of one of the producers of tonight's show. We have a view of the TV tower from here, and at night, it not only sparkles from the white lights but its antenna pulses red.

I'm getting cold, but I haven't had a chance to speak to the producer. Her name is Petra, and when she leaves to get a drink, I chase after her. In the kitchen, as she pulls out a bottle of white wine, I say in German, "Thank you for having us here tonight. Your apartment is beautiful."

"You're welcome," she says. "More white wine?"

"Yes, please." She pours. "Can I ask you what you thought of my performance?"

"First, *Prost*." She smiles without wrinkles around her eyes, and we clink glasses. "It was a good performance."

"Awesome!" I exclaim, but then she places a hand on my shoulder.

"But there were notes you didn't sing correctly," she says. "I had the impression that you didn't practice enough. Excuse me." She leaves the kitchen, and heads back to the terrace.

Karsten comes to my side. "How did it go?"

"Bitch doesn't know what she's talking about," I say. "Let's go." I'm silent as we take the glass elevator downstairs. Karsten wants to hug me again, but I cringe away from him. I practiced my ass off.

On the street, we hail a cab. We pass Kit Kat Club, where there's still a line to get in. "The scenic route back, please," I say to the cab driver. He nods, and I place my hand on Karsten's lap. Karsten wraps his arm around me, and it feels tender as we drive. We pass the former checkpoint from West to East Berlin, the glitz of modern Potsdamer Platz, and the golden spire that is the Siegesäule.

I was not like the other singers on stage tonight. They told me how they've practiced since their childhood, learned instruments that I have only read about, have parents that are musicians and spend every waking fucking moment breathing music. One even joked that her breathing technique is so good she can hold her breath for five minutes. I can't do any of that.

There are also the stares when I walk into a room of just singers. I'm handsome, and many of them are not. I once entered an audition and heard a baritone joke that the auditions for the boy band are next door. And when I sing my audition, I see some of them sneer.

"This is my favorite time of day," Karsten says as we pass Brandenburger Tor. I peek at the rising sun through the columns. The chariot is basked in soft orange, and I feel like it belongs to me because at this time, the hordes of tourists are gone. We're stopped at a light even though there is no traffic.

"Berlin at dawn is beautiful," I say as the traffic light turns green.

21. Kay

I sit in my office with dread. There's a meeting in twenty minutes, but instead of preparing, I stare at the email from Timothy's mother. "We have arranged for Timothy to be transported to London where the funeral will be held. We request that you and your kind remain in Berlin. If you respect our family's traditions, you will do us this honour. We request his passport, his wallet, and any photos at his residence to be mailed to us. Please help the family mourn with dignity and forget the travesty in Berlin."

After work, I'm supposed to go to Timothy's apartment and clean it. Did he intend that night to be his last? I sift through the events of the evening. Does it even matter if he did?

It matters to you. Intentional means it could never happen to you. You'd never kill yourself. Unintentional means it could. Your vices let loose in Berlin could be your own undoing.

The five-minute alert for the meeting pops up on my screen.

Out of habit, I tighten my tie and head to the meeting room. What is the point of this? I sit as introductions are made and stare at faces. There are those who talk too long, citing unrelated facts. There are those busy on their phones, and answer every email ASAP because everything is urgent. Only a few seem to be focused and aware to be helpful.

Today, I am the weirdo in a room full of normals. Or is it the other way around? I see these faces in business attire, and I try to imagine what their home lives are like. I care about you as a person, don't you care about me as a person? Don't you care that a friend of mine died?

Anton pours me a cup of filtered coffee. Its steam rises above my eyes, and when I focus on Anton, he catches my eye and his chin points to the presentation.

During the break, Anton ushers me to a bathroom far away from the meeting room, used by the building's maintenance staff. Although clean, it hasn't been renovated since the 1970s with beige and brown colours which are a little too dark to be modern. "What's wrong with you, Kay?" he demands. "You're a high flyer and need to comment on the proposals. We need to align."

"Why does it matter to you?" I say.

"I've vouched for you so my reputation is on the line," he says.

"A friend died over the weekend," I explain.

"I don't care," he says. "Wake up and get your act together."

Wake up? Anton has said that to me before, once when we had an urgent meeting at his apartment in Schöneberg. Then I think back to Timothy and his confession, and remember the pipette bottle. The stupor of both evenings felt the same. "Why don't we ever have urgent meetings at your place anymore?" I ask.

He dismisses my question with a wave of his hand. "This is irrelevant."

"No, it isn't," I say. I step closer to him. "After CSD, I was still jet lagged from our trip to Indonesia, and thought the tiredness came from that. But you laced my drink with GHB. If I didn't have to meet my friends, I probably would have fallen asleep on your couch. I almost had to push you off to leave." He steps back but I step in unison. "What would you have done with a knocked-out Kay?" I see sweat on his forehead.

"You can't prove anything," he says. "No evidence shows up in blood."

"Not blood," I say, "but hair." Anton's eyes grow even wider. "I haven't cut my hair since. I'll get the strands analyzed and prove it. What will the other board members think when you're found guilty of attempted rape?"

Anton screams and with hands like claws, reaches for my head and hair. I feel a surge of adrenaline course through me. I push him back, and he falls onto the ground. There's a tearing sound.

"I almost trusted you as my mentor," I say. I notice the rip in Anton's grey slacks revealing pink underwear. His eyes narrow and I see his hands clench into fists. I have no future at CoExcel, I realize. "I quit," I say. Try explaining the rip in your pants during the rest of your precious meeting.

There is nothing like adrenaline to help you overcome fear. I rush from the CoExcel complex and head to Timothy's apartment. During one of our drunken evenings, we had exchanged spare sets of keys in case of emergency. I put the key in the main door, and sigh. It did.

"Are you Kay Hung?" someone says.

I turn around and see a man. It's summer, but he's wearing a formal suit. But then I look at myself, and remember that so am I. "Who are you?" I ask.

"I'm Edmund Goodall," he says. "I'm Timothy's father. From the email address, I thought it was you." This is what happens when I switch emails from hotboii69@hotmail.com to something respectable like my name. He staggers closer, and I can smell the whiskey on his breath. "Could you let me into Timothy's flat?"

"OK," I say.

Mr. Goodall leans on my shoulder and we wait for the elevator. "At the hospital, I had to confirm it was Timothy," he says. "My boy, my boy, he was my boy but he didn't look like it." Images of that night flash in my mind. As Thomas cradled Timothy's naked body, arms limp, chest so thin I could see his ribs, I glimpsed into Timothy's eyes staring off toward a world I could not see. Maybe it was heaven.

"I shouldn't have to bury my own son," Mr. Goodall says but is wracked with agonized sobs and I feel like I'm cradling a wounded soldier.

The elevator opens. A man in a business suit walks out. Mr. Goodall stands on his own as if embarrassed, and gets into the elevator. "I'm sorry," he says when the doors close, and wipes the tears on his sleeve.

I want to say that it's OK, that we need to grieve in our own way, but I've never had to deal with death until this moment. Timothy was his son, and the pain is much more than I've ever experienced or could ever imagine. I grab his hand, and his eyebrows rise in shock. I squeeze, and he squeezes back. There's strength in his grip, and he seems to understand the need for strength now—we arrive at Timothy's floor. We are slow with each step in the hallway. We stop in front of apartment seventeen. "Are you ready?" I ask.

Mr. Goodall nods, and I open the door.

I feel like I am entering Timothy's mind. I've never been to Timothy's before, but I had imagined something organized, almost meticulous. I had imagined an original piece of art as the centerpiece, something dramatic painted on a two-meter canvas. I had imagined a library with leather-bound classics, a plush reading chair, and a table adorned with a book and a vase of lilies.

Reality is different. Berlin reality is always different.

The room with its paper veneer furniture looks like a room at a one-star hotel close to an airport, but without maid service. Paper and empty bottles cover every surface, save the sofa bed. The orange curtains are drawn, and everything is tinged with this coloured light, as if the scene were a photograph from decades ago, left to bleach in the sun. All the furniture is pushed against a wall. Mr. Goodall walks to the window. He screams as he pulls the curtains downward and the cheap cotton rips from the hooks and falls to the floor. The light that enters is bright, now unadulterated.

"Do you want me to call your wife?" I ask.

"No," he says. "This would break her." He walks and examines the papers. "Your email explained Saturday night in great detail, and for this, I'm grateful," he continues. "One aspect, however, isn't clear." I hold my breath in expectation that he'll ask how I found Timothy, where in the club it was exactly—or why I didn't arrive sooner.

"Did Timothy intend this?" Mr. Goodall asks. I breathe again and he holds the side of the desk as he continues to speak. "The autopsy concluded it was cardiac arrest due to a cocaine overdose. But it doesn't answer what I need to know. Did Timothy commit suicide? I need to know!" Mr. Goodall smacks a pile of paper, and sheets of A4 float into the air. He crumples to the laminate flooring.

If it was a suicide, wouldn't there be a note? I help Mr. Goodall on the couch and his breathing slows.

I search for anything that could give insight to Timothy's thinking. The papers are flyers, bills, unopened letters, including ones from the *Finanzamt*. There were some with the heading, "Business Plans," but the end of the page would inevitably be a drawing of a penis. I collect the sheets of paper that were more parent-friendly, as well as the identification that Mrs. Goodall requested. I hand them to Mr. Goodall. "I don't see a suicide note," I say. He nods while clutching his face with his hands. I give the collection to him. "There are also a few letters from the tax agency," I say.

"I have my barristers looking into his finances," he says. "I don't expect any good news there. Kay, where do you suppose is the bed?"

"I think you're sitting on it," I say.

Mr. Goodall then sees the pillow, and he buries his face in it. "It doesn't smell like Timothy," he says, and looks at me with sadness. "Nothing here reminds me of Timothy."

"Maybe the closet?" I ask.

Mr. Goodall rushes to the wardrobe, opens the door, and breathes in. He buries his face in a brown wool coat that muffles his sobs. I see a suitcase on top, and carefully take it down and lay it beside him.

"Do you want help packing his clothes?" I offer.

He takes his head from the coat, and says, "I need to do it myself." With care like he's tucking a four-year old Timothy into bed, Mr. Goodall folds and lays coats, suits, and ties into the suitcase. As he does this, I notice a briefcase and check inside.

"Timothy's laptop is here," I say. "There may be a way to access the hard drive." The ghastly implications occur to me. "What will you do with Timothy's online accounts?"

"I've never thought about that," he says.

"I don't think anyone has," I say. Including the websites. What is the social norm in this situation? Does he put a status update for his dead son? Do the Goodalls close the account, or keep it open as a memorial?

"Do you have Timothy's phone?" I ask.

Mr. Goodall pulls a black phone from his pocket. "It was on his person, and the hospital gave it to me. I don't know the password." I take the phone from him, and try to remember where Timothy's fingers tapped, but I never paid attention.

"I've seen Timothy unlock his phone a few times, and can try but I don't know," I say.

"You're the best chance we have," Mr. Goodall says.

I see a free outlet by the window and balcony door. I plug the phone in, and after a few minutes, the lock screen appears. I swipe to unlock. At least his SIM card wasn't locked. I picture Timothy's fingers. Left of the screen, right of the screen, and two double taps. I remember the rhythm of the sound effects. I try 7, 9, and double 5s. I shake my head. I'm about to hand the phone back to Mr. Goodall when I notice the light reflect off the screen. There are smudges on the surface. I stare closer, and hold the phone to catch the light better. The bottom half is where the keyboard is, and it's a patchwork of smudges. But the upper half has three distinct spots. 1655. The home screen appears.

"1655," I say. I peek into the gallery, and the last thing is a video from Thursday. I hand it to Edmond, and he presses play. It's filmed on a couch, and a German guy is laughing while holding the phone, and there's a line of cocaine on the guy's thigh. Timothy comes into view, and inhales before reaching for the camera man's underwear as the German says, "*Du Schlampe.*" The video stops.

"I'm sorry you saw that," I say.

Edmond tucks the phone carefully into his pocket. "I pressed play." He shakes his head. "What is the favourite memory you have of Timothy?" Mr. Goodall asks.

I have to be honest, I know, but I don't have to be brutally honest. "My favourite memory of Timothy was when we spent a day at Volkspark Friedrichshain. We set up a grill, and in between rounds of eating and drinking, we just laughed. Timothy could tell the funniest stories. That was a good day." I don't mention that Timothy disappeared for an hour while cruising the bushes.

Mr. Goodall nods. He wipes more tears from his eyes, then whispers, "I think I should go."

"I'll call my friends and we'll clean up the rest," I say.

"Before I depart," he says, "I'd like you to have this." He hands me a hat. It's one of those handcrafted, posh hats that I never thought I'd ever wear, but when I try it on, it actually looks good on me.

"I have a big head," I say. "Hats don't usually fit me."

"Timothy has," Mr. Goodall says, then corrects himself. "Timothy had a large head, too." He leans in, and gives me a hug. "Thank you, Kay." I escort him to the elevator, and when he enters, I take off the hat in salute and say goodbye.

I grab garbage bags and begin cleaning. It's my third round going to the dumpster, and when I leave the apartment with hands full, I see Anna. She stares at me and freezes with her key in her door lock.

"Hi Anna," I say. I stand still.

She looks away, and bolts inside her apartment. But just as quickly, she returns. "Kay, the man who's seen me naked."

"Yes, the man and idiot who tried having sex with you," I say. "Like trying to play billiards with a rope."

"You should have folded it in half and stuck it in." She smiles like Margaret Cho, and we laugh. It feels so good to laugh. "Is Timothy making you do his housework as well?"

I drop the garbage bags. "Timothy is dead. From a drug overdose. It was an accident." I think. I want to believe.

"Oh God no," Anna says.

And just as quickly, I'm crying again. Anna rushes to me, and hugs me. "I'm sorry," I say.

"It's all right, it's all right," she says.

Am I sorry to Anna? Am I sorry to Timothy? Anna clutches me tightly. Timothy—I failed him. I was selfish and I failed him. And in failing Timothy, I failed myself. I think about the risky situations I've put myself through.

"I need to go," I say.

Anna breaks the hug. "OK, but let me help." She walks into the apartment.

I'm outside, and as I walk to the dumpster, I see Berlin's TV tower. The sun's light is reflected like a *t* on the disco ball. It resembles a cross.

"I need to go," I say through sobs. *"Berlin, ich liebe dich aber ich muss Tschüss sagen."* After throwing away the remains of Timothy's life, I blow a kiss as a goodbye.

22. Thomas

It has been a time of many firsts. My first flight across the Atlantic, first time seeing mountains, first time dipping my toes into the Pacific Ocean. Kay and I sit on rocks, and gentle waves lap at our toes. The water is cool.

"Vancouver is beautiful," I say. "How could you have left Canada?"

Kay sits beside me and feels the waves with his hand. "You were in Winnipeg. In November. With Arctic winds freezing your eyelids closed. And a freak snow storm that delayed our flight. You were anxious about getting to Vancouver." He uses one arm to hug my waist. "But my parents liked you, especially my mom. She kept feeding you her best dishes."

"She liked that I stayed with her in the kitchen," I say. "When we get back to Germany, would you like to visit my family?"

"Yes, I'd like that."

Kay stares into the distance, and I stare with him. English Bay stretches wide, the blue water calm, and off to the right, green mountains frame a view that is not just picturesque but epic. The pictures I've seen of Canada have always shown a pristine and untamed landscape. I thought I'd feel powerful in a country with untouched nature, as if I were an explorer with no borders or limits, and I was one to tame it.

The feeling, however, is something else. The cold, a bitter wind so powerful that my ears froze in minutes and the skin flaked off like dust, that I shook deep within my body almost to the point of seizure.

This is -40C. This is what it truly feels like to freeze. I began to fear the outdoors. In Vancouver, although in the same country, the landscape is completely different. It's warm at 12C, but when I crane my neck to see a redwood or the snow on a mountain peak, I feel, for once, small and insignificant.

"Hey guys, come on, dinner's ready!" It's Michael, and he waves at us.

We slowly make our way from the rocky outcrop back to the sandy beach. Michael has set up a picnic blanket. "Roger should be coming down soon," he says. He hands me a silver thermos, and says with a wink, "Please enjoy your grape juice responsibly."

"Grape juice? I thought it was wine," I say.

"Shhh," he says. Oh yes. It's against the law to drink in public so I drink without saying *Prost*. I hope it doesn't mean seven-years bad sex. British Columbian white wine is good.

Roger comes holding two white bags in either hand. He's broad shouldered and stocky. And Asian. Michael kisses him on the cheek, and I learn there is such a thing as sticky rice.

"Samurai Sushi's party tray," he says. "I hope you're hungry."

The sushi looks delicious. Not only are there varieties that I've never seen in Germany—what's inside a BC roll?—the salmon and tuna sashimi slices are half a centimeter thick, and I need to take two bites to finish a piece. I don't know if I could ever go back to bad sushi at the Asian Imbiss on my street in Berlin.

"Thank you," I say to Roger.

He smiles back. "You're welcome. Anything to celebrate a successful interview. When will you know?"

"In two weeks," I answer. "I've already heard from the University of Zurich. I've been accepted there."

"Will you move to Zurich or here?" Michael asks.

"This morning, I went to get a cappuccino," I say. "She asked if I wanted fun in it. I was so confused. What do you mean by fun, and I felt like an idiot that I didn't understand. But she was patient and friendly, and explained fun was whipped cream. I said, 'No fun for me.' She laughed. If I move here, I know I'll have more of these moments."

"Is that a yes to Canada?" Michael asks.

I look at Kay, but he looks off into the distance. "It's a yes," I say.

I lay my chopsticks on a Styrofoam box. I place my head on his lap, and look up at his face. "Will you move with me to Vancouver?"

"To Canada, the place I left years ago?" he says while raising his eyebrow, but in the end, smiles. "Yes. I love you, and love is more important than anything else." He opens his lips to say more, but stops. English Bay is now awash with orange, pink, and purple. I shift my head and stare into the orange and red water. Sunset, sushi, and the sea. Kay caresses my cheek. He knows I love him, too.

23. Kay

My thirty-fourth birthday, and I can't imagine spending it any other way. The theme is cabaret that's fabulously spectacular. Thomas stands in the living room of my apartment, even taller than usual—as a drag queen with a blond rococo wig and thrift-store high heels with chest hair poking from her cleavage. The dress is too short to cover her hairy calves.

"*Willkommen meine Damen und Herren,*" she says as her arms part open with a flourish as if she were to hug the entire crowd, "*Ich bin Paulette Liebewurst und unsere Show fängt gleich an.*" Without missing a beat, she wags her index finger and scolds, "Expat bitches who still don't know German, tonight you better learn."

Lights off. Rustling. Spotlight—er, flashlight, and I see Paulette sitting on a stool with a white cardboard cut-out of a guitar. Cue music, and I recognize the song immediately. It's from Eurovision, a 1982 ballad for which Germany finally won the contest after decades of attempts. Paulette plucks imaginary strings as she sings about love and freedom, but halfway through, there's a twist.

"I am the real Wurst!" comes a high-pitched scream from behind. All eyes twirl back to look at my friend, bearded, with a long cream dress and shoulder-length wig, swing open the double doors and enter the living room with an entourage of cellist and violinist. Alex, or Conchita Wurstchen tonight, clutches a microphone studded with rhinestones. The violinist and cellist start to play, and even without a full orchestra, I recognize *Rise Like a Phoenix*. Conchita fills the room with a voice like warm chocolate coating a *Schwarzwalder* cake.

My Berlin friends—what a contrast a year makes. At this party in this mismatched Berlin apartment, there is sass but no class—men, women, and those in between wearing ill-fitting, second-hand suits. Each person's face sports fierce attitudes which convey the message with just a glance, "I am poor but fuck you, I'm sexy."

This is my last birthday in Berlin and the pageantry is beautiful. This is my last birthday here and the warmth of so many friends fills my heart to almost bursting; we were rejected misfits with eccentricities from all over the world, and in a once-divided Berlin, we finally found a place to unite us.

Karsten is dressed in a respectable suit, but I forced him to wear one of my pink ties to gay it up. David and Georg wear black and white suits with opposite ties. Anna is with a man from Munich named Sascha, and they look respectably normal in a dress and suit.

On the window sill, a candle flickers in front of a photo of Timothy and me, the selfie we took while he was in drag and we were in a taxi. The flame sways to the slow melody of the bows sliding across strings.

When the song ends, Paulette rushes over and they hug. There's a round of glorious applause, and Paulette asks in German, "Are you the real Conchita Wurst?"

The bearded drag queen snaps back, "As real as my boobs," grabbing them and shaking them like maracas. She introduces the next performance, an Argentinean piece in which the cellist plucks her cello strings like a guitar. Hips and shoulders dance to the rhythm.

There's a loud buzz of the door intercom and I make my way to the hallway. I see two men enter the bathroom, and without much thought, knock and say in the politest tone I can muster, "Blow jobs fine but no drugs in the bathroom, please." Alex's friends from music school.

I reach for the buzzer, then say, "Front house, second floor." I am a bit annoyed that someone would show up so late, and am shocked that I may be turning German. I wonder if Canada is ready for an abrasive Kay.

I head to the kitchen to grab another beer. Kitchens in Germany are a peculiar thing—apartments don't come installed with them. This kitchen was just a room with tiles and a spigot, and after multiple trips to Ikea, is now furnished haphazardly like the writings on a schizophrenic's notepad. With the party noise muted by distance, I ask myself: Why am I leaving? I take a gulp of my beer.

I love Thomas and can't imagine being without him. I think about Timothy and close my eyes—and when my eyes open, I see the late guest entering the hallway and drop my bottle. It doesn't shatter, but beer spills everywhere.

Helmut rushes to me. The man who kissed me six years ago as we were drinking beers on the street outside of Heile Welt in Schöneberg. The man who loved me, and the man I betrayed. Helmut picks up the bottle and hands it to me. "Hi, Kay."

"Hi," I say and wipe the mess with a rag. I squeeze the rag dry over the sink. "I was meaning to call you back, but…" What did I want to say? That I was afraid to talk to him? That it was easier to go to the next party instead of talking to him?

"The light," he said. His English is more halting than I remember. "That's why I came up. I remembered your birthday and you had emailed me your address to forward your mail."

"Do you want something to drink? I have red wine."

He coughs with his hand covering his mouth, and wipes it on his jeans. "As long as you have a glass with me." The eighteen-year age difference is even more stark today. Helmut's eyes are still a bright blue, and he still dresses in expensive clothes that fit perfectly. But the sagging skin around his eyes, the pallor of his cheeks, the hair now completely white—this is a man who has become old.

I reach far into the back of the cupboard where I have hidden the good wine, away from the drunken, fumbling hands of friends who wouldn't appreciate the difference between a fine red and a dusty *Späti* bottle. As I pour the Italian wine into tall stem glasses, I think back. "Do you remember when we were hiking in Italy, and among the mountains and apple trees, there was that sign saying 'Good wine for sale'?"

Helmut smiles at that. "When we finally got past the dogs, the farmer looked so drunk. And it was only noon. *Prost.*"

"*Prost.*" I show him the bottle. "You can buy it online now."

"You have a beard now," he says. "You look more mature." I realize he's being very un-German in describing how I look.

"You look slimmer," I remark.

He shrugs. "Yes. Thanks."

There is a pregnant pause, and we both look away like there's something terrible to say. "I'm leaving Berlin," I blurt.

Helmut looks at me. "Oh. Where to?"

"Vancouver," I answer.

"You've never lived there," he says. "Are your parents happy about it?"

"Yes. They've put the Winnipeg house on the market."

He takes another sip. "Why?"

I take a big gulp. "My boyfriend is moving to Vancouver for university."

"Moving for love," Helmut says. "It's a habit of yours."

Paulette walks in. "Darling, it's almost time for your birthday cake, complete with frosting," she says. Paulette sees Helmut and purses her lips.

"Helmut," I introduce, "this is…"

"Thomas," he suddenly says, his voice back to its normal bass. He offers a firm handshake. His eyes narrow when looking at Helmut, but relax when he faces me. "I'll try to hold off the crowd, but don't be long." He turns around and with giant strides that hit the hardwood floors, walks to the living room.

"Of course, you're having a party," Helmut says. "We never had this many shoes when I had a birthday party for you. I hope your cake is home made."

"It is," I answer, "even if it's not as good as one of yours." Alex tried to bake something, but kept mixing metric and imperial measurements for his favourite cake recipe.

Helmut downs the wine in one final gulp. "I won't keep you. I just wanted to see how you were doing." He gets up.

I walk toward him, and he holds out his hand. I think a handshake too impersonal, and almost fall into him for a hug. Helmut hugs me back. "I'm sorry." I breathe him in, and he smells mildly sweet, like baking bread.

"The years we were together," he says, "were a gift."

"All my happiness, I owe to you,"I say. It wasn't just Helmut that brought me to Berlin, but every freedom I know as a gay man, every kiss and love, were the result of older men like Helmut who fought for these freedoms. Some are still alive, but many are not.

We break our embrace, and he says, "I wish you success in going home to Canada." He leaves, and I sigh.

Conchita Wurstchen, aka Alex, comes in. "You better hurry."

I grab another beer and gulp it down like I'm deep throating it. I head back to the party where a rendition of "Happy Birthday" in English greets me. When it's time to blow out the candles, arranged as a misshapen three and four, I first don't know what to wish for. But then I see Thomas, and even in ugly drag, his smile is handsome. I blow and the flames dance to a puff.

Later that evening, with the bedroom doors closed and two alarms set, we strip. "Our last night in Berlin," I say as I get into the bed. I look at our suitcases. Mike will pick us up from the airport in Vancouver, and already has helped us find an apartment on the Hastings Sunrise with a view of the mountains and water. In his car. He was very excited to drive again.

"I want dim sum as my first meal," Thomas says as he gets in. "Are you sad to leave?"

"No," I say. "Are you?"

"I'm excited," he says. He spoons me, and rubs my belly. "Canada, our new home."

"Home," I repeat. Thomas kisses the back of my neck. He turns off the nightstand light. "Wait," I say.

Thomas turns on the light with concern in his eyes. "What?"

"My birthday blow job," I say.

"Leaving Berlin with a bang," he says. He lifts the bed cover from me, and starts licking my cock.

"Who said birthday blow jobs are only about receiving?"

Thomas lays flat on his back to be the six, and I position myself as the nine. He climaxes first, and his moans are muffled by my cock still in his mouth. Just like my moans as I suckle on his soft and spent dick. I fall asleep spooning Thomas in a feeling approaching bliss.

24. Alex

I've overslept. I hate saying goodbye at airports, but I jump out of bed. Karsten is still sleeping. I head down the hallway, past the living room where a mess greets me. The door to the other bedroom is open, and I see an empty bed and no suitcases. They've left.

There's a note on the chest of drawers. "Thank you, Alex, for being a wonderful roommate and friend. Visit us in Vancouver. Love, Kay and Thomas."

I walk around the quiet room. I've always been the one to leave, and for the first time, I'm the one who's been left behind. The feeling is shitty. I wish the year could have lasted forever. I break the silence with a song. *Una furtiva lagrima*, a furtive tear.

Am I doing the right thing? Am I fulfilling my passion? There is Vicki, Josh, and the growing child inside her to think about. I need to get my act together for the child. I want to be there for them, but I'm not sure how. I need to have a stable job that keeps me in one place. Did Kay do a MBA program in Berlin? If I had a MBA, I could start as a mid-level manager at Anders Trucking—and back to middle America.

I finish the song, and notice Karsten standing by the door. He has tears in his eyes. "That was beautiful," he says. He comes toward me and hugs me. "Kay and Thomas left already?"

"Yes." I'm alone, I want to say, but his arms feel good.

"Let's go have brunch, I invite you," Karsten says. I'm still not sure about what's next. When in doubt, brunch.

Glossary

A novel set in Berlin wouldn't be complete without German. Here is my definition for these words:

abspritzen – to ejaculate. It's a split verb, so when I say I come, it's *"ich spritze ab"* unless it's part of a long sentence and is the weaker clause so it's *"Ich bin müde weil ich abspritze."* German is hard.

Analverkehr – anal traffic, i.e. anal sex. A country known for its automobiles has a fascination with all things *Verkehr*.

Apfelschorle – apple juice mixed with sparkling water. Unavailable in Austria and Switzerland.

Arschloch – a beautiful word, asshole.

Aufgüsse – infusion or extraction used in saunas, although in Thermea in Winnipeg, Aufguss is also used. Sometimes it's the other way and German words enter the English language. Like *Schadenfreude* and *Blitzkrieg*.

Bier – beer silly. The first word to learn *auf Deutsch*.

Bitte – the second word to learn. Please learn.

Blasen – to blow, especially for dicks. I don't know why in English it's a blowjob but we suck dicks. German is more consistent.

BVG – *Berliner Verkehrsbetriebe*. Public transport authority in Berlin with the motto, *"Weil wir dich lieben."* Check out the Youtube video *"Ist mir egal."* I am not kidding about what happens on the subway in Germany's capital.

Currywurst – a sausage doused in a ketchup-like sauce. Perfect for a late-night snack.

Dankeschön – thank you beautiful.

Döner – another perfect late-night snack except with vegetables and meat. It may or may not be chicken.

Du – the familiar form of you.

Einzelfahrschein – single journey ticket on the BVG. Don't forget to stamp it to validate it otherwise you're screwed when your ticket is checked.

Endlich – finally. *Endlich* is more satisfying to say to friend who's late.

Erguss – bruise, extrusion, emission, discharge, or ejaculation. I have an *Erguss* on my face. How embarrassing.

Fabrik – Europe's economic powerhouse has factories galore

Fahrscheine, bitte – ticket please.

Ficken (and variants) – to fuck. Sounds as powerful in German as it does in English, except only used for intercourse. Fuck this shit does not translate to "*Fick die Schieße.*" Unless you're at Lab on a particular night.

Finanzamt – a dreaded word in Berlin. It's the tax authorities.

FKK – *Freikörperkultur.* Be nude in nature and be happy.

Geil – originally it meant horny, but it now means cool. It's cool to be horny.

Geschlechtsverkehr – sexual intercourse. *Ficken* sounds better.

Gymnasium – high school for those planning to attend university.

Hartz IV – welfare, social assistance, and a Berliner way of life.

Hinterhaus – the house in the back.

Hochschule – tertiary education.

Imbiß – a snack stand and a play on words. *Bissen* means to bite so it's like to bite in.

Laufbier – why walk sober when you can have a beer in hand?

Laugenstange – a pretzel-like pastry.

Oralverkehr – intercourse with your mouth.

Ordentlich – orderly. It's a very common word in Germany ... outside Berlin.

Ossi – someone from the former East.

Pendler – someone who commutes on weekends to a second home.

Germany has tax breaks for these people.

Prost – cheers! Eye contact is imperative when toasting.

Sau – sow, or pig. *Geile Sau* is a complement.

Scheiße – shit or general term Germans scream when things go badly.

Schwanz – cock or tail. I'm not into bestiality so it almost always means cock for me.

Schwarzwald – black forest. Berlin has more discos.

Sehr – very, as in *sehr sehr geil*.

Sekt – sparkling wine from Germany. Delicious, especially Rieslingsekt.

Späti – a convenience store, and a Berlin word.

Spucken – spit out.

Tschüss – goodbye and used in northern Germany.

Tut mir leid – sorry. I forgot to define this.

Typisch Deutsch – the German stereotype according to Germans

U-Bahn – subway. Really, check out that Youtube video.

Thank you

My first thank you is to Guillermo, who was the first to read my book while on the beach. This book has gone through a few permutations, but you have helped.

I also want to thank my friends. Brian, Joe, Pete, Sarah, Desmond, and Matthew. Aimee, thank you for a brilliant title. Amarins, thank you for the book cover. Markus, thank you for the corrections. Adonis, thank you for the song. I'd also like to thank the MK Enjoyers gang, and Nico for the creative encouragement.

A particular thank you to John who not only gave input to the different permutations of this book, but gave me emotional support when I needed it most.

Last but not least, I'd like to thank you, the reader. I hope you've enjoyed the party, and it's true, it's all true. The party's only fun when it's earned. If I've earned your trust, please add an honest review on Amazon because each and every review helps others find this book. If you write a review and send an email to jin@jindeluong.com, I'd like to thank you by sending a bonus from Naked Love Berlin. Once again, dankeschön!

About the Author

Jin De Luong has moved fifty seven time zones, and has more than a decade love affair with Germany. He graduated with a Bachelor's of Science in Pharmacy from a Canadian university, and he received a dual master's degree from Hamburg University and Fudan University.

He speaks three languages well, two additional languages with enough wine, and can order more wine in another. *Naked Love Berlin* is his first book and tribute to his love of a city that didn't always love him back, but Berlin did always offer him a beer and a blowjob, even when it wasn't Jin's birthday.

www.ingramcontent.com/pod-product-compliance
Lightning Source LLC
Chambersburg PA
CBHW071431200726
48294CB00002B/598